A Dance to Die For

by

Rebecca Lee Smith

This is a work of fiction. Names, characters, places, and incidents are either the product of the author's imagination or are used fictitiously, and any resemblance to actual persons living or dead, business establishments, events, or locales, is entirely coincidental.

A Dance to Die For

Contact Information: info@thewildrosepress.com

Cover Art by *Kim Mendoza*

The Wild Rose Press
PO Box 708
Adams Basin, NY 14410-0708
Visit us at www.thewildrosepress.com

Publishing History
First Crimson Rose Edition, 2012
Print ISBN 978-1-61217-027-5
Digital ISBN 978-1-61217-049-7

Published in the United States of America

Something zinged past Annabel.

It cut and ruffled the new growth of hickory leaves beside her shoulder, like a bird soaring through the trees at warp speed. Her head jerked around. Trent was running toward her with his arms airborne, his beige raincoat ballooned behind him like a cape.

He pushed her off the path, then hit the ground sideways. He slid into the underbrush, shoulder first, and roughly pulled her down on top of him.

Another high-pitched crack echoed across the meadow.

Trent's hard body jolted beneath her.

He enveloped her in his arms and rolled her to the side, pressing her head into his broad chest. The musky scent of his aftershave mingled with the pungent tang of dried weeds and earth sent her senses into overload. The weight of his muscular thighs pushing against her equally muscular thighs sent a shudder pulsing through her. "It's okay," he whispered. "I've got you."

They lay motionless in the tall warm grass, side by side, for what seemed an eternity. Until the only sounds she could hear were the soft, protesting whir of insects and the rapid, steady thumping of his heart.

Annabel lifted her head and stared at the line of dark stubble along his chin. "What the hell was that?"

"Probably a poacher."

"A poacher? Are you serious? *Here?*"

He loosened his grip on her shoulders. "The forest across the road belongs to the inn. There's no fence. All we can do is post *No Hunting* signs and hope for the best."

"So, how do your guests feel about dodging bullets? I bet this place stays packed."

Dedication

For Smith.
Thanks for still hanging around
and showing me the world.

For Jared and Bryan,
my best editors on the page and in life.

And for my mother,
who never went to bed without a book.

Prologue

The Park Square Theater's old gas furnace could crank out more heat than a honeymoon in hell. The first number hadn't begun, and already Annabel Maitland was breaking a sweat.

"Five minutes," the stage manager called. He glanced up from his clipboard and frowned. "You gonna be okay tonight?"

"Sure, Murray." To prove it, she leaned forward and stretched her left leg out behind her, then swept her fingers across the hardwood floor, as if she were a prima ballerina. She couldn't hide it much longer; people were beginning to notice. If her physical condition filtered up to the suits who signed her paycheck, the managing producer would send her packing before she had time to hang up her sequined Wonderbra.

She stretched again and winced. Once the adrenaline kicked in, she would be all right. The blistering pain in her hip would dwindle to a dull, steady throb, a level of annoyance she was used to tolerating. She straightened up. Her head felt woozy—three margarita woozy.

Maybe her blood was too thin again. She'd have to start eating liver and soybeans, one of Aunt Lou's vile but effective remedies. Maintaining her health through the rigors of an all dance show like *Moondance* was a priority, but she refused to be one of those fitness obsessed dancers who swallowed a handful of herb and vitamin supplements before every performance. She already swallowed enough ibuprofen to choke a plow horse.

Her dance partner took his place beside her and smoothed his gray silk tie. "Hey, sweet-stuff. You look terrible."

"Well, thanks, Byron."

Her gaze did that funny distorted thing again accompanied by an acute hit of nausea. Orange-flavored saliva rose in her throat. A film of perspiration misted the back of her neck. She grabbed the edge of the prop table, shadowed blue beneath the dim backstage light.

"I'm serious, Annabel. Are you sick?"

"I don't know. I was fine ten minutes ago." She looked past his shoulder to the back curtain where a line of couples stood waiting for their entrance cue.

The houselights dimmed. A stray cough echoed from the balcony. Two soft taps from the conductor's baton, and the overture began to play.

"Quinn doesn't look any better than you do," Byron whispered. "What did you girls do after the matinee? Go to Hannigan's and get plastered?"

Annabel glanced across the stage. Quinn stood in the wings, slumped over the stair railing, blotting her forehead with a workout towel. "We didn't do anything. We were—" A wave of vertigo darted in front of her eyes. She took a deep breath and clutched his arm.

"That's it," Byron said. "I'm telling the dance captain to get one of the swings ready to go on for you after the opening number." He put his arm around her shoulder. "Just hang tight."

She took Byron's hand and pointed her right toe. "If I throw up on your shoes, you'll never let me live it down, will you?"

"No, ma'am. These puppies cost two hundred bucks." Byron tightened his grip. "It's okay, kid. I've got your back. I won't let you fall."

The downbeat sounded. Annabel moved forward. A bright spotlight shimmered across her face. *Step, touch, slide together.* She could do it if she concentrated. *One hitch kick. Two.* Not bad for someone seeing double.

She took another step and executed a shaky pivot turn. Then she caught sight of Quinn.

"Look at that," sniffed one of the dancers. "I knew Quinn would screw this up for the rest of us."

Quinn stumbled to a stop at the edge of a platform. She grabbed her throat with both hands. Even above the pulsating music, Annabel could hear her wheezing and gasping for air.

Why don't they help her? Annabel thought. *Someone has to help her!*

She spun out of Byron's arms and twirled past the dancers separating her from Quinn. One by one their faces registered surprise, then horror. The audience gasped. A trombone player climbed on his chair. From the wings, Murray made throat-cutting gestures to the conductor.

Quinn clutched her chest and cried out. The bloodcurdling scream silenced the left side of the orchestra. She crashed to her knees inches from the platform edge, then swayed forward and back in agonizing slow motion.

Annabel raised her arms. She pushed off and took a flying leap into the air. Her foot touched Quinn's platform and her ankle twisted to the left. She grasped the first thing she could reach—Quinn's white sequined collar—and yanked hard. Her fingers held onto the slick fabric long enough to pull Quinn away from the edge.

Quinn toppled backward, splaying the bulk of her weight onto Annabel's side with a spongy thud. Annabel's hip wrenched, then snapped. Pain shot down her leg. The sound of her own voice shrieked in her ears.

Someone must have closed the curtain and sent for the nurse playing gin rummy in the green room, then made a quick, impromptu speech reassuring the audience the show would go on. But Annabel couldn't tell who or when. The piercing ache in her hip, signaling the end of her dancing career, barely registered. All her brain could process was the panic glowing in Quinn's green eyes and the rattle of each labored breath as the air gurgled and hissed in Quinn's throat.

"Someone did this to me," Quinn rasped.

"Don't try to talk. No one could've—"

"You have to find out." Quinn's fingernails dug into the back of Annabel's palm. Her eyes squeezed shut. "Mama, I'm sorry. Tell Selena...*Sheffield*."

"What are you trying to say?"

Quinn focused her gaze on Annabel's face. Her mouth opened and closed. "Promise me—*promise me!*"

"I promise. But I don't think—oh, God—*Quinn!*"

Quinn's eyes rolled back in her head. Her body stiffened, then arched, then jerked. With each convulsion, she thumped against the hollow platform like a battered marionette. Her long blond hair tangled into a nest, her thin rigid arms flailing upward. Her delicate hands flopped, unhinged, up and down, as if they were waving goodbye.

Chapter 1

Two Months Later

Annabel had been wrong about the Sheffield Inn. It was anything but flea-bitten. Ruth's description had prepared her for the worst, something along the lines of the Bates Motel meets Petticoat Junction, not a rundown, miniature version of Tara.

The urge to escape washed over her, a gutless fantasy she couldn't seem to shake. In her head, she was already sprinting down the blacktop driveway, flying past the curve where the rhododendron grew wild, galloping across the stone bridge at the edge of the forest like a spooked palomino. She handed the airport limo driver his tip and wondered what he would think if she shoved him aside and clambered back in the car. He looked old, seasoned. He'd probably seen fares change their minds and bolt. He probably had nightmares about it.

A bellman materialized from behind a potted plant and scooped up Annabel's bags. He tossed them onto a metal cart as if they were made of Styrofoam.

"I'm looking for Mr. Sheffield," she said. "Where would—"

"In the lobby."

She pressed some dollar bills in his hand. "Thanks. Go on ahead. I'll catch up."

"Yes, ma'am," he drawled.

The sharp April wind cut through her quilted jacket. She wrapped her arm around a not-so-white column and clenched her teeth to keep from shivering. The Blue Ridge Mountains encircling the hotel were more beautiful than she'd imagined. Everywhere she turned, it looked like the Bob Ross painting her mother had hung over the parlor daybed back in Indiana.

It wasn't too late to back out. People reneged on promises all the time, especially to the dead. She could run after the bellman, grab her bags off the cart, and forget the last two months had ever happened. If she could still manage to run, the cowardly part of her might have considered it.

"Calm down," she muttered to herself. "No one knows why you're here. Just calm the hell down." She pushed the front door open and stepped into the lobby. If she could make it across the hardwood floor without falling on her face, she might be home free.

"Miss Maitland?"

Annabel turned.

"Hey, there! I'm Gil Sheffield. Welcome to North Carolina."

She'd expected an older, more sophisticated man, a man who wasn't afraid to ask the imperious Ruth Donovan to find him a dance director for his hotel, a man with nerves of tempered steel. But the guy walking toward her, shaking a shaggy wisp of dark hair out of his smiling brown eyes, didn't look old enough to buy his own beer.

He pumped her hand up and down. "So, you're the gal who's gonna put a supper club show together for us and make us a big pile of money."

"I'm going to try."

"Ruth said you'd be perfect."

"Yes...well." She shifted her hip, fighting the impulse to wince. The ibuprofen was wearing off fast. The old familiar ache had returned with a vengeance. She tried to concentrate on Gil's face.

"I wish my brother Trent could've been here to welcome you, but he's on one of his trips. Doesn't matter, though. The supper club is my project."

"When can I see it?"

"After lunch. It's not quite ready. The carpenters still have a few things left to do." A matching set of dimples creased the sides of his cheeks. "But it's gonna be great! I'm trying to work out a deal with the little jazz combo that plays for us in the Laurel Room. But I guess Ruth explained all that to you."

"Not really." Had she even taken the ibuprofen? She couldn't remember. She had to have taken it. She never would have made it through the Asheville airport without it. "To be honest, I've only spoken to Miss Donovan once, briefly."

"But she gave you such a great recommendation. I thought she knew you."

"She's seen me dance a few times. I guess she thought of me for this job because I was friends with her niece."

The blood drained from his face. "You knew Quinn? Quinn Wolcott?"

"We danced together in a musical off-Broadway. So far off, it was practically in Hackensack."

"You were in *Moondance* with Quinn? That's amazing." Pain settled in his eyes. "I'm sorry. It's just that I...she stayed here sometimes." His gaze shot to the top of the stairs, as if he thought she might still be standing there. "She camped out here when she and her mother weren't getting along. Which was most of the time."

"Quinn said her mother lived in Black Mountain. Is that near here?"

"About fifteen miles away. Quinn's two sisters live there too. And her nephew." His voice betrayed more emotion than he could handle. He took a deep, ragged breath and smoothed the shirttail flap on his plaid flannel shirt. "Can you excuse me for a minute? I need to check on something, then we'll get you moved in." He ducked behind the front desk and disappeared through a doorway.

Annabel blew out a long sigh. She'd only been at the Sheffield Inn for three minutes and already she was in over her head. Why had she mentioned knowing Quinn before she'd worked out a game plan? She'd seen the shattered look on Gil's face. Did she think she could just waltz in and start asking questions about Quinn without dredging up painful memories? People who had known Quinn were still grieving. What right did she have to intrude on their lives?

She shifted her weight to her left leg and looked around the spacious room. The years had taken their toll on the once elegant lobby. Plush furnishings dripped with tattered old world charm. Velvet drapes, marble-topped tables, high-backed Victorian loveseats, an open cage elevator straight out of *Thoroughly Modern Millie.*

"You gonna stand there all day, or do you want your key?" A young African-American woman, sporting a mass of intricately braided hair and an impressive pair of biceps straining beneath the sleeves of her green tailored jacket stood staring at Annabel from behind the front desk. The name plate said, *Keisha Releford, Day Manager*. "Most of the employees stay in the staff cabins down by the lake, but you get to sleep upstairs in the Rose Room." The slight lift of her eyebrow told Annabel how she felt about that piece of news. "It's on the third floor, so you'd better be careful. There's a lot of construction still up there. How long you here for?"

"A few weeks. Just until I get the floorshow up and running."

"Uh, huh. Well, I sure am glad I'm working tomorrow."

"Why is that?"

"'Cause that's when Mr. Trent gets back." Her coal black eyes twinkled. "And that's when things around here are gonna get mighty interesting." Her gaze darted toward the office then back to Annabel. "Can I give you a piece of advice?"

"Sure. Go ahead."

"I heard what you were saying to Gil, and if you know what's good for you, you won't mention that bitch's name around here again."

"What bitch is that?"

Keisha lowered her voice. "Quinn Wolcott. No one around here wants to be reminded of her. Especially Gil. That man went to pieces when she died."

"I didn't know—"

"I heard what happened to her in that play, *Moondance*. And I'm glad—*damn* glad. Quinn was a ballbreaker and proud of it. She used up people like cheap toilet paper. She got what she deserved. You know what I'm sayin'?"

Heat surged across the back of Annabel's neck. The image of Quinn's twisted face flashed behind her eyes. She tried to keep her voice steady. "Well, I was there, Keisha. And believe me, nobody deserves to die the way Quinn did."

Keisha shrugged and pulled the metal basket from beneath the electric shredder. "I think you're wrong. I think some people get *exactly* what they deserve." She dumped the tangled paper strips in the trashcan and looked at Annabel. "I heard Quinn said she thought somebody had tried to murder her. Is that true?"

Annabel nodded.

"Well, I can understand why," Keisha said. "A couple of months ago, there was a time when, if I thought I could have gotten away with it, I would have killed the bitch myself."

****

Wire-framed glasses inched their way down the damp slope of Annabel's nose. She pushed them up and repositioned her throbbing hip on the ladder's top rung. She was almost done. One more PAR can light to attach and she could close her burning eyes and climb down.

A row of miniature spotlights hung across the metal grid. Once those bad boys were lit, the room would stop looking like a dilapidated carriage house. A few strategically placed beams of light would soften the timber and stucco walls and transform it into magic. Below her, the carpenters—two brothers named Ham and Leon—sat taking a break on the edge of the stage.

"I like it with the lights turned down," Leon said. "It looks like nighttime, don't it?" He squinted up at Annabel. "Where'd you learn to do this stuff?"

"I volunteer at a theater workshop for inner-city kids off Houston Street. You ever been to New York, Leon?"

"Nope."

"Well, it's big. Too big."

"Thanks for setting the lights," Ham said. He wiped his neck with a folded bandana. "We were worn out when you showed up and offered to help. I hate climbing that durn ladder."

"I've been here for almost two days," Annabel said. "And anything's better than sitting in my room counting wallpaper roses. I was up to two thousand and four when I—"

"You count roses?" Leon asked, blinking up at her. "I like roses."

Ham laughed. "And don't we wish you smelled like one."

"Can somebody hand me a dry rag?" Annabel said. "This blasted light has too much grease on the joint. I can't keep it from slipping."

Ham got up and lumbered to his toolbox.

The outside door crashed open and slammed shut, echoing through the drafty room like gunfire. Annabel grabbed the lighting grid above her head.

"*Gil!*" a deep, rich baritone shouted. "*You in here?*"

"Not here," Ham replied.

"Do you know where he is?"

Uneasy silence filled the room.

Annabel glanced down. The blurred image of a man stood in the white circle of stage lighting. The carpenters turned toward the pool of light. They stared at the man in wonder, as if he were an alien who'd just beamed down from the mother ship.

"You might try the kitchen," Annabel offered. "He is the assistant chef."

The man stood with his hands on his hips, like Yul Brynner throwing his weight around in *The King and I*. "Will somebody please tell me what the devil's going on?"

Annabel swore under her breath. "Hit the house lights, Ham. Leon, could you climb up and hold this lamp for me while I get down?"

In a few seconds the house lights popped on. Leon climbed the wooden ladder and waited for Annabel to swing her bare foot over the top. She held the lamp steady until they could safely change places, then slowly descended the other side.

She took off her insulated gloves and walked toward the man, wondering if the trickle of perspiration sliding between her breasts was visible through her cotton T-shirt.

"I'm Annabel Maitland. You're looking for Gil?"

The searing light had blinded her. All she could make out was a pair of broad, taupe-colored shoulders and a set of flashing white teeth. He could have been a Rottweiler in a raincoat and she wouldn't know the difference.

"I don't care who you are," the man said. "Or what you think you're doing here." He stopped and gazed around the room. "Oh, God. This looks like a dinner theater. Tell me this isn't a dinner theater."

"It's Fred and Ginger's," Annabel said. "Or it will be when it's finished. Isn't that a great name for a 1930's supper club?" She pointed behind her. "Tables will sit along those platforms in front of the bar. Over here, we'll drape chiffon curtains on French doors and wrap tiny white lights around fake palm trees. The orchestra will play on that platform—big band, jazz, swing. The little spotlights will make everything look dreamy and romantic. Very retro. The bartender is learning how to make vintage cocktails like sidecars and pink squirrels and gin rickeys."

"I want you out."

"What?"

"I want you and your incompetent friends packed up and out of here in ten minutes."

"Hey!" Annabel said. "You can't just come in here and—"

"Ten minutes or I'm calling the police." He turned on his heel and walked out, banging the heavy door behind him.

Annabel looked at Ham. "That wasn't—"

"Trent Sheffield." Ham put down the rag and picked up his Mountain Dew. "And from what I hear, he pretty much calls the shots around here."

"Then you'd better wish me luck." Annabel slammed out the door into the bright sunshine. "Mr. Sheffield!"

He stopped halfway up the path.

"Can I talk to you for a minute? Please?"

He let out an exasperated sigh, then turned and retraced his steps.

Annabel cupped her hands over her eyes. "Would you mind moving into the shade? I've been staring at 300 watt bulbs for the last two hours." She pushed her glasses on her head, which is where she usually wore them, and rubbed the tender indentations on either side of her nose.

He glanced at her feet. "Where are your shoes? Doesn't the carpenters' union frown on working barefoot?"

"It frowns on falling off ladders. My toes keep me anchored."

"Well, don't step in the poison ivy."

They left the path and walked to the nearest tree. Annabel blinked, willing him to slide into focus. "You're a tall person, aren't you?" she said, laughing. "Are you sure you and Gil are brothers? He can't be more than five-foot—"

"Same mother, different fathers."

"And you share the same last name?"

"Don't ask. It's complicated."

The ghost light swimming across her line of vision began to fade. In its place stood the disconcerting image of Trent Sheffield, a towering, more intense version of his younger brother, Gil. The same matching dimples slashed the contours of his angular cheeks, the same unruly dark hair curled around his temples. But the resemblance stopped there. Gil's brown eyes were warm and trusting. Trent's hazel eyes appeared guarded and suspicious, and so crystal clear, they reflected the colors of the woods surrounding them. They watched her intently, sizing her up, while an involuntary shiver danced the length of her spine.

"Look, Miss...uh—"

"Maitland. Annabel Maitland."

"Annabel." His soft western Carolina drawl melted each vowel. "That's an old-fashioned name you don't hear every day."

"You would if you hung out at the Dairy Queen in Marshall Hill, Indiana. You'd also hear Sue Ann and Mavis. And Rita. I know three Ritas. One with the first name of Margo."

"Margo Rita?"

"There's not a lot to do in Marshall Hill."

"I see." The trace of a smile twitched the corners of his perfect, sculptured lips. "Look, I don't know what Gil's told you, but there's been a mistake. A big one."

"Oh, no mistake. I'm not really a carpenter. I work here at the inn. I'm the person Ruth Donovan found for you and Gil. You know, to choreograph the dance routines for the floorshow? At the supper club?" He stared at her. "I'm also going to teach a couple of dance classes to the guests in the morning—swing and salsa. Salsa's very big right now, especially with the senior citizen crowd." She laughed uneasily. "You don't know anything about this, do you?"

"You say Gil called Ruth Donovan?"

"She recommended me. For the job you seem to know nothing about."

He raked a hand back through his thick brown hair. "I've only been gone a week."

"A week and two days."

"Then I should know better. The last time I was gone for a week, Gil dug up the south lawn and installed a swimming pool."

"It's a lovely pool," Annabel said lamely. "You don't see many shaped like a flower pot."

"No, you don't. Last month he hung a wrought iron fence gate from the kitchen ceiling to use as a pot rack. It took five people to lift it. Last fall, he hired our plumber's mother as a cook. Mrs. Rosetti, who doesn't speak a word of English and doesn't care to learn any. When I came back, I tried to fire her, and she handed me a slice of pizza. It's a game we play now. I tell her she's leaving, and she hands me pizza. Every damn day—pizza."

"I haven't tried her pizza yet. Is it good?"

"Well, yes, but—"

"Her cannoli is incredible. And her minestrone soup is—"

"I don't believe this," he said to the tree. "Half the third floor is filled with scaffolding, and Gil's decided we need a supper club? Now, *that's* realistic. How long can I keep posting little signs over missing stairwells that say *Please Pardon Our Dust*?"

"If you'll just talk to Gil, I'm sure—"

His eyes flashed. "Talking to Gil isn't a good idea right now. I might do something I'll regret. Like disown him. Or dismember him."

"Can't you just—"

"No, I can't." His brow furrowed into a single ridged line. "Gil agreed never to spend the inn's money again without consulting me."

"But the majority of your guests are senior citizens who...who like to dance in the Laurel Room. Even though it's way too small." She was rattling sentences off the top of her head. "And who...have cataracts. Cloudy, cloudy cataracts. After dark, I'm sure they'd rather not have to drive down the mountain to Asheville in order to find some decent entertainment. A supper club is the perfect solution. Catering to seniors can be a goldmine. But if you want them to keep coming back, you need to offer them something more stimulating than prune juice and bran on the breakfast buffet."

Trent directed his gaze back to Annabel's eyes, scalding them. "You should be in sales."

"Fred and Ginger's could be something special—live music, great food, a floorshow with professional dancers."

"Which is where you come in, right?"

"Gil thinks a club will keep the inn from going under."

"Things are fine," he said tightly. "It's true we

could use some more bookings, but when the weather gets warmer—"

"This place needs more than warm weather, it needs an overhaul. The lobby and the Laurel Room are nice, but I've heard complaints."

"What kind of complaints?"

Annabel met his gaze without flinching. "That the inn is on its last legs. That your Aunt Margaret let the old place fall into disrepair before her death, and neither you nor your brother have the resources or the vision to restore it. That the only reason people pay to come here, besides the killer mountain views and the slow but impeccable service, is the food. I would've found out more, but I've only been here a day and a half."

"You don't know what you're talking about."

"Maybe not. But I've worked in enough dinner theaters to know if the food is the main attraction, Mrs. Rosetti won't stay here long. Some big hotel or restaurant will quadruple her salary and snatch her out from under you."

The carriage house door swung open.

"Everything okay?" Ham asked. "I heard shouting."

"This is Ham Newland," Annabel said. "He and his brother Leon are building your supper club."

Ham sidestepped a large pile of two-by-fours and stood twirling a baseball cap in his large callused hands. "I hope you're not mad about Annabel helping us."

"No," Trent said. "I just don't want her to get hurt."

"Oh, I wouldn't worry about Annabel," Ham said. "She's a way better carpenter than Leon. Of course, Leon only has eight fingers, and his—"

"I get the picture," Trent said.

Ham cleared his throat. "We want to thank you for giving us this job, Mr. Sheffield. It's been hard finding work, what with my wife sick and all. No company will hire me when I can't give them a full day, or take on Leon because he's a little slow. Gil took a chance on us. He gave us back our self-respect."

Trent nodded.

When Ham had gone, Annabel said, "Why didn't you tell him you're letting them go?"

"Are you kidding? I'd sooner send a couple of kittens out into a snow storm. I'm gonna let Gil tell them. Gil hired them, he can fire them. Let him be the bad guy for once."

Annabel looked at the sky. Not a single cloud marred the sweeping expanse of robin's-egg blue. *Severe clear*, the Air Force called it. And if she had any sense, she'd be flying through it on her way out of town.

Trent wasn't going to budge. She could see that now. The stubborn set of his jaw told her it was time to cut her losses and resort to Plan B. If she had a Plan B. If there was information to be gleaned about Quinn's death at this hotel, she might still discover it. After two months, the trail was probably ice cold. It wouldn't be easy, but she could try—stay in the area, get some kind of job. She had brains. She was resourceful.

She pulled herself up to her full height, which was considerable, and stretched her classically trained body until her lips were inches from Trent's face. She was so close, she could smell the faint, sweet trail of his aftershave floating between them. Her heart squeezed against her ribs. "I have a signed contract promising me employment until Fred and Ginger's opens."

"Are you threatening me with a lawsuit?"

"No, but I think you owe me at least a week's severance pay and airfare back home."

"Fair enough."

"All right. Well." She took a step back. "I guess this is goodbye. Good luck, then."

"Because I'm going to need it, right?"

She didn't answer.

"Look, I'm sorry I insulted your friends, Ham and...what's his name. Will you apologize to them for me?"

Annabel planted both feet in the soft earth. "No, Mr. Sheffield, I won't. You apologize to them. You're the one who called them incompetent."

His eye color seemed to change by the minute. As he turned toward the light, a tiny streak of blue darted across the edge of the brown-green iris like a miniature flash of electricity. He looked formidable standing there, frowning at the ground. He also looked sexy as hell.

"Fine," he said. "I'll go apologize."

"Good." Their eyes locked, but this time she was ready for it. A wave of heat shot from the back of her neck to her solar plexus. "Then I...I guess we're all done here."

"I guess we are."

She turned and started up the path, stubbornly weaving her way barefoot through a maze of jagged stones. As long as he was watching—and he was, she could feel it—she had no choice but to put one foot in front of the other.

Well, let him watch, she thought. If there was one thing she knew how to do it was make an exit. Shoulders back, head held high, ass to the wind.

****

Trent watched Annabel thrash through a thicket of mountain laurel as she headed up the path to the inn. Her bare feet kicked out little streams of dust. He'd noticed her feet before he noticed her silver eyes. She had those ugly, knobby feet that all dancers had, with protruding bunions the size of radishes and red overlapping lumps on her toes and heels that would never soften back into normal flesh.

But her eyes—eyes the color of the sky just before it rained—had pushed her misshapen feet right out of his mind. There was something behind those eyes. Something he couldn't put his finger on. Her eyes had taken him by surprise. And not many things surprised Trent Sheffield.

He sat on a freshly cut tree stump and rubbed his neck.

Christ, he was tired.

He'd had the old elms cut down to make room for the new additions—bright new bungalows that would bring in enough money to pay off their debts and build more bright new bungalows. But until he sold the lots he and his father owned jointly, those plans were on hold.

Everything was on hold.

And now he had to deal with a supper club. What the devil had Gil been thinking? How could he have called Ruth Donovan—Quinn's aunt, for Christ's sake—and asked her to send them a dance director? For what? To put together some stupid show in an old carriage house that still reeked of hay and horse manure?

Now he'd have to call Ruth and apologize, explain it had all been a mistake. Oh, Ruth was going to love that. That's all he needed. Something else to make her hate him.

Resentment rose in the back of his throat. What was he going to do with that boy? How many times had he been forced to make similar calls on Gil's behalf, clean up after one of Gil's escapades, bail Gil's butt out of an expensive jam? And Gil's jams were always expensive. Didn't the kid understand the inn's bank account was draining faster than a keg of beer at a Panthers' game?

Trent stood and brushed a streak of crusted leaves off his all-weather coat. A dark stain smeared across the hemline. Great. Now he'd have to get it cleaned. Another expense.

He shoved his hands in his pockets. God, he was beat.

The trip to New Jersey to search for his father had been a waste of time, a waste of money they didn't have. Things were unbelievably tight. If the inn went under—and that was a real possibility—he'd have no one to blame but himself. The two things in the world that meant the most to him were his brother and the inn. And he'd made a royal mess of both of them.

Why did a new set of problems always crop up before he'd finished solving the old ones? Why couldn't he have just one day to stop and take a breath? He could handle Gil, but his father was a different set of wheels. Even if Trent could track him down and come to a reasonable agreement over the property settlement, it might be too late to save anything.

His gaze shot to the top of the hill toward the inn. He stood on his toes and craned his neck, but she'd already gone.

Annabel Maitland. Who was she anyway? She'd said she was a dance instructor, but those feet did more than teach a few classes. He'd seen the toned muscles expand from one side of her back to the other like wind across water, the delicate way she held her fingers. She was a dancer, all right. A hard core, class-every-day/show-every-night dancer. Just like Quinn had been. She probably knew how to lie like Quinn too. But what did he care? She'd be gone soon. Just like Quinn. Gone and forgotten.

He rubbed his temples and yawned. Twenty hours on a Greyhound bus hadn't done much for his disposition. He was too old to go without sleep. It made him say things he shouldn't. Made him think things he shouldn't.

He stepped over a thick patch of poison ivy.

Before he confronted Gil, and passed out from lack of sleep, he had to make nice with the carpenters. Apologizing wasn't something he did well. Or often. But the place was a mess, and he might need their help someday. No use burning any bridges.

He sighed and yawned.

His hands were on the carriage house door when the gunshot reverberated above his head.

Chapter 2

Something zinged past Annabel.

It cut and ruffled the new growth of hickory leaves beside her shoulder, like a bird soaring through the trees at warp speed. Her head jerked around. Trent was running toward her with his arms airborne, his beige raincoat ballooned behind him like a cape.

He pushed her off the path, then hit the ground sideways. He slid into the underbrush, shoulder first, and roughly pulled her down on top of him.

Another high-pitched crack echoed across the meadow.

Trent's hard body jolted beneath her.

He enveloped her in his arms and rolled her to the side, pressing her head into his broad chest. The musky scent of his aftershave mingled with the pungent tang of dried weeds and earth sent her senses into overload. The weight of his muscular thighs pushing against her equally muscular thighs sent a shudder pulsing through her. "It's okay," he whispered. "I've got you."

They lay motionless in the tall warm grass, side by side, for what seemed an eternity. Until the only sounds she could hear were the soft, protesting whir of insects and the rapid, steady thumping of his heart.

Annabel lifted her head and stared at the line of dark stubble along his chin. "What the hell was that?"

"Probably a poacher."

"A poacher? Are you serious? *Here?*"

He loosened his grip on her shoulders. "The forest across the road belongs to the inn. There's no fence. All we can do is post *No Hunting* signs and hope for the best."

"So, how do your guests feel about dodging bullets? I bet this place stays packed."

"As far as I know, this is the first time it's happened."

"Then how do you know it's a poacher?"

He untangled his legs from hers and rolled her off him. "I don't. But I'd rather believe that than believe someone's taking potshots at me."

He helped her to her feet then scanned the mountainside behind them, cool as you please. Her heart was racing, her mouth as dry as the black soil he dusted off his sleeve.

She pointed to the cell phone dangling from a metal clip on his belt loop. "Aren't you going to call someone?"

"Who?"

"Oh, gee, I don't know. Maybe—the *police*?"

"It wouldn't do any good. Any self-respecting poacher would be long gone by now."

She took a step and wobbled.

"What's wrong? You're limping. Did I hurt you?"

"No, it's just an old war injury." She took a deep breath and tried to ignore the pain radiating through her hip.

He glanced at her bare feet. "Let's cut through the sundial garden. It's a little further, but the path is sloped, and there aren't as many rocks."

"What if someone is waiting for us to come out in the open?" She stared at him. "You don't even look upset. Someone just shot at us. Doesn't that bother you at all?"

"Of course it bothers me. I plan to look into it

when we get back. And the sooner we begin walking...."

"Okay, okay."

She kept one eye on the hill across the road and started down the path, navigating the dips and turns like a drunken mountain goat. She'd been lucky. The tumble in the grass hadn't seemed to make her hip any worse. After two months of excruciating therapy, the pain had dwindled to a dull, steady throb. By the time they reached the inn's office, she was barely limping.

He motioned for her to sit in one of the wingback chairs. "Keisha keeps a stash of water behind the desk. Something about keeping her system flushed."

He crossed to the front desk and knelt down. The muscles in the thighs she'd felt rub against her less than fifteen minutes ago strained against his khaki pants. They were strong but normal, not grotesquely distended like every male dancer she knew.

She reached for a Sheffield Inn brochure lying on his desk, glanced at it, then flipped it over. Trent and Gil had been posed beside the grand staircase in the lobby, arms looped in a casual, brotherly embrace. Gil's expression was smiling and open. Trent looked like he wanted to break the photographer's jaw.

"Here." He handed her a bottle of water. "It's the least I can do after throwing you to the ground like a linebacker."

"What? No vodka tonic?"

"I'll send one up after dinner." He hung his raincoat on a hook behind the door. "Or maybe you'd rather have a pink squirrel?"

She laughed. "Now, about that poacher. Are you—"

"Hey, man, you're back!" Gil stood in the doorway, wiping his hands on his black apron. "I see you've met Miss Annabel. She's gonna save this old mausoleum from rack and ruin."

Trent crossed his arms over his chest and stood with his feet wide apart, scowling.

"When did you get here?" Gil asked.

"Half an hour ago," Trent said. "But you know that already."

"How was your trip?"

"Fine. How was hiding in the pantry?"

"I didn't—"

"Keisha said you ducked out the service entrance when she told you I was here, then locked yourself in the pantry. Don't deny it. She saw you."

"Well, so much for Keisha's raise. How was Jersey? Did you find your dear old dad?"

"Not yet. But I found the supper club. Clever of you to hide it in the carriage house."

Gil grinned sheepishly. "Sorry, Trent. I'd forgotten how much you hate surprises."

Annabel stood and moved to the door. "You know, I should go. I have a zillion things to do—pack my clothes, pick the splinters out of my feet, wash the gunpowder residue out of my hair. So, you guys enjoy the day. I know I will." She toasted them with her water bottle, then pulled the door closed and left.

****

"What's she talking about?" Gil asked.

"Someone fired a gun at us from Sourwood Hill."

"Jesus, Trent. Did you call the police?"

"I want to check with Selena first. Make sure that nephew of hers isn't hiding in the woods again when he's supposed to be in school."

"Yeah, well good luck finding out anything about Eli. He is one sneaky brat."

"Sneaky seems to be the order of the day." Trent tried to keep the anger out of his voice. "Dammit, Gil. What the devil were you thinking? I thought we agreed I would run the business, and you would—"

"—manage the creative part. That's what I'm doing."

"By throwing our hard-earned money down the toilet?"

"Pipe down. I didn't use our money."

"The hell you didn't."

"You know, if your voice was a little higher, and a lot more shrill, you'd sound just like Aunt Margaret right before the flying monkeys landed on her windowsill."

"How long has this plan to turn the carriage house into a club been in the works? Since the day you found out I was going to New Jersey?"

"Kind of."

"You've got some nerve, little brother. Do you ever listen to a word I say?"

"Of course I do."

"Then why did you call Ruth Donovan and ask her to send a dancer down here? I told you I was through with the life I left behind in New York. And I don't want a living, breathing reminder of it shimmying up and down one of my ladders."

Trent knew he should temper the things he said, but he couldn't help it. He could see Gil's defenses gathering strength like an activated force field. If Trent was going to get through this argument without battle scars, he would have to tread lightly. "A supper club, Gil? You're building a supper club? Not a techno club, or a hip hop club, or a pub club?"

"That's right."

"*Have you lost your friggin' mind?*" So much for treading lightly.

"Look, I've studied all the angles. Asheville's got some great jazz bars, but nothing like this. We'd be tapping into a new market. With a swanky little retro supper club attached to the inn, we'd be right up there with the big boys. We'd finally get the kind of classy clientele who stay at expensive hotels like the Grove Park Inn. We'd be more affordable—sort of Grove Park Lite. And yeah, we're low on funds, but—"

"You got that right."

"We're lucky to have Annabel. Ruth could have sent one of those artsy-fartsy performers like our mother used to run with, but Annabel isn't like that. She's down to earth. Real."

"Just like Quinn was real?"

Gil opened his mouth to fire back a reply, then closed it. The pain that filled his eyes cut Trent to the quick.

"Sorry," Trent said. "You were engaged to marry the girl. I was out of line."

Trent sat in the swivel chair and rested his elbows on the desk. He rubbed his burning eyes with the heels of his hands until tiny lines and circles pulsated behind his eyelids. It had been weeks since he or Gil had mentioned Quinn. But it was always there between them, lying just below the surface, threatening to bubble up like molten rock to singe the soles off their shoes.

"Gil, we can't do this. I'll admit your idea has merit, but we can't pour money into a project this huge. One wrong move and we could lose this place. Is that what you want?"

"When are you gonna stop treating me like I'm a twelve-year-old with the IQ of a dead plant? Aren't you ever gonna trust me? I know I can make this work."

"By risking everything we have? The inn is finally starting to get a reputation we can be proud of. Things have started to pick up. But we have to be careful."

"What about you? You spend our money on trips looking for your father."

"Don't throw that up to me. I travel by bus. I stay in cheap motels. I live on peanut butter and diet soda. If I find my father, our financial problems could be over. Be sensible."

"Sensible is your middle name, isn't it? Well, that's fine. *Be* sensible. But we both know you owe me this chance."

"Here it comes."

"Eight months ago, I gave you all the money I had in the world. All the money I'd been saving since I was seventeen. I just handed it over, no questions asked."

"I know you did, and I'll pay you back."

"I'm not asking for it back. I'm asking for a say in what goes on around here. We own this inn equally. I may be ten years younger than you, but I deserve a chance to prove myself."

"Just tell me one thing. Of all the crazy schemes you could've come up with, why this? Why a supper club?"

Gil blinked at him. "Because I promised Quinn. She said if I built her a place to dance, she would stay here. With me. Forever. And even though she's gone, I'm keeping my word to her."

Trent sighed. "Okay. Fair enough."

Trent's heart ached for his brother. He wondered if he would ever be able to stop feeling like a parent toward him. He looked at the kid and smiled. Gil didn't look much different than he had the morning they'd woken up and discovered their mother had left in the night without saying goodbye. He'd protected Gil for so long, it was second nature. But the kid wasn't a kid anymore. He was a grown man. A man who had barely survived a broken heart and had been so depressed, Trent worried he might never bounce back. This supper club thing, impractical as it was, had sparked the first sign of life in Gil since Quinn's death.

"All right," Trent said. "You have the right to make some decisions where the inn is concerned.

Your timing is lousy. But you have the right. You want a chance to prove yourself? Then go ahead."

Gil pulled Trent into a bear hug. "Thanks, Trent. I mean it." He stepped back. "And you'd better be nice to Annabel. She doesn't know your history. She doesn't know how much you detest theater people, and probably wouldn't understand if she did."

Trent nodded, then forced himself to smile.

The kid had a terrible temper, always had. But he was sharper than Trent gave him credit for. And more compassionate. His little brother was turning into the kind of man Trent could, on a good day, like and respect. Maybe he hadn't done such a bad job raising him after all.

Chapter 3

"I tried to call your cell," Byron said. "But I can't get through."

"My phone died," Annabel said. "It fell in the toilet when I was packing, and I haven't had time to shop for another one. God, what next? I can't seem to catch a break." She switched the phone to her other ear and rolled onto her back. "Sorry. You know, if Quinn were here, she'd ask me if I wanted some cheese with that whine."

"Well, hell, darling. *I* can do that!" He laughed. "So, how are things in Hooterville? Found Quinn's murderer yet?"

"No, but it looks like I'm going to have to find another job. Seems the Sheffield Inn's budget can't quite fit me in."

"Then get on a plane and come back to New York."

"You know I can't. Not until I'm satisfied there's nothing to discover about her death."

"Sweetheart, why are you doing this? Quinn's dead. What's it going to matter?"

"We've been through this a hundred times."

Byron sighed. "Okay, okay. But I hate the thought of you there all alone. I'm getting some time off. Maybe I can come down and help you interrogate the locals."

"What do you mean time off? From *Moondance*?"

"They're closing the show temporarily to work on the big expansion. After all those weeks of rumors, we finally got the news last night. *Moondance* is moving to Broadway."

"Oh, Byron, that's wonderful," she said, and tried to mean it. A lump lodged in her throat. A jealous, resentful lump. The kind Aunt Lou always said would eventually strangle her.

"If your hip heals in time, you can rejoin the show."

"Sure. Maybe."

"I'm worried about you. Ditching physical therapy the second Ruth calls, agreeing to take a job at that ramshackle old inn just because Quinn used to go there. You're not being rational."

"*Sheffield* was one of the last words Quinn said. It has to mean something. And the inn is not ramshackle, it's...charming. Ruth did me a favor setting me up with this job."

"Maybe. But I'd be careful accepting favors from a woman like Ruth Donovan. It's like eating meat. It's nourishing and tasty as long as you don't spend too much time thinking about where it came from."

Annabel laughed. Byron always put everything in perspective. For the last two months, his friendship had kept her sane, and he was as dear to her as a brother. Annabel's own brother didn't care that she'd never dance professionally again. Drew Maitland lived in another world. The real world, according to him. He was more concerned with the price of cattle, and getting the foals ready for the summer horse auction, and calculating how many jars of pickled okra his wife Linda could sell in a year. And now, with the new baby due in July, Annabel doubted if he ever thought of her at all.

"So, how's the hip?" Byron asked.

"Not bad," she lied, stretching her right leg into the air, pointing her toe toward the ceiling. After the long walk back from the carriage house, she had tried to relax, but her body felt old and out of shape.

The flat stomach and the strong, taut muscles in her arms had softened into curves. Her calves no longer bulged when she wore her Capezzio dance shoes. In eight weeks she had gone straight to seed. She hardly recognized herself.

"Well, you'd better take care of yourself if you want to be strong enough to dance in Freeman Saunders' new piece. His assistant showed me a rough step sheet, and it's extraordinary. Best thing he's ever done. You haven't heard from him have you?"

"Who? Freeman?"

"He's supposed to decide soon whether the lead will be a man or a woman. You know it's come down to the two of us, don't you?"

"Which one will you play, the man or the woman?"

"Very funny. I don't mind if he chooses you. I'm flattered to even be in the running. I love my little number in *Moondance*, but I would do *anything* to dance the lead in one of his shows. Do you know how lucky you are?"

Pride kept Annabel from saying anything. It was foolish to hang onto the illusion she might actually resume her old life someday. There was plenty of time to tell Byron and Freeman Saunders she would never dance in anybody's musical again, no matter how extraordinary it was.

"I heard something about Quinn today," Byron said. "Did you know that right before she took over Rachel's part in *Moondance,* she was engaged to a man who owned a hotel?"

"No, I didn't. We shared a dressing room, but Quinn didn't really confide in me."

"Well, she did say the word *Sheffield* before she croaked. Do you think he might own the place you're staying at? I may have actually met the poor guy at a rehearsal once—tall and dark and very hunky. He had these strange eyes that looked right through me. Quinn didn't introduce me, of course. She was probably afraid I'd take him away from her." He paused. "That was a joke, Annabel. I don't hear you laughing."

The man's description sounded like Trent Sheffield. Had Quinn been engaged to Trent? It made sense. Trent was exactly the type Quinn would have gone for—handsome, polished, educated. But aside from Quinn's physical attributes, which were legendary, why would a man like Trent Sheffield fall for her? Quinn was beautiful but abrasive, as rough around the edges as Trent seemed refined. Maybe rough around the edges was what he liked. Maybe that's what floated his boat up the river and back. Besides chemistry, and the capricious pairing of pheromones, who ever really knew why one person was drawn to another?

Four rapid-fire knocks on the door made her jump.

"Miss Maitland? Are you in there?"

"Gotta go, Byron. My pink slip is here." She looked around for her glasses and cursed softly. They were never where she thought she put them.

"Annabel? It's Trent Sheffield. Can I talk to you?"

"Just a minute." She found the glasses dangling from the towel rack in the bathroom and pushed them on her head. She thought about changing out of the inn's complementary bathrobe, but decided not to bother. She would be out of there soon enough. She flipped the lock and swung the door open. "Hi. Have you found the poacher yet?"

"No, but Keisha's on it."

"Keisha, the desk clerk?"

"If you're gonna work here, never underestimate Keisha Releford. I learned that a long time ago."

"Am I working here? I thought you fired me."

She looked into eyes that were as clear and deep as winter pond water, framed with a fringe of jet black lashes she would have given her right arm for, and smiled. He smiled back, a kind of sweet, lopsided smile that flashed the dimpled crease on the left side of his face and caused her to go a little weak in the knees. She pulled the terrycloth belt tighter.

"I've changed my mind about the supper club," he said.

"You're kidding." She dropped onto an antique velvet chair. The worn metal springs twanged softly. "I'm surprised. You don't seem like the kind of guy who changes his mind."

"I'm not—I don't. Unless I have a good reason."

"Like a deep, abiding passion for torch songs and tap numbers?"

His dimples deepened. Late afternoon sunlight spilled through the blinds, streaked across the front of his white shirt like burnished gold. "I won't lie to you, Annabel. I think this idea of Gil's spells financial suicide."

"Then why are you going ahead with it?"

"Gil can be very...determined."

"Family trait?"

"You could say that. We're both stubborn. We've had our share of head-butting sessions."

"I know what you mean. If your relationship with Gil is anything like the one I have with my brother, you can't decide whether to hug him or throw a hubcap at his head."

"I know he has the inn's best interest at heart, but he...he's—" Trent's gaze landed on the front of her robe, then quickly shifted to the wall behind her.

Annabel glanced down. Her robe was falling open. Not exactly the end of the world for someone used to dancing in fishnet stockings and a satin bra, but still.

She pulled it closed and re-secured the belt, then tried to pretend she hadn't caught him staring at her chest with his mouth open. Her chest was hardly concave, but she'd spent most of her adult life feeling inadequate in the headlight department. Since forking over two or three paychecks for plastic surgery had become the norm in the dance world—and every other world—it wasn't easy being one of the last breast augmentation holdouts in a dance company full of perky 38-C's. She'd looked like a boy next to Quinn, although she knew the male dancers in *Moondance* appreciated the fact they could triple spin her without getting their noses mashed with silicone.

She leveled her gaze at him. "You were saying?"

"Gil is in charge, but I'm not letting this thing spin out of control. I want the costs held down." He stopped and took a breath. "Which brings me to the rules."

"The rules?" The bulky terrycloth lapel slid off to the side.

****

Trent's gaze shot to her bare shoulder.

"There...there are ground rules," he said. "And I expect them to be followed."

"Such as?"

Annabel crossed and uncrossed her legs. Her slender ankles swept to the side in one fluid motion.

Christ, her legs were long.

The image of them wrapped around his waist blazed across Trent's mind for an instant, and in spite of everything, he felt that old familiar tightening in his groin. She'd seen him eyeballing her legs like a hungry mountain lion. Those big gray—or were they blue? Those big eyes of hers didn't miss a thing.

"The rules?" she prompted.

"Right. The rules." He swallowed the sudden

knot in his throat. "I don't want the dancers or musicians near the guests. Gil says they'll be living in the staff cabins, but I don't want them in the main lobby, or the Laurel Room, or in the kitchen begging food off Mrs. Rosetti. And I don't want them hanging around the bar or the pool before ten p.m."

"Do you want me to put little bells around their necks so you can hear them coming?"

"I'm serious, Annabel. This is non-negotiable. If you don't like it, then—"

"No! No, it's fine. I'll get my stuff moved down there tonight."

"I didn't mean *you* had to go."

"It'll be a little hard for me to avoid the lobby if I don't. Unless you're planning to put a ladder outside my window."

"This isn't a joke. There have to be rules. You know that." Gil had said for him to be nice, and he was acting like a pompous ass. He took a slow, silent breath and tried not to stare at her skin. It was luminous and smooth, and so transparent, a hint of blue crisscrossed the ridge near her collarbone. How could anyone pull off luminous in broad daylight?

He cleared his throat. "I let the staff stay in the old bungalows down by the lake so they won't have to drive the mountains at night to get home. The cabins are nice enough, and the college kids can't really hurt anything." He glanced at the fragile Queen Anne desk, the canopy bed festooned with ecru lace. "Not like here."

"I understand." She straightened her back, elongated her graceful neck, and gave the robe an impatient little yank. Then she blinked at him with her silver eyes until he had to look away.

"Keisha said one of the busboys wants to audition for your show. I told her I'd tell you."

"That's great," she said. "If I can find the dancers we need without putting an audition notice in the paper, it will save money."

"How many dancers are we talking about?"

"Three is the absolute minimum—two women and one man. I'd really planned on using five or six, but—"

"Three will be fine."

Annabel stood and gave the robe another tug, closing the gap for the umpteenth time. She looked at the robe, then looked back at Trent. They both began to laugh. "One-size-fits-all, huh?"

"That's what the packing slip said."

"Yeah, well, I hope you got a discount."

"Look," he said warmly. "I wish you'd stay here at the inn. In this beautiful room. It suits you."

"We just met. How do you know what suits me?"

Why was she being so stubborn? The Rose Room was his proudest accomplishment so far. It had taken him weeks to restore it. Hadn't she noticed how smooth the plaster ceiling was? How great the crown molding looked? He'd smashed his thumb twice putting that stuff up.

Trent stepped back. Oh, man. What was he doing? Worrying that a woman he barely knew wasn't creaming over his crown molding? He was officially losing it.

He needed to get a grip. And fast.

"Trent!" Gil shouted, rapping on the door. "Trent, you in there? Annabel?"

Trent opened the door, and Gil burst in. Annabel held her robe lapels in a vise grip.

"The news ain't good," Gil said. "Mrs. Wolcott is making a scene in the lobby."

Trent felt the tension bunch in his neck. "Quinn's mother is here? Are you sure?"

"Oh, yeah," Gil said. "She's here. And she says she's not leaving until she sees Annabel Maitland—the girl who killed her daughter."

Chapter 4

"*That's her!*"

Quinn's mother stood at the bottom of the stairs, pointing a crooked finger at Annabel as if she were picking a rapist out of a police lineup.

Annabel had only seen Mrs. Wolcott once. Most of the images from the days following Quinn's death were wrapped in the blessed fog of painkillers and shock. But the memory of Phyllis Wolcott's stunned, tear-streaked face as she stood in the alley behind the theater, clutching her daughter's white wool coat to her chest, had stayed sharp and relentlessly clear.

Mrs. Wolcott closed her eyes and clasped her hands to her chest. "*Thank you, Je-sus.*" Her voice quavered. "*Wash away her sins, Lord. Save her wicked soul from eternal damnation.*" She rocked her body back and forth. Strands of reddish gray hair flew about her face. "*Save her, Almighty God. This girl's a sinner!*"

A crowd had begun to gather.

"Mrs. Wolcott," Trent said quietly. "Why don't we step into my office where it's private."

A spark of recognition flickered in Mrs. Wolcott's eyes. She leaned on her wooden cane and let Trent guide her across the lobby. Annabel and Gil followed. The last thing Annabel saw before Gil closed the door was Keisha standing behind the brochure rack, rolling her eyes.

Mrs. Wolcott lowered herself into the wing chair beside the desk and folded her large weathered hands in her lap. The double row of black buttons straining across her large stomach threatened to pop off her skirt one by one and ricochet around the room.

The only noticeable resemblance between Mrs. Wolcott and Quinn were their eyes; round, slightly slanted, and the same pale shade of green. Some obscure likeness must have linked them forever as mother and daughter, but Annabel couldn't see it. Quinn was never the tallest dancer in the company, but she must have towered over her mother, a stocky, solid woman who waddled when she walked. Quinn had never waddled in her life. Quinn's slender frame had moved across the stage like quicksilver, her nimble feet barely touching the ground.

"Now, Phyllis," Trent said gently. "Why don't you tell us what this is all about."

"Last night, I heard that Annabel Maitland was here. She's Quinn's friend, the girl what killed her."

Trent's eyes darted to Annabel.

Mrs. Wolcott patted her chest as if she were five seconds away from cardiac arrest. She stretched her arms to the ceiling. "*Blessed Jesus! Praise His holy name!*" She grabbed Annabel's hand and crimped it between her pudgy fingers. "You listen to me, girl. I'm gonna redeem your soul for what you done. You sent my Quinn's soul to glory, and it's my holy obligation to release yours into the Father's loving arms."

Annabel jerked her hand away.

Mrs. Wolcott stared into space. Her eyes glowed hot and feverish. She looked like Carrie White's mother from the Stephen King movie when Carrie finally spilled the beans about going to the prom.

"I'm sorry for your loss," Annabel said. "But my soul doesn't need releasing right now."

Mrs. Wolcott began to cry. "Stop dancing, I told

her. Stop whoring with every man you meet. The fires of hell will devour you and there'll be no turning back." She swayed from side to side. "My Quinn is dead because of *you*."

Panic rose in Annabel's throat. She looked at Trent, then back to Gil. "She's wrong. I would never have hurt Quinn. Quinn was my friend."

Mrs. Wolcott held onto the desk and pulled her bulky frame up until she was standing. Her gaze, suddenly clear and razor-sharp, zeroed in on Annabel's face. "You sent her to Jesus. You gave her them pills that killed her, so don't go adding deceitfulness to your other sins. The Lord will forgive you, but first you have to—"

"Mama?" The office door clicked open. A young woman with long brown hair and a worn-out version of Quinn's face stood in the doorway. She was on the plump side, softer and curvier than Quinn, carrying the extra thirty pounds Quinn was always afraid she would gain.

"Come on in, Selena," Gil said.

"You're causing trouble again, aren't you, Mama?" Selena crossed the room and placed a hand on her mother's shoulder. Selena looked at Trent. A faint tinge of color swept across her face. "I'm sorry, Trent. I swear, I didn't know she was going to do this. Ham's wife goes to Mama's church. She told her about Annabel being here, and it got her all upset. I didn't think she'd actually come over here and make a scene."

"It's all right," Trent said.

"We can't seem to keep her at home. She's always running off somewhere. How'd you get here, Mama? Did you call another taxi? Did Miss Ellen bring you?"

Mrs. Wolcott nodded. Her gaze, distant and fuzzy again, drifted to a spot on the corner of Trent's desk.

"You must be Annabel," Selena said, smiling at her. "I saw you in *Moondance* when it was in previews. You were wonderful, especially at the end. I cried like a baby."

"She's another sinner!" Mrs. Wolcott spat.

"Now, Mama," Selena said calmly. "Everyone is different. If we all believed the same thing, the world would be a pretty boring place, now, wouldn't it?"

Mrs. Wolcott glared at her daughter. "Someday, you'll find out just how boring fire and brimstone can be."

"Yes, well," Selena said. She smoothed her baggy blue corduroy jumper. Her thin ponytail, pulled straight back from her round face, hung down her back like a frayed rope. "Where's your cane, Mama? Let's find your cane so I can take you home."

"I'll do it," Gil said. "You go on back to work." He squatted beside Mrs. Wolcott's chair. "You'll let me drive you home, won't you, Mrs. Wolcott?"

"My baby's dead, Gil. My little girl's gone to heaven."

The stricken look on Gil's face made Annabel want to cry. Gil squared his shoulders, then handed Mrs. Wolcott her cane and slowly led her out.

Selena's eyes seemed to come alive when she looked at Trent. "I'm sorry about Eli shooting the gun this morning."

"That was Eli up on Sourwood Hill?" Trent asked.

"He was positive you'd seen him. The school called me at the bank and said he'd skipped class again. Seems he decided to borrow Mama's old Winchester and go hunting in your woods. You said he could hike up there anytime he wanted."

"I said *hike*, not shoot at anything that moves."

Selena shook her head. "I know. I swear, if Sarah doesn't get back from Atlanta soon, I don't know what I'm gonna do with that boy."

"He's a handful," Trent said.

"Don't worry," Selena said. "I made him swear to stay off your property. And it'll be easier to enforce now that I've hidden the car keys until his mother gets home."

"Good for you," Trent said.

Selena turned to Annabel. "You know, I'd really like to get together sometime to reminisce about Quinn. It's...well...I'm just never with anyone who really knew her."

"I didn't know her well," Annabel said. "But I do have a few stories."

"I'll bet you do," Trent said.

"Mama has Bible study Saturday night. Can I come by the inn about seven? We could have a drink in the bar."

"Great," Annabel said. "I look forward to it."

"Taking care of Mama is a fulltime job. I only get Saturday nights and Sunday afternoons off. I'd like to hire someone, but Mama won't hear of it." She glanced at Trent. "So, I guess I'll be going." The desperate smile she flashed his way before she left seemed to bounce off him. *Was the man blind?* Annabel wondered. *Or was he just pretending to be?*

Annabel started for the door.

"Not so fast," Trent said. He reached over her shoulder and pushed the door closed. "Okay, Miss Annabel Maitland. I want to know exactly why you're here. And this time, I want the truth."

****

Trent couldn't help feeling a little pleased that Annabel's face had gone ashen. Of course she was friends with Quinn. He should have figured that one out the second he'd met her.

"I told you the truth," Annabel said. "I came to choreograph the floorshow and teach a group of seniors how to do the rumba without screwing up their hip replacements."

"Ruth Donovan sent you down here to spy on me, didn't she?"

"That's ridiculous. I'm here because I needed a job."

"Couldn't she find you one in New York?"

"That's beside the point. But no, she probably couldn't. I'm not exactly on the A-list anymore."

He should have trusted his instincts. The moment he'd found out she was a dancer, his gut should have told him she was hiding something. Women like her were always hiding something. Whether it was the amount of chocolate they wolfed down when no one else was in the room, or the offhand way they lied about where they spent the weekend. Annabel Maitland was no different from any of them.

"Why didn't you tell me you knew Quinn?"

Her gray eyes blazed at him. "I told Gil I knew Quinn the first day I got here, within the first five minutes. He didn't have a problem with it. Why does it bother you?"

"Bother me? It infuriates me. I should have known you had a hidden agenda the minute I found out Ruth set this up."

"Ruth Donovan is a formidable force in the dance world. She has the connections to make or break careers. I'd be crazy to turn down a job offer from her no matter where it was."

"So you took this piddling little job in the backwoods of North Carolina to further your dancing career? Oh, Lady, I don't think so." She crossed her arms over her chest and blinked at him. "I want to know why you're here. And don't pretend that the fact you were friends with my brother's dead fiancée doesn't enter into it at all."

"*Gil?* Quinn was engaged to Gil?"

"You sound surprised. How long had you and Quinn been friends?"

"Not long. We met at auditions for *Moondance*. She started out as a swing."

"A swing?"

"A dancer in the company who's prepared to take over another dancer's part in case they can't go on. Like an understudy."

"But you knew Quinn was engaged, didn't you?"

"Not until today. I just assumed—I mean, I thought it was you."

"Gil was engaged to Quinn until she broke it off last December." He tried to ignore her eyes following his every move, judging every word, making him wish he could trust her.

"I'm sorry," she said. "I should have known it was Gil. He's the one grieving for her."

She failed to add *and you're not*, but Trent knew she was thinking it.

"Why did they break up?" she asked.

He laughed harshly. "You come right to the point, don't you?"

"Saves time."

He sat on the edge of the desk and ran his hand back though his hair. "Gil and Quinn were very different. But Gil worshipped her, and Quinn loved to be worshipped."

"How long were they engaged?"

"A couple of months. After Quinn called it quits, I don't think Gil ever stopped hoping they'd get back together. When she died, he took it pretty hard. For a while, I was worried he might do something stupid, like try to join her."

Pretty hard was an understatement. Gil had gone on a four day bender. He'd kicked in the kitchen door, broken two cabinets full of dishes, and taken a sledgehammer to the new retaining wall before disappearing without a word. Two days later, Keisha found him passed out in the alley behind Bernie's Bar. If she hadn't hoisted him over her shoulder and carried him to her car, he would have drowned in his own vomit.

Annabel curled her fingers around the back of the chair. "So, why do you think Ruth Donovan hired me to spy on you? Why would she do something like that?"

"Because she despises me. She'd love to ruin me, and what better way than to sneak someone into the inn to dig up a little dirt. I know Gil called her, but Ruth's never been one to let an opportunity pass her by. The inn is my Achilles heel. She knows how much it means to me."

"Well, I hate to ask the obvious. But why does she hate you?"

Trent walked to the arched window and looked out at the slate gray sky. The wind had picked up. A ring of mist had wrapped itself around the middle of Peg Leg Mountain.

He turned back to Annabel. "A long time ago, when I lived in New York, Quinn and I dated for a short while. It got pretty serious. At least, I thought it did. And then, it ended badly. Ruth knew I would do whatever it took to keep Gil from making the same mistake. And she was right." He picked up a brochure and set it back down again. "So, if you're not here to spy for Ruth, why are you here?"

"Because I owe Quinn."

He looked at her with renewed interest, then immediately got lost in her eyes. He'd thought he was strong enough to keep a cool distance, but he found himself drowning in them. He cleared his throat and tore his gaze from her face. Wouldn't it be nice if the simple act of looking into someone's eyes could grant him the ability to distinguish integrity from lies? What a miracle that would be. But so far, he'd never been able to separate fact from fiction where the women in his life were concerned.

She looked upset. He wasn't equipped to handle

upset.

She wrapped her arms around her waist and pressed her full, perfectly shaped lips together to keep them from trembling. Tears pooled in her lower lids. Brownish blond hair flew around her face like wisps of twisted silk. The unyielding set of her jaw told him she would rather die than cry in front of anyone. Especially him.

Oh, God, she was getting to him. And he couldn't let her know it. Because once a woman knew she'd crawled under a man's skin, she thought she could make him do anything she wanted. And pretty soon, before the poor guy knew what lightning bolt had hit him, she started wanting things he just didn't want to give her.

"You don't owe Quinn anything," he said gently. "Quinn is dead."

Annabel shook her head vehemently. "Doesn't matter."

"Honey." *Did he just call her honey?* "Quinn always made sure the people around her stayed obligated to her. She kept a running tab. That's how she controlled them. But she's gone. And I think you should consider yourself very lucky to be off the hook. I'm sure you're not the only one she exacted a promise from."

"Maybe not. But I was the last one."

"What do you mean?"

"Quinn begged me find out the truth if anything happened to her. I promised her I would, and two minutes later she died." Her eyes searched his. "Could you ignore a request like that? Could anyone?"

"So, that's why you're here? To play girl detective for Quinn? Carry out her last wish?"

"My Aunt Lou has a plaque in her kitchen that says, *Search for the truth, Look for the good, Hope for the best.*"

"And that's your philosophy? What you live by?"

"Well...yes."

He sat in the swivel chair and leaned back. "Look, I admire your loyalty, but you're wasting your time here. It's April. Quinn hasn't stayed at the inn since December. Most of the seasonal staff is new. I doubt if anyone remembers her except for Keisha, and maybe Donald, the night clerk.

"As for Quinn's family—well, you've seen two of them. Phyllis is a delusional, Bible-thumping fanatic who sailed right over the edge the day her daughter died. And Selena, the sanest of the lot, is a senior loan officer with the largest bank in North Carolina. She takes care of her crazy mother, a sister who can't keep a job more than three days, and a surly fifteen-year-old nephew I wouldn't trust with a dog I liked. Are you going to question them too?"

"I had planned to, yes."

"I realize that the Wolcott clan is, for the most part, certifiable, but they just lost someone they loved." He softened his tone. "If you want to find out what happened to Quinn, then go back to New York. Question the people in that play—*Moondance*. Like that girl who jumped onto Quinn's platform and tried to save her. Did you talk to her?"

"That was me."

He stared at her. "Oh, Christ," he whispered.

"Mrs. Wolcott was right about the pills. I saved Quinn from falling, but she died from anaphylactic shock. From an allergic reaction to codeine."

"You gave Quinn codeine?"

"Not on purpose. We thought we were taking an over-the-counter, aspirin free pain reliever called Curenol. The pills in Quinn's bottle looked like regular strength tablets, but someone had switched them with Curenol-C, one of the strongest acetaminophen/codeine tablets they make. We took four each."

The haunted expression in her eyes pulled at his heart, made him want to shut the hell up and let it go. But for Gil's sake, he had to find out what happened to Quinn from someone who was there. Then, if he had to temper the truth, he'd do it to save his brother from more heartbreak. "Why did you take so many pills?"

"Quinn had had a headache for two days, ever since the dressing rooms were painted. I have chronic muscle pain. Anti-inflammatory medicine bothers my stomach, so during the show I try to get by on ibuprofen. I would have taken it that night, but my ibuprofen bottle was missing."

"Didn't that seem odd?"

"I just thought someone had borrowed it and forgotten to bring it back. If you dance eight shows a week, sooner or later you're going to get hurt—pull a muscle, micro-tear a ligament, sprain an ankle. And most of the time, you just keep dancing. Ibuprofen is usually the drug of choice, but if you need something stronger, it's always available. Quinn had serious allergies. Curenol was one of the few things she could take."

"And Quinn was never one to suffer in silence," he said. "If her head was hurting for two days, I'm sure everyone knew it. Maybe whoever filled Quinn's bottle with the codeine Curenol figured she'd need them sooner or later for her headache. And they got rid of your ibuprofen to make sure she didn't take it instead. Not a bad plan. Who do you think did it?"

"Well that's the big question, isn't it? No one except the cast is allowed backstage after the stage manager calls half-hour. It's a small theater, security is a little lax, but an outsider couldn't navigate the halls without being noticed. Before warm-ups, everyone's door is open. People are in and out of each other's dressing rooms. It's chaos. It's normal."

"Maybe someone used that normal chaos as a cover."

"Maybe."

He loved watching her. One minute she looked as unsure as a newborn colt, the next strong enough to take on an army. "I don't want to upset you," he said. "But has it ever occurred to you that you might have been the target instead of Quinn?"

"I'm not allergic to codeine."

"How much did you take that night?"

"Each tablet contained 60 mil, so 240 milligrams."

Trent whistled through his teeth. "And what did that do to you?"

"At first it made me dizzy, then I got sick and broke out in a cold sweat. They said if it hadn't been for the adrenaline rush, I would have blacked out." She walked to the window and looked out. "Do you really think someone didn't want me to dance that night, and Quinn got caught in the crossfire? I've considered I may have been the target—I'd be stupid not to—but I can't seem to wrap my brain around it."

"I think it's a possibility you shouldn't rule out." She sat on the edge of the wide windowsill and held onto the curved edge with both hands. "So, you're the girl who jumped on Quinn's platform and pulled her away from the edge while the other dancers stood and watched? That was very brave."

"Yep," she said faintly. "But what good did it do? She died anyway."

The rain that had held off all afternoon began to fall in torrential sheets. Wind slammed against the side of the building, pounded the shutters Gil had promised to secure, and rattled the loose glass in the windowpanes until it shook.

Forks of lightning streaked across the sky, followed by a deafening crash of thunder. Trent jumped to his feet the same moment Annabel catapulted off the windowsill. And by some miraculous glitch in the universe, he caught her in his arms.

She landed against him with a soft thud, and as the seconds ticked by, her head instinctively nestled into the crook of his neck. He could feel her shoulders tremble, which for some reason, filled him with an astonishing urge to protect her. Her hands clutched the muscles in his upper arms, and her head rested beneath his chin. Her short, loose curls tickled his nose. Her hair smelled like Charleston in the spring—jasmine and honeysuckle and sunshine.

He stood, holding her like an idiot, stone still, afraid that if he moved a centimeter in either direction, she would take it as a cue to extricate herself. And he didn't want her to leave.

"Sorry about that," she said. "Not so brave in a storm, I guess."

"No problem," he said, suddenly unable to control the sound of his own voice. "I'm just as jumpy as you are." His baritone had dropped to a growl. Like an old dog with a bone.

His biceps contracted, heating up beneath her touch, and he wondered if the imprint of her delicate hands would stay branded, long after she had released them.

She looked up and smiled, but still didn't let go. "This is the second time today this has happened—you, me, in a clinch. Do I detect a pattern here?"

He opened his mouth to reply, but nothing came out. He didn't have enough spit left to swallow, much less answer her. His face was inches from hers, her lithe body so close he could feel the toned muscles in her abdomen rise and fall with each silent breath. He couldn't take his eyes off her—the soft curve of her cheek, the half-moon fringe of dark lashes sweeping her smooth, pale skin. He was not a spontaneous man—Quinn could attest to that—and he had always hated being a stuffed shirt, every move carefully thought out and analyzed to the point of being mind-numbing. And yet, here he was, going with the flow, standing as close as he could to the kind of woman he had no business whatsoever being attracted to. And giving in to it. It felt dangerous. Liberating. How many times did he actually do what he wanted when he wanted, without weighing the consequences?

He didn't know who this woman was. He had only known her for half a day. But he was helpless around her—emotionally, physically. He'd never felt that way about Quinn. Ever.

And impulsive. When he was near Annabel Maitland, he felt as if something had knocked him just a little off center and no matter how hard he tried, he couldn't regain his equilibrium. Two scotches and a beer did the same thing.

Without thinking—and God, it was a relief not to think—he lifted one hand and slowly stroked the length of her face with the back of his fingers. She felt like silk. The corners of her mouth curled upward, and he wondered what they would feel like moving against his.

"What are you doing?" she murmured. "Exactly?"

"I'm not sure. I think I wanted to find out if your skin was as soft as it looked."

He heard her quick intake of breath, then the slow exhale, felt it slide across his chin. "And is it?"

"No. It's softer."

She laughed. "I guess sleeping with a vat of Oil of Olay beside my bed has finally paid off." She pulled out of his arms and stepped back, breaking the spell. Her eyes narrowed. "Wait a minute. How did you know the other dancers just stood and watched?"

"Selena told me. She and her mother were at the

theater that night."

"That's right, they were. It was terrible. I heard her mother fell apart when they told her Quinn was dead." She stopped. "You know, Quinn didn't mention anything about them coming to the show. Do you think Quinn knew they were there?"

"I don't know." Trent crossed his arms over his chest and held them tight. They felt cold, empty. He didn't know quite what to do with them. "Selena said her mother balked at the front door and wouldn't go in the theater. Selena stayed with her while they waited in the lobby."

"Well, they didn't have long to wait. Quinn died during the first ten minutes."

A muted thunderclap echoed above Peg Leg Mountain. "Sounds like the storm's moving on." Trent hesitated, then decided to pursue it for Gil's sake. "Can I ask you something?"

"What?"

"You were there when Quinn died. Did she...say anything?"

****

The image of Quinn's last moments flashed behind Annabel's eyes. She swallowed and took a deep breath. She forced the words, when she finally said them, to sound calm and impassive. "Before Quinn died, she said, *Mama, I'm sorry*, then *Selena*, then *Sheffield*. When Ruth called and offered me a job at the Sheffield Inn, fifteen miles from where Quinn's family lived, I took it as a sign I should come here."

"You believe in signs, do you?"

"Yes, don't you?"

"I don't think the universe is that sneaky. Things are either the way they are, or they're not. Yes or no. On or off. Black or white."

"Then how are things?" she asked quietly. "Because I would really like to know."

He raised one dark eyebrow and cocked his head slightly to the left. His eyes regarded her with amusement. His dimples deepened, and she had the distinct impression they weren't talking about Quinn anymore. His clear hazel eyes caught the light, and her heart gave a little lurch. A tingle shot down the back of her neck and across her shoulders where he had touched her. For an instant her gaze dropped to his chest, to the soft mound of muscle beneath his collarbone, to the little indentation in his throat where her cheek had felt the steady, reassuring flicker of his pulse. His lips fascinated her. She could almost feel the air between them crackle.

This is crazy, she thought. He was giving her important information about Quinn, and she was wondering what kind of kisser he was. She glanced at his face and focused on his nose—that was safe enough—and shoved the urge to nestle into his arms again as far away as possible, all the way to the back of her head, and her heart, where it could dissipate on its own among the other hopeless cobwebs.

"I might as well tell you this," he said, leaning back against his desk. "When Quinn said the word *Sheffield*, I don't think she was talking about the inn. I think she was referring to me. That's what she always called me—Sheffield."

"Then I guess that brings us to the next big question, doesn't it?"

"Which is?"

"In the last moments of Quinn's life, before a grand mal seizure stopped her heart forever, was she longing for the people she loved most? Or was she naming murder suspects?"

"Leave it alone, Annabel. Let the dead stay dead. You'll only end up hurting people. You'll hurt Gil, and he's been hurt enough. I can't allow that."

"Don't you think he'd want to know the truth

about Quinn's death? He loved her. If someone I loved died like Quinn, I wouldn't rest until I knew what happened and why."

"Do you know why Gil is so determined to turn the carriage house into a supper club? Because he promised Quinn he would build a place for her to dance, even though Quinn never had the slightest intention of moving back here. Not for Gil, not for anyone. Stirring everything up is only going to prolong his grief. *Please*, Annabel. Leave it alone."

"I can't," she said simply. "I understand you want to protect Gil, and you can fire me again if you want me to leave. But I have to do this. I gave Quinn my word."

Trent put his hands on his hips and stared at the floor. "Dear God, will she ever be completely out of our lives?" He glanced up. "Ironic, isn't it? You and Gil keeping a promise to Quinn Wolcott, when she never kept a promise to anyone in her life?"

"I'm not Quinn."

"I hope not, Lady. Because that's exactly what I'm counting on."

Chapter 5

Trent threw the Saturday paper on his desk and walked to the window. If he stood beside the left sash and squinted, he could see the path leading down to the carriage house. He glanced at his watch. In a few minutes, Annabel would walk by. She usually stopped beside the fence to stretch her leg and rest. He'd never asked about the limp she seemed determined to hide. He figured it was the result of her onstage heroics to save Quinn. He also figured it had something to do with the two month lapse between Quinn's death and her showing up at the inn.

He sat in his swivel chair and waited. Just like he had every morning for the past three days. Every morning at 9:55, he took his mug of coffee into the office, propped his feet on the desk, and pretended to read the paper. He wasn't sure who he thought he was kidding. Not Keisha, anyway. The look she'd shot him over the rim of her sludge-colored power shake told him she was on to him but good. He was pathetic. In three days, he'd become addicted to the rush of warmth that traveled the length of his spine whenever she was near. He'd feel it, savor it, then begin to question it. How could he stay racked with regret while the sight of her lifted him to a place he swore he'd never see again?

The thing was, he liked her. Besides being sexy as all get out, she seemed sweet and smart and guileless, with the kind of personality he'd always wished he could at least fake. She chatted up the wait staff like she'd known them all her life, told off-color jokes to the freezer repairman until the man wept with laughter, and charmed Mrs. Rosetti into force-feeding her chocolate chip cannoli. Except for Gil, Trent had never seen anyone charm Mrs. Rosetti. It was like charming a slab of Italian marble.

Gil was right. Annabel was the real thing.

And it scared the hell out of him.

He needed to apologize to her for accusing her of being in cahoots with Ruth. He should have done it before now, but during the day she spent most of her time helping those two carpenters. And at night, if he wasn't holed up in his office, or taking a quick turn through the Laurel Room, he was sitting on the side of his bed with his head in his hands, wondering what was wrong with him.

"Trent?" Gil strode into the room and plopped into a chair. Gil could never stay still. Even as a kid, he'd always been in motion, jiggling his foot, drumming on his knee, tapping out some secret rhythm only he could hear.

"You're up early," Trent said. "Going for a run?"

"In a minute."

Trent leaned back. "You didn't come in here to stretch your hamstrings. What gives?"

"I'm worried. Annabel's been asking questions about Quinn."

Trent shrugged. "So what? They were friends. She knows Quinn stayed here. Maybe she wants to talk to someone who knew her."

"No, it's more than that. She's talked to Keisha, and the maids, and Mrs. Rosetti. She's talked to the busboys, the gardener, the guy who drives the pastry truck. It's like she's going down a list and crossing people off."

"Has she talked to you?"

"No. She knows it still hurts me to talk about Quinn. I think she's afraid to say anything." He played with his shoe lace. "I don't know, Trent. After Mrs. Wolcott accused her of causing Quinn's death, I keep wondering if I should ask her about it, get her side of the story."

"Did you know she was the girl who jumped onto Quinn's platform during *Moondance* and pulled her back from the edge?"

Gil's head jerked up. "She did *what?* How long have you known this?"

"She told me after Mrs. Wolcott left."

"And when in the hell were you gonna tell *me?*" Gil jumped to his feet. "God, Trent! I am so damned tired of being kept in dark around here."

"I didn't want to upset you."

"I've never been able to believe anyone in this goddamned family. Not *my* father, not *your* father, not dear, sweet Aunt Margaret. And our mother—didn't she tell enough lies for all of us?"

"Gil, I—"

"She lied about leaving. She lied about coming back. She lied about my father. And all of it to protect me." He grabbed the edge of the desk. "Well, I'm sick of being protected. If there's something to feel, I want to feel it. If there's something to know, I want you to friggin' tell me."

"Fine. I'll friggin' tell you."

"Does Annabel think somebody murdered Quinn? Somebody here at the inn? Is that why she's asking all these questions?"

"Calm down." Gil's temper could shoot through the roof in a nanosecond.

"*Tell me,*" Gil demanded.

"Annabel isn't sure. But she was there. She saw Quinn die. I think she's just trying to make some sense of it."

"Jesus, Trent. She doesn't suspect me, does she?

I mean, I was in New York the day Quinn died. We both were. If she thinks for one minute I would hurt Quinn, she—"

"I'll talk to Annabel. Get her to stop." Trent sighed. He knew this would happen.

Gil looked down and slowly shook his head. When he finally spoke, the anger in his voice had disappeared. Now he just sounded sad. "No, leave her alone. Let her ask her questions."

"Are you sure?"

"Yeah. Maybe she'll find out something. If someone at the inn caused Quinn's death, I want to know. I want to know who, and I want to know why." Gil regarded Trent solemnly. "Annabel—she's not what I expected. She's not like Quinn at all."

"Give her time."

"Is that what you think?"

"I think you should go for your run."

After Gil left, Trent sat looking out the window, watching the wind move through the trees one branch at a time. He'd never felt so conflicted. Why was he trying to push the image of Annabel's face out of his mind while his eyes scanned the yard for a glimpse of her? He might as well be on a bus with no brakes, careening down the side of Peg Leg Mountain. Take her lips, for example. He couldn't stop looking at them. He calculated their softness, measured their pull, imagined how they'd feel moving against his.

"Trent?"

He looked up, and his heart lurched.

Annabel stood in the doorway with the morning light spilling across her face. The faint, sweet scent of cucumber aloe soap drifted toward him. He'd smelled it thousands of times, ordered it by the caseload for the guests, but he never knew how intoxicating it could be.

"Gil's not here? I thought Keisha said he—"

"You just missed him."

"Oh." She hesitated. "Well...sorry I bothered you."

"Come on in."

"No, I—"

"I'm not gonna bite you, Annabel." His head was pounding. Where was that bloody control he'd always counted on?

She walked across the room—floated, actually—and set a brown paper bag on his desk.

"What's this? Breakfast?"

"I found it on the front porch of my cabin."

She opened the bag and pulled out a square white box, the kind the gift shop used for souvenir mugs. She opened it and lifted out a small red and white plastic bottle. Her hands were trembling. He wanted to take them in his, but instead, he took the bottle from her and gripped it as if it were a grenade he might lob though the window.

"It's a Curenol bottle," she said flatly. "Someone besides you knows why I'm here."

He popped open the child-proof cap and shook out a curl of white paper. He unwound it and read the scrawled message.

"You're looking in the wrong place."

Chapter 6

"Miss Maitland? Do you want me to do the combination again?" Craig Girard pulled a handkerchief out of his pocket and dabbed at the beads of sweat glistening on his forehead.

"No, no," Annabel said. "It was fine."

"Is that *all?* Just *fine?*"

"Why don't you run through it again?" Annabel stifled a yawn.

"Okay. But this time I'm using my lucky top hat." He held the brim with both hands and snapped it open. "It's an antique made out of beaver fur." He waggled his thick eyebrows at her. "Usually, when I tell that to the ladies, they laugh."

"Do they?"

She waited until Craig reset the CD track and began soft shoeing across the stage before she let her mind rocket back to the Curenol bottle. Was it a joke? A warning? Had someone been trying to scare her? She rubbed her throbbing temples and tried to concentrate on Craig's routine, but twenty-eight bars of "All I Need is the Girl" didn't have enough clout to hold her focus.

All she could think of was Trent Sheffield.

Why had he thought Ruth Donovan had sent her to spy on him? Did he have something to hide? A powerful woman like Ruth had every conceivable resource at her fingertips. If she wanted to dig up information on Trent, she would hire the best private detectives in New York, not some washed-up dancer who could barely make it up a flight of stairs.

As the music crescendoed, Annabel leaned back. Her head pounded with the beat.

Craig would do, she guessed. Twenty-one, athletic build, waves of black, mousse-tamed hair. He would look Gene Kelly handsome in a tuxedo and fuel the fantasies of the older female guests. She glanced at his résumé and wondered how he'd managed to snag the role of Curly in *Oklahoma*. Chances were he'd lied about that one. But maybe she was too cynical. Maybe Craig Girard had been the best tenor the Brownsville Apple Tree Theater could find.

"Are you sure you'll be able to fit this into your schedule?" she asked.

Craig smoothed the rim of his top hat. "Miss Maitland, this is a dream of mine. You don't know what it's like to come from a little town in the middle of nowhere and have dreams that don't have a chance in hell of coming true."

"Well, actually, I do, but—"

"It would be *so* awesome to work with you. I Googled you and—wow!—you've done a bunch of shows. And you've worked with my idol, Byron Patrick. Just being able to learn from you would be the most amazing, the most—"

"You're hired," she said, laughing. "You don't need to blow any more sunshine my way."

"Annabel?" Ham poked his head around the door. "Some girl is out here looking for you."

"Does she want to audition?"

"I don't think so. I found her wandering around the garden looking for the carriage house."

A willowy redhead stepped inside. Skintight jeans hugged her bony hips. High-heeled ankle boots clicked sharply across the wooden floor. She hoisted a large leather bag off her shoulder and set it beside the table of sheet music.

Annabel stared at her in disbelief. “Rachel Finley?”

“Hey, Annabel.” She twisted a long lock of hair around her index finger.

“What are you doing here, Rach? It’s Wednesday. Shouldn’t you be in New York warming up for the matinee?”

“I’m moving to my aunt’s house. Like tonight.”

Rachel’s high-pitched voice always took Annabel by surprise. Betty Boop on helium, Byron always said, and it was true. But that same woman could do twenty-seven fan kicks then belt out a ballad the second mezzanine could hear. Without a microphone.

“You mean your aunt’s house in Georgia? I thought you hated your aunt.”

“I do. But my parents won’t let me come home. They think I’m a bad influence on my brother. I mean, *now* they throw me out? The day I graduate from rehab, all sparkly clean and sober, they throw me out? I mean, Jesus.”

“What about *Moondance?* Aren’t you staying with it until it goes to Broadway?”

Rachel glanced at Craig. He was hanging on every word.

“Rachel and I danced together in New York,” Annabel said.

“Awesome,” Craig said.

“I’m sorry about the blower still being here,” Ham said. “I’ll take it away tomorrow, and I’ll come back tonight and vacuum up the sawdust. I know it’s a mess, but my wife has a doctor’s—”

“It can wait til tomorrow,” Annabel said. “Can you give Craig a lift back to the inn?”

“Sure thing,” Ham said.

“And thanks, Annabel.” Craig grabbed his jacket and followed Ham outside.

Annabel scrutinized Rachel. The girl wasn’t as

emaciated as she had been in *Moondance*, but still long and lithe, and probably just as unpredictable. "I can't believe you're here, Rach."

"Me either." She managed a quick smile. "Hey, you cut all your hair off."

Annabel ran her fingers through the short stubby curls. "I was going for an early Meg Ryan kind of thing, but I don't think Meg woke up every morning looking like a wet chicken. Or maybe she did. Now there's a comforting thought."

Rachel glanced around. "Is this the supper club? I saw the sign in the lobby."

"I'm putting together the floorshow. Simple but showy. That's the plan, anyway."

Rachel reached into her tiny shoulder purse. "Okay if I smoke in here?"

"Not with all this sawdust lying around. We'd go up like...well, sawdust."

Rachel nodded and bit her lip. Her thin hands trembled.

"Come on," Annabel said. "We can go in the green room and slide the back door open." She picked up one of Ham's empty soda cans. "I'll bring the ashtray."

Annabel sat cross-legged on the dilapidated sofa. Once Rachel's cigarette was lit, and she was puffing away, she seemed calmer. She smoked silently for a few minutes.

"You look good, Rach."

"Bullshit. I look like hell, and you know it. I've gained twenty-three pounds, my skin thinks it's in puberty again, and my hair is coming out in clumps. I'm a train wreck." She smiled. "But I'm a clean and sober train wreck."

"I can tell," Annabel said, and meant it. Rachel's bright blue eyes appeared clear and alert. The far-off, bewildered look was gone.

"Yeah, well, it sucks." Rachel stood and blew a

coil of gray smoke into the air. "They fired me from *Moondance*. Did you know that?"

"No. I'm sorry."

"I thought Byron might have told you." A trace of contempt crept into her voice. "I thought Byron told you everything."

"He was probably just protecting me. You know, after everything that happened."

"Yeah, well, I'm out on the street. Since Quinn's death, there's a new zero tolerance drug policy in place." Rachel tossed her cigarette butt onto the concrete step and ground it with the toe of her boot. "Aren't you gonna say something about my smoking? You always said it would kill me one day."

"I guess it's better than doing pills and cocaine."

"That's what my counselor says." She glanced up and laughed. "But some days I just ain't so sure."

For a second, she was the old Rachel. The one who could slay Annabel with a filthy joke then turn, walk onstage, and sing a solo so tender and heartbreaking, it moved an entire audience to tears. The old Rachel—the pre-uppers and downers Rachel—would have had the guts to skip the amenities and cut to the chase about why she was there. The old Rachel wouldn't have been afraid to call first.

"When did we stop being friends?" Rachel asked. "When I started self-medicating myself? Or when Quinn took over my part in *Moondance*?"

"It all happened about the same time." Annabel studied her for a moment. "How'd you get here, Rach? You don't have a car, do you?"

"Jesus, no! I took a bus." She pushed a mop of straggling red curls back from her face. "Don't worry. I'm not staying. After I say what I've come to say, I'm boarding another Greyhound for Atlanta."

A slice of late afternoon sun streamed through the open doorway, making Rachel's hair shimmer like strands of copper wire. Rachel's pink translucent skin, splattered with hundreds of salmon-colored freckles, was the one thing she detested even more than her hair.

"Can you dance?" Rachel asked. "Are you gonna be able to go back to work?"

"Nah. It's over. My hip is shot."

"Oh, God, Annabel. I'm so sorry. I wish I could've—"

"Why are you here, Rachel?"

"To make amends. It's part of my twelve-step recovery program, and I wanted to do it face to face. I thought I owed you that."

"You don't owe me anything."

"I stole money from you to buy drugs."

"Well, maybe you owe me that. But that's all."

Rachel wrapped a bony arm around her waist. She pulled out a new cigarette and gripped it between her thumb and index finger like a joint. "It was my stash of pills that killed Quinn."

"*What?*"

"About a year ago, I got a prescription for Curenol-C for an abscessed tooth. Remember my abscessed tooth? When we were doing that jazz workshop for the Manhattan Dance Project?"

Annabel remembered it well. Rachel had written a bad check to pay for the endodontist and hadn't been able to eat anything but potato soup and milkshakes for three days.

"But Rachel, you weren't there when Quinn died. Murray made you leave the theater before the matinee because you were—"

"—stoned out of my gourd." Rachel's eyes filled with tears. She wiped them away with the heel of her hand. "Ignore this. I'm raw. These days, I cry at hemorrhoid commercials." She puffed her cigarette. "I couldn't go in your dressing room because Quinn was there. We'd had a fight the day before when she said I ruined the timing on her big solo. She forgot it used to be *my* big solo."

Annabel kept silent.

"All right. I deserved to lose my part, but I would never have screwed up her dance number on purpose. I'm a professional. I loved *Moondance*."

"I know you did."

"Anyway, I had a bad headache from the paint fumes. So, instead of borrowing your ibuprofen, I got some Curenol from Frank. Then I took Frank's bottle back to my dressing room."

"Why?"

"I don't know. I guess I was too trashed to think clearly. No, wait a minute. The water was off in Frank and Louis' dressing room. That's why I went back to my own room, to get some water so I could take the pills." Rachel slid to the floor. She dropped her head onto her knees. "See, this is where it all goes to hell. I had my Curenol-C stashed in the back of my locker inside an old tampon box. I stood in my dressing room, holding Frank's Curenol, and my skull was pounding, and I thought, Jesus, taking regular Curenol will be like taking spit. I need something stronger. So, I opened my locker to get the codeine pills—my lucky seven, I called them—and they were gone. It was all gone. The bottle, the pills, everything."

"What did you do?"

"I freaked out. I took Frank's bottle back to him, but he and Louis had already gone downstairs for warm-ups, so I set it on his makeup shelf. At least I think I did. But I must have wandered into your room by mistake and set the bottle on your shelf instead of Frank's. The side hallway was like a rabbit warren. The dressing rooms all looked alike. People were always walking into the wrong one."

"That's true. I've done it myself. Did you tell the police?"

Rachel's eyes widened in fear. "No! I didn't tell anyone. I was too scared. Do you think the police are still asking questions about her death?"

"No. They're calling it an accidental homicide. Quinn's family never filed a wrongful death suit, and once the cops found out how many injuries we deal with, and the amount of prescription medicine floating around a dance company on any given day, they dropped the investigation. Wait a minute—you said you only had seven codeine pills, right?"

"Yeah, why?" Rachel took a final drag and flipped her cigarette out the door. A tiny shower of sparks danced across the stone landing.

"Because I took four, and Quinn took the same amount, which means someone must have added more pills. You've got to tell the police. They have to know. It could change everything. They might reopen the investigation."

"And they might decide I murdered Quinn." Panic settled in her eyes. "I don't want to open up anything. I just want to forget about it."

"But Rachel—"

"The police don't care. They have all the explanation they need. I screwed up, okay? I should never have kept those pills in my locker. It was a mistake, and that mistake killed someone. Don't you understand? I have to live with that every single day."

"But if they reopen the investigation, they might find out who did this. Don't you want to know? Whoever killed Quinn is still out there."

"Look, I am one day out of rehab. I'm barely treading water. I'm too shaky to dredge all this up again. I have to think of myself now. I have to stay strong."

"I know," Annabel whispered. "I wasn't a very good friend to you, was I, Rach? When you lost your way, I turned my back on you. I am so sorry."

"Don't be." Rachel pushed a curl of copper hair out of her eyes. "I'm the one who let drugs and Quinn Wolcott take away my life." She opened her bag and fished in the side pocket for an envelope. "This is for you—the three hundred bucks I took. You can count it if you want." She zipped her bag closed. "I've gotta catch a bus. Do you think the front desk will call me a taxi?"

"What are you going to do in Sylvester, Georgia? Pick peanuts on your uncle's farm?"

"It's an honest living."

"Wouldn't you rather be dancing?"

"Well, sure, but who's gonna hire me? Everyone knows I'm bad news. And I'm the worst kind of bad news: the kind that's trying to stay sober. There are too many temptations in New York. I can't go back there to live until I've been clean for at least six months."

"You could work here, dance in the floorshow. You already know most of the routines. It won't pay much, but you'll get your own cabin, lots of fresh air, and all the Italian food you can eat. It may not be glamorous, but it's a long, long way from New York."

"You don't have to do this."

"I want to."

"Annabel!" Gil shouted.

"Back here, Gil." She looked at Rachel. "That's funny. I didn't even hear him come in."

Gil barreled through the doorway and stopped. His mouth dropped open.

"Gil, this is Rachel Finley."

His chocolate brown eyes lit up. "Well, hello, Rachel Finley. I can't understand why Annabel didn't tell me she was auditioning angels back here."

Rachel laughed. A slow pink flush spread across her high cheekbones.

"Rachel, Gil Sheffield. Your new boss."

"And I'm the boss's brother," Trent said,

appearing behind him in the doorway. "Looks like you've got two Sheffields for the price of one."

"Not a bad deal," Annabel said. She smiled at him and tried to ignore her heart flopping around in her chest. "Trent, Rachel's an old friend from New York. She's agreed to be the headliner in your supper club."

"I had to say yes," Rachel said, still looking at Gil. "She promised me Italian food. And these days, I am so all about the carbs."

"Come on," Gil said to Rachel. "I'll show you to your cabin. Then we'll get some lunch." He put his hand on her lower back as he guided her out. "So, how do you feel about gelato?"

Rachel grinned at him. "Almost as good as I feel about your hand on my ass."

"Sounds like a match made in heaven," Trent said after they'd left.

"Wouldn't that be something?"

He patted the back of the sofa. "This looks familiar. I think I had it in my first apartment."

"Really?" Annabel raised her eyebrows. "And if this old couch could talk, what kind of tales would it tell?"

"Mostly PG-Rated ones. Except for that night after the homecoming dance. I almost made it to a good solid R. But then my date started throwing up the strawberry daiquiris and..."

Annabel laughed. "Yeah. I hate it when that happens."

He sat beside her on the sofa and twisted in the soft cushions until he was facing her, with one long leg crooked beneath him and the other stretched out across the floor. He had changed out of his khaki pants, shirt and tie uniform, and Annabel couldn't take her eyes off him. His jeans were worn in all the right places. He had unbuttoned the top two buttons of his blue plaid shirt and rolled the sleeves up over his wide forearms. A small vee of dark curly chest hair peeked out of his collar. He stretched and sighed, then smiled at her, creasing the slash of dimples on his angular face. It was the most casual and relaxed she had seen him. And judging from the sudden rush of heat spreading like wildfire through her solar plexus, he had never looked sexier.

She shifted in her seat.

"Need to ask you something," he said. "I've noticed you limping. The old war injury you mentioned—was it from trying to save Quinn?"

"My hip was messed up before that, but yes, catching Quinn finished it off. Its days were numbered anyway. I have what they call 'dancer's hip.' Which isn't as much fun as it sounds."

"Is it painful?"

"It can be. It's an inflammation of the psoas tendon, like tennis elbow, located where your leg hooks into your pelvis." She demonstrated by interlacing her fingers and twisting them.

"What causes it? Too much tennis?"

"Too many fan kicks. Chronic strain and fatigue from dancing."

"Is there something you can do for it?"

"Yeah, stop dancing." She looked into his eyes. At least they weren't full of pity. She didn't think she could stand seeing that from him. "But it could be worse. I mean, I'll still be able to dance, just not eight shows a week. I'll never be able to do that again."

The end of the road. She'd arrived earlier than most. But time was what every dancer fought, with every performance, through every year, until the punishing schedule finally took its toll on flesh and blood bodies that were never built to last.

"You're going to miss it," he said softly.

"Yeah." She tugged at a string on the ragged knee hole of her jeans. "But you'd be surprised how many things I won't miss. Hoofing it through eight shows a week when I can barely walk, soaking my hip in ice just to get it through a matinee, watching my career go down the tubes show by show by show, and hiding it from everyone I care about. Little things like that."

"Is it because of your age? I know a dancer's shelf life is limited."

"Not so much. These days, if you're careful and stay injury free, you can dance well into your forties. Stage floors are cushioned to save knees and backs. Shoe support is state-of-the-art. My problem, besides having a weak hip, is that I started too late. I'm thirty-four. I've only been dancing pro for four years. Too soon to have an exit plan in place. I was a pretty good dancer, but I had to work three times as hard to keep up. The twenty-year-olds were light-years ahead of me."

"What do you mean you *were* pretty good? Past tense?"

"Yep. Past tense. My career is dead." She leveled her gaze at him. "I'm not a fool, Trent. Not about this, anyway." Her voice shook a little, betraying her. "I've lived on a farm, buried family. I've dealt with death before, and believe me, I know the drill. When people and things die, they leave cold turkey. And they never come back."

He leaned over and took her hand, then held it tightly between both of his. Nothing had prepared her for the jolt of electricity that shot through her, or the head-to-toe shudder that followed. It ran the length of her like lightning, leaving a cold empty streak in its wake.

He pulled her toward him and put his arms around her. She dropped her head onto his chest, then nuzzled into the sweet spot between his shoulder and neck. She breathed in his scent, musky and clean, felt the strength of his jaw and the soft stubble of beard rub against her forehead. He held her loosely, as if he were giving her the option to draw back or bolt. When she didn't, his long fingers trailed heat down her arms until they cupped her elbows.

"Oh, Annabel," he whispered hoarsely. His slow, southern drawl slid across each vowel like warm honey. "What am I gonna do with you?"

She lifted her head and looked at him. "That depends. What do you want to do?"

With one hand, he slowly traced the curve of her chin and jaw, then trailed his fingers around her collar, up the back of her neck, and threaded them through her short curls. She shivered and made a little noise in the back of her throat, followed by a sharp intake of breath. She felt like time was spinning her in slow motion, then speeding up. Going faster and faster until she couldn't breathe. He pulled her toward him and lowered his lips to hers, stopping just before he reached them. "What do I want to do? I guess I want to kiss you."

She reached for his face with both hands and drew it toward her, closing the gap between them. His lips were soft and endearingly hesitant at first. But as the attraction crackling between them exploded, they became fueled with an urgency that surprised them both. A flare of pure sensation engulfed her. The kind where time stops and cathedral bells chime in the distance, and what little breath is left escapes the lungs in short, whimpering pants. His tongue found hers, setting it on fire. And for one crazy moment, she thought she was flying through space. She wrapped one arm around his neck, as if she were grabbing on to an anchor, and pulled him close, pressing her breasts against his broad chest. His mouth slid languidly down her throat, then kissed its way back up to her ear. And just before the heat he was generating wiped the last coherent thought from her brain, somewhere in the stratosphere, she thought she heard a floorboard creak.

Trent froze, then pulled his lips away and glanced behind him.

"Oh, shit." Rachel grabbed her leather bag and slung it over her shoulder. "I am so sorry. I left my bag in here and...and I...oh, shit."

"It's okay," Trent said.

"No, no," Rachel said, backing toward the door. "It's my fault. I should have knocked."

"Rachel, it's all right," Annabel said, laughing.

Rachel swiped a cloud of red hair back from her face. "I was always doing this in rehab. I zero in on something and keep my head down. Tunnel vision." She smiled brightly. "So, I guess all I can say is...carry on." She turned and ran out.

"Rehab?" Trent said. "When was she in rehab?"

"Um...until this morning?"

He moved back and stared at Annabel. "You aren't serious?"

"She's an old friend. She needs a job." He untangled his arms from Annabel's and stood up. "Don't go away. What's wrong?"

"Well, for starters, you've completely lost your mind."

"I know." She smiled at him, feeling heat flood her cheeks. "Kissing you was pretty mind-blowing."

"What was she in rehab for? Alcohol? Drugs? Sex addiction?"

"Drugs. Cocaine, mostly."

"And she's gonna be working at my hotel?" He ran his hand back through his hair and stared at her. His beautiful green-brown eyes had turned cold and accusing. "Well, that's just great. What the hell were you thinking?"

"Rachel is clean and sober. I can tell that by looking at her. She's trying to turn her life around, and she needs a job. She needs to dance. And we need a strong dancer in the floorshow. She'll be great. We're lucky to have her."

"That's what Gil said about you. And I thought he might be right. But now I'm not so sure." He blew out an exasperated sigh and paced to the door and back. He stopped and stood looking down at her with his arms crossed over his chest.

"My father used to stand like that," she said. "Every Saturday night, when my brother Drew staggered in three hours past curfew, reeking of cigarettes and Blue Ribbon beer."

Trent shoved his hands in his jean pockets.

Annabel stood and faced him. If she was expected to defend her decision, she was damn well going to look him in the eye. "I don't think Rachel will be a problem," she said. "If she is—"

"If she is, then—*what?* That girl is a loose cannon. Who knows what she'll do? This is another risk you and Gil expect me to take. And I'm supposed to feel better about it because you're vouching for her? Who, besides Ruth Friggin' Donovan, has vouched for you?"

"No one." She took a deep breath and tried not to look as hurt as she felt. "I'm not stupid, Trent. I know the bottom line with you is money. So it should make you feel better to know that Rachel Finley is an award winning dancer with a New York résumé I would die for. With the right publicity, and the support of all those Asheville theater snobs Keisha's been telling me about, Rachel could pack this place on weekends. I can't guarantee she won't screw up—that's what people do. But I know she'll try not to. I have faith in her. I have faith in Gil too. But you don't. You don't seem to have faith in anyone."

Trent glanced down. A knot in his jaw tightened then released. Inside his pocket, she saw his hand curl into a fist. His gaze shot back to her face. The pain that had filled his eyes raked across her heart like broken glass.

"I used to have faith in people," he said flatly. "But not anymore. These days, I can't afford to." He started for the door then turned back. "And what we just did here? The...uh...uh—"

"Kissing?"

"The kissing." He wasn't even looking at her. He was talking to himself. "It was a mistake. A crazy, careless mistake." He shook his head. "Christ, I know better. And I can promise you one thing, lady, it will never happen again."

Unexpected tears stung behind her eyes. "Don't worry. I'll make sure it doesn't."

"Your friend has one chance. *One.* If she falls off the wagon or behaves in any way that might be construed as questionable, both of you are out of here. Got it?"

Annabel raised her chin and looked at him. "Oh, yes, Mr. Sheffield. I've definitely got it. "

Chapter 7

Trent stood at the Laurel Room door, scanning the room for Gil.

The comforting aroma of tomatoes and basil and freshly baked garlic ciabatta bread engulfed him. If he hadn't been so angry, it would have made his mouth water.

He strode across the parquet floor, almost leveling one of the waiters, then zigzagged through a maze of linen-covered tables. The Blondes—Gil's name for the groups of single women over-seventy who thought blond was the new gray—tried to get his attention by waving their napkins in the air. He ignored them and sailed up the ramp to the lobby. People emerging from the elevator stopped in mid-sentence to watch him take the stairs two at a time. He didn't care. He had only one purpose in mind—to find his brother and put things back the way they were.

He banged on the door to Gil's suite, counted to three, then flung it open. He tramped across the floor and stood, gulping in air. His heart pounded in his ears. Hadn't stopped pounding since he'd left Annabel alone in the carriage house. Holding her like that, kissing her, touching her—had filled him with a hunger so profound, it threatened to swallow him up. When he was around her, he felt desperate and irrational and out of control. And sexy. And hard. It was crazy. *He* was crazy. And worse, he was helpless.

It had to stop.

Gil sat perched on the edge of his desk, talking into his cell phone. "Sorry, Keish. I'll have to call you back. A wild man just broke into my room."

"You and I have to talk," Trent said tightly.

Gil snapped the phone closed and stared at his brother. "What's wrong? You look like something big and nasty chased you down the street."

"I can't do this."

"Do what?"

"This supper club thing. I—we can't do it."

"I see."

"No, I don't think you do."

Gil slumped into the wobbly Windsor chair beside his desk. "This is great. Just great. You want to tell me why you're going back on your word? This isn't like you, Trent."

"It's a mistake. We need to face facts. I know you loaned me the money, but I don't think we can risk it."

"You want to know what I think? I think you can't stand not being in control for more than five minutes."

"That's not fair."

"Maybe not, but it's true." Gil took a deep, measured breath. "I appreciate the fact that you took care of me all those years after Aunt Margaret dumped me on you, but I'm a grown man now. I'm not your responsibility anymore. Our fathers are gone. Our mother is gone. Aunt Margaret is rotting away in a tiny room somewhere in hell."

"But you know what Aunt Margaret's will said. We have two years to break even or the entire estate goes to her favorite charity. And unless you want to hand over the inn to the Reverend Bertram P. Sloop's Church of Abundant Living, we have exactly six months left to make it pay for itself."

"That's what I'm trying to make happen," Gil

said. "Which is more than I can say for you. You've been using our precious revenue to look for your father. I mean, come on, Trent. Tracking down Nolan Sheffield won't change anything. You're still your mother's son. Even if you find the selfish bastard, do you really think he'll let you sell the lots?"

Trent bit back his reply. God, he was tired of this argument. Trent's father, and their differing views on his treatment of their mother, was an open wound between he and Gil.

"I'm worried about Annabel's lapse in judgment," Trent said. "That girlfriend of hers—"

"Rachel."

"Rachel. You should know she's only been out of rehab for one day."

"I know. She told me."

"And this doesn't bother you? Christ, Gil. We don't have the resources to cope with this kind of thing. We have enough problems of our own."

Gil catapulted out of his chair. "What's wrong with you? Where's all that bleeding-heart sympathy you haul out for Mrs. Richmond, and Mr. Landis, and the other pathetic old coots who can't pony up with their bills? How can you be so compassionate toward them and so cold toward Rachel? At least she's trying to get her life back together."

"That girl has a serious problem, and I question Annabel's wisdom in hiring her."

"Annabel and Rachel are friends. If you had any friends, you'd know what that felt like. I like Rachel. She'll be great. She said she's going to stay clean and sober, and I believe her."

"You've known this girl for less than three hours. How can you be so trusting?"

"How can you not?"

"Okay," Trent said. "Let's just look at the facts. To prevent the inn from plunging into bankruptcy, we've employed a dancer who's still so shaky from rehab, she has trouble making eye contact, and a choreographer who can't take three steps without limping."

"Rachel said Annabel hurt her hip. She can't help limping."

"Annabel Maitland is useless to us. I saw her dancing with Mr. Landis in the Laurel Room last night, and it was like watching Olive Oyl and Bluto at the junior prom."

The second the words were out of his mouth, he regretted saying them. Images of Annabel flashed behind his eyes: Long slender legs stretching languidly to the ground, small, firm breasts visible beneath her cotton T-shirt, silky curls framing her gentle face, a face he had the urge to caress every time he saw it. He didn't know her very well. And because of the Quinn connection, he would probably never trust her. But the thought of her quick, unsure smile made him ashamed he'd insulted her. Made him wish he'd never opened his big mouth.

"Rachel danced with Quinn," Gil said. "In *Moondance*."

"About that." Trent jumped back into the fray. "Don't you think it's strange they're both here—Annabel and Rachel? That out of the blue, two months after Quinn died, two of her dancer friends show up here to work?"

"No, I don't think it's strange. I think it's great. The fact that they shared Quinn's life is a comfort to me. It's like having a part of Quinn back again."

"But don't you wonder—"

"Trent, shut up. Go downstairs and have a beer. Let me take care of things for once. Who knows? You might just find you like letting someone else drive the bus."

Trent clenched his jaw until it ached. He had to stop bringing up Quinn's name in front of Gil. The truth had a nasty habit of slipping out when he least expected it, and he couldn't risk that. If Gil found out why Trent had ended his relationship with Quinn, it would devastate the boy. Gil had been disillusioned enough by the women in his life. The least Trent could do was spare him one more.

He left Gil's room and stared down the gloomy hall. It was depressing. Stained carpet, strips of brown, curling wallpaper, the faint, unmistakable scent of mildew. A plastic flap covered the opening near the demolished stairwell, the construction abandoned until they could accumulate more funds. Trent and Gil had plastered and painted until they couldn't move their arms, but they weren't fooling anyone. One look, and it was clear the Sheffield brothers had bitten off more than they could chew.

Trent yanked open the door to his room, then stopped and cursed softly. What was he doing? He still had to make an appearance in the Laurel Room. The Blondes—and, no matter how sparse the guest list was, there was always a table of Blondes—wouldn't leave until he'd said hello and steered a couple of them around the dance floor. His dancing skills left a lot to be desired, but The Blondes didn't seem to mind. They vied for his attention as if he were the sexiest man alive instead of a moody, thirty-six-year-old bachelor too set in his ways. Invariably he reminded them of someone—their son, their late husband, a young Gregory Peck. He had to admit, he liked The Blondes. They were an easy remedy for a battered ego.

Annabel had been right about the Laurel Room dance floor being overcrowded. But so what? A full house made the place look successful. Bookings were up thirty percent, and last month's review in the *Citizen-Times* praising the Laurel Room's authentic Italian cuisine had given him a glimmer of hope. If the plumbing and the roof held out through another harsh Blue Ridge winter, they might be in the black by the end of the year. And if he could locate his father and secure permission to sell off the lots on the south side of Peg Leg Mountain, the inn might make it after all. Which was exactly why he didn't want something as uncertain and costly as a supper club hanging around the inn's neck like a money-sucking albatross.

At least that's what he told himself.

Trent hurried and changed clothes. He left the collar of his white shirt open and pulled on a navy sport coat, then straightened his lapels, shot his cuffs, and checked his watch. He wondered if Annabel had shown up at the bar to meet Selena.

The thought of Annabel—any thought of Annabel—sent a shaft of heat coiling through him. Maybe she was already there, sitting on one of the high wooden stools, sipping wine and chatting with the bartender while she crossed those amazing, long legs of hers.

He rounded the railing at the top of the stairs and met Donald on the landing, wringing his hands. His Adam's apple quivered up and down like a whiffle ball.

"We've got trouble," Donald said. "That rancid Mrs. Richmond fell on the dance floor and twisted her ankle, and she swears she's not going to the ER in an ambulance."

"Call Annabel. If it's a foot injury, she'll know what to do."

"I did, but she isn't in her cabin."

"Try the bar. She and Selena were meeting for a drink."

"I did that, too. But she isn't—"

"What about the carriage house?"

"I went to the bluff and looked down, but the lights are off. She isn't there, Mr. Sheffield. She isn't anywhere."

****

Annabel hurried along the slippery path. Her leather flats slid off the packed dirt into a thick bank of ivy. She threw out her hand and grabbed on to a dogwood limb. Her hip twinged, and she sucked in air. But at least she didn't fall. She should have driven the inn's utility shuttle and come the long way around, which was what most of the Sheffield Inn guests would have to do to get to the supper club. She couldn't imagine the majority of them trying to navigate such a treacherous walkway. If Gil and Trent expected The Blondes to tromp down it for a couple of slow dances and a free apple martini, they needed to install sturdy railing and foot lighting.

At the bottom, a green, sloping meadow spread out low and wide, reminding her of the south field beside her father's farm in Indiana. Except for Peg Leg Mountain's hulking silhouette in the distance, it could have been the view from her old front porch at twilight.

Home.

Just thinking about it made her heart burn with a slow, familiar ache. It had been four years since she'd seen her father. Two since she'd seen Aunt Lou and Drew. This was the first time in her life none of them knew where she was, and it felt strange. She had been selfish not calling them and telling them she'd stopped dancing, but she didn't think they would understand the magnitude of her loss. And even if they did, she couldn't bear to face them until she'd figured out the rest of her life. The first thing they would ask is, *What are you going to do now?*

Quinn almost seemed like an afterthought.

And yet, Quinn's death was the reason—and the catalyst—for everything.

Annabel knew what kind of person Quinn had been. Growing up in rural Indiana hadn't insulated her from the assholes of the world, it had taught her how to deal with them. Quinn had been self-centered and callous and cunning. She'd hung around Annabel, pretending to be her friend, so when Annabel's hip finally gave out, she could swoop down like a vulture and pick the part clean. It was only a fluke that Annabel had been the one to leap to Quinn's rescue and hear her last terrified request. Maybe it was also her destiny.

Keeping Quinn's promise didn't make Annabel a saint. Or a loyal friend. On the surface, it looked like the most noble, honorable thing one person could do for another. But in the darkest chambers of Annabel's heart, she suspected her true intentions were as manipulative as anything Quinn had ever done. Because, after all, wasn't the one thing her father respected and valued most in the world was a person who kept their word? And wouldn't it be a miracle if she showed her father she was that person?

But even that was a crapshoot. She wished she could make her father proud of her for at least one thing while they were both still on the planet, but it didn't seem likely. Odds were, Henry Maitland would never forgive his daughter for leaving the farm after her mother had died to try to make it as a dancer. She might as well have joined a circus. His sister, Lou, had been more sympathetic. And practical. Before Annabel left for New York, Lou had sewn pockets into Annabel's bras to hide her money from potential muggers, made her promise to call home once a month, and given her a lucky buckeye to keep her alive.

Annabel curled her fingers around the smooth brown buckeye that hung on a silver chain around her neck. She didn't really believe it could bring her luck, any more than she believed its powers had abandoned her like a spurned lover the night her hip gave out. It was just a thing to remind her of home. A secret bridge to connect her forever with the people she'd left behind.

She stopped to rest beside the carriage house and thought about the cryptic message Selena had left for her at the front desk. *Meet me at Fred and Ginger's. I have something to show you.* Annabel wished she could muster some enthusiasm for Selena's surprise, but her temperament had pretty much been shot the moment Trent said he regretted kissing her. The image of him lowering his head to capture a kiss, his dark eyes smoldering with desire, seared its way across her brain. She shoved it away.

When she got to the door, she found the padlock dangling open. Ham had probably come back to pick up the blower and forgotten to lock the door behind him. She pushed the door open and flipped the light switch. Nothing. *Great,* she thought. Another circuit overload. That was twice in two days. Ham didn't have any faith in the electrician Gil had hired and thought it was time Gil told him to rewire the faulty lighting or find someone who could. Maybe she could reason with Gil. He seemed to trust her judgment.

Annabel edged her way into the lobby, then grappled in the dark until she found the flashlight Ham kept inside the box office window and turned it on. A wedge of dim, amber light barely illuminated the space in front of her. She moved along the aisle, feeling her way between the tall plywood risers. The tang of paint thinner and fresh, woody sawdust pricked her nose.

"Selena? Are you in here?"

Annabel's toe bumped something hard.

Something long and tube-like slithered across her ankle.

The quick movement threw her off balance, sending her spiraling backward. Her free hand pawed the air. It flailed back and forth until it hit the edge of the platform railing. She righted herself and pointed the fading flashlight beam at the floor. The air blower cord, thick as a double twist of licorice, looped around her ankle. She extracted her foot and kicked the cord aside.

The light flickered. She banged the flashlight against the railing, and for one glorious moment, it flared into brilliance before dimming again. After years of navigating her way across badly lit backstage terrain, she wasn't afraid. Her eyes quickly became accustomed to the dark.

She slid between the blower's grillwork and the bandstand, then felt her way along the edge until she found the gray metal box hanging on the wall beside the restroom. Not the most convenient place for a breaker box, but that was always the way in theaters. Things were never where they needed to be, and no one ever seemed to know why.

She found the bottom lever and flipped the breaker. The ceiling lights flashed on. White hot glare filled the room.

"Thank God," she whispered.

And then she turned around.

The stacks of sheet music and dance diagrams she had so carefully categorized before leaving New York had been trashed and strewn around the room. Songbook covers stared up at her—Ella Fitzgerald, Fats Waller, Judy Garland, Billie Holiday. She couldn't believe what she was seeing. The music couldn't have fallen over on its own. Gravity would have toppled the song sheets against the stage, not scattered them across the floor like Bourbon Street the day after Mardi Gras.

A chill raced down her spine. This was no accident. It was a deliberate act of vandalism directed at...who? The inn? *Her?*

She picked up a wrinkled song sheet. Why hadn't she taken the time to make copies? She'd borrowed most of them from Byron. He'd been collecting old tunes for years. Many were out of print, some extremely rare. If they were ruined, she didn't know how she would replace them. It would take the rest of her life to track them down on eBay.

Could an electrical short have caused the blower to cut on by itself? She had enormous respect for air blowers. Directors were always using them to create the dreaded windblown effect, and she'd never met a dancer who didn't loathe them. The cold air dried the mouth, burned the eyes, and made keeping an already half nude body decently covered virtually impossible. Heavy blowers were hard to manage. The velocity on a large one could launch a stack of sheet music into the air like confetti.

Annabel blew a film of sawdust off "The Way You Look Tonight." She pushed open the hinged plywood door and crawled under the bandstand to gather up the rest.

The house lights dimmed, then flashed back on. The blower fan began to whir softly, rapidly changing to a high-pitched squeal as the giant blades gained momentum.

Annabel's head swung around.

When the first spray of sawdust hit her face, she was still on her hands and knees, clutching a stack of crumpled sheet music to her chest.

Chapter 8

Trent pushed his way through the group of onlookers.

Rachel sat on the dance floor with Mrs. Richmond's swollen ankle resting in her lap. She was the last person Trent would have asked for help, but it looked like he didn't have much choice. According to Keisha, who was never wrong, the girl had spent the afternoon telling anyone who would listen that she was in the process of turning her life around.

One day at a time.

At his hotel.

Maybe he and Gil should turn the place into a freaking halfway house. Mountain views, clean air, kindhearted employers. What could be more soothing? The entrance fees alone would pay their heating bill.

Trent shook his head and sighed. Gil was right about him sounding like Aunt Margaret. When had he become so cynical? When had he turned into someone he couldn't stand?

Gil was also right about him lacking compassion for people who claimed they were trying to get their lives back together. What did that mean, anyway? That something had come sneaking out of the night and blown their screwed up lives apart like a toy tank, excusing them from all further responsibility until they glued it together again? Well, he was sorry. But in his opinion, that was just an excuse to buy more time while they pushed their problems off onto someone else. Someone like him. As long as they said they were getting their lives back together, they didn't have to actually do it.

Why was he never granted that luxury? Why was he always the capable one, the one who had to do the gluing for someone else? He'd developed a low tolerance for people who refused to accept the lives they created for themselves. Everyone made choices, every minute of every day. And most people had to live with them.

He glanced at Rachel. Her ripped jeans and *Broadway Baby* T-shirt had some of the older women staring. Her squeaky voice sounded like a shovel on concrete, and the pungent scent of her grape bubble gum permeated the air every time she opened her mouth. But he had to admit she seemed to know what she was doing.

She wrapped her fingers around Mrs. Richmond's ankle and gently pressed the tendons and bones. "Hey!" she yelled. "Can we get some ice over here?"

Mrs. Richmond eyed her suspiciously. "Are you the doctor? Because I don't like people poking at me who aren't qualified."

Rachel laughed. "Are you serious? You think I look like a doctor?"

"No," Mrs. Richmond said tersely. "You do not!"

"I'm a professional dancer," Rachel said. "I see this kind of sprain all the time."

"What happened, Mrs. R.?" Trent asked.

Mrs. Richmond glared up at him. "Nothing too earth shattering. I was doing the foxtrot and fell off my shoes. I'll be fine. All I need is an Ace bandage and a stiff drink."

"And a new pair of shoes," someone said from the crowd.

"I heard that, Myrtle Lawson," Mrs. Richmond

said. "And I don't find it amusing."

"You need to get this X-rayed," Rachel said.

Mrs. Richmond closed her eyes and sighed. "Oh, all right. But someone needs to check on my dog. Someone needs to walk Precious."

"We'll take care of it," Trent said.

Mrs. Richmond opened one eye and scowled at Rachel. "My daughter lives in Boston. She can do the tango. Can you tango?"

"I don't have the patience for it," Rachel said, smiling. She looked up at Trent. "She'll be all right in the backseat of a car if she can prop her foot up. Can you get us to the ER?"

"I'll drive you," Gil said, appearing beside Rachel. Trent wasn't surprised. As soon as someone else had the crisis under control, it was just like Gil to materialize out of nowhere.

Gil helped Rachel to her feet. Their gazes locked. Trent noticed their fingers lingered together a few seconds longer than was necessary.

So that's the way the wind was blowing.

He guessed it could be worse. Rachel came with enough baggage to fill up a stateroom on the *Queen Mary*, but Gil already knew that. Everyone within shouting distance knew that. Trent would have to persuade the girl to curb her confessional impulses where the guests were concerned, but he had to admire her guts. That kind of raw, in-your-face honesty always made him uncomfortable. Made him want to charge through the front door and keep on running. But who was he to say it was wrong? Maybe that's what it took to overcome an addiction.

Gil and Donald slid their arms beneath Mrs. Richmond's shoulders and lifted her solid frame until it was upright. She hopped on her good foot to the nearest chair.

Trent turned to Rachel. He was going to ask if Mrs. Richmond needed a pillow for the car, but the panic-stricken look on Rachel's face stopped him cold. He followed her gaze to the lobby entrance.

A man stood in the doorway, scanning the crowd. He wore tight jeans, a crocheted scarf looped twice around his neck, a brown Indiana Jones hat, and a leather shoulder purse. He tipped his hat to The Blondes at the front table and winked. They twittered and giggled and waved, women from a generation of moviegoers who still refused to believe Rock Hudson was gay.

The man started across the floor. His posture was youthful and straight, even though the deep creases on either side of his nose betrayed the fact he was probably pushing forty. His deep-set eyes were positioned beneath a protruding forehead like something hiding under a cliff.

Rachel ducked behind Gil. By the time the man had navigated his way around two tables and a waitress pouring coffee, Gil and Rachel had disappeared into the crowd.

"Mr. Sheffield?" The man held out a manicured hand for Trent to shake. "*Gorgeous* place you have here."

"Thanks," Trent said. "And you are...."

"Byron. Byron Patrick. Don't you recognize me?"

"I don't get out much," Trent said. Did the man have on lipstick? It had been a while since Trent had seen that. A long, long while.

"I'm a friend of Annabel's. You and I met in New York at the 53rd Street Rehearsal Hall. Quinn Wolcott introduced us."

"Oh, yeah."

It was all coming back to him now. Byron Patrick. Quinn. *Moondance*. One of the worst weekends of his life. He'd gone there to beg Quinn to leave Gil alone, but it had only made her more determined to get her claws into him.

"Well, Quinn didn't really introduce us, but I did

say hello, and—" His gaze slid over Trent's right shoulder. "Holy mother of—shit!—is that Rachel Finley?"

"You mean the redhead running out the door?" Trent glanced at The Blondes to see if they'd heard Byron's expletive. For all their outrageous behavior, the old gals were still a conservative bunch.

"Does Annabel know Rachel's here?"

"Annabel hired her."

"Oh, dear Lord." Byron lifted the third and fourth fingers of his right hand and placed them gently over his right eyebrow. Then he closed his eyes and sighed. Suddenly his eyes fluttered open. "Annabel is still working here? I thought you fired her."

"It was a misunderstanding." Trent glanced at Donald, who shook his head. "Could you excuse me for a minute? Why don't you wait for me in the bar. Drinks are on the house."

"A bar? Oh, thank God. Who said the South wasn't civilized?"

Trent stuck his head in the back storeroom. Keisha was zipping up her leather bomber jacket. She stopped and stared at him, her dark eyes taking in everything at once. "What's up?" she said. "Boss?"

"Find her for me."

"Who?" Keisha regarded him for about half a second. "Oh, Annabel."

"No one seems to know where she is. I'm a little worried."

Keisha nodded. "Then I'm on it."

He went back to the bar and sat at Byron's table, positioning himself so he could watch all the entrances.

"*Very* nice bar," Byron said.

"So, you and Annabel danced together in *Moondance*?"

"Eight shows a week. Have you ever seen

Annabel dance, Mr. Sheffield?"

"Not really. Is she any good?"

Byron sipped his whisky. "She was wonderful. Electric. You couldn't take your eyes off her. She's always been a little taller than the other dancers. And older. She started *way* too late to pull any kind of long-term career out of the hat. By the time she'd managed to get off that damned farm, she was too inexperienced to land anything except back row chorus. Until *Moondance*."

"You talk like it's all in the past—her dancing, I mean."

"A lot of people in *Moondance* think she's never going to dance professionally again, but I believe they're wrong." He smiled, showing a bottom row of yellowed, overlapping teeth.

"Why?"

"Because I know how stubborn and brave Annabel is. If she can leave a soybean farm and move to a city where she doesn't know a soul, then try to break into a profession where she's already past her prime, working her way back from a hip injury will be cake." He folded the corner of his cocktail napkin. Then folded it again. "So, how *is* her hip? She ditched physical therapy to come down here, you know."

"You'd have to ask her," Trent said. He didn't want to tell Byron how many times he'd seen her hobbling to and from the carriage house when she thought no one was looking, her face twisted in pain.

"She'd better heal fast." Byron downed the last of his whisky and signaled for another. "Freeman Saunders is champing at the bit to get her back in New York. He's creating a new dance piece, and he wants Annabel to dance the lead in it." He smiled again. "I can't tell you how jealous I am. It's like having Sondheim call and ask you to sing for him."

"Sondheim. He writes musicals, right?"

"Yes...he does." Byron shuddered, clearly believing he was in the presence of someone who thought live theater was one jump away from professional wrestling.

And that's the way Trent liked it. It was an easy way to keep the curious at bay. Once people found out he'd spent the first ten years of his life hanging out with his mom in the greenroom of a string of crummy dinner theaters, they bombarded him with personal questions. And if there was anything he hated, it was having his past trotted out and shoved in his face.

Trent's gaze flicked from entrance to entrance. Still no sign of Annabel or Keisha. He clenched his fists under the table. If Annabel was on the property, Keisha would find her. Keisha had never let him down. Why the hell was he so worried? Annabel was probably just lying low, avoiding him at all costs. He couldn't blame her. After kissing her—and oh, God, he had loved kissing her—then telling her it would never happen again, he wouldn't want to see him either.

That was it.

She was avoiding him. She was all right.

But what if she wasn't?

He glanced at his watch, then at Byron, who was blathering on about torn cartilages and shin splints. Good thing he was only half-listening, or he might be in danger of losing his lunch.

He glanced at his watch again. He'd give Keisha ten more minutes, then he'd go look for her himself.

****

Sawdust churned toward Annabel.

It spattered her glasses and filled her mouth the second she opened it to scream.

She covered her face with her hands. The sheet music she was holding tumbled to the ground. It flapped and twisted in the air, then flew against the platform bracing. Shards of paper pushed through the openings to fly around the room like crisp autumn leaves.

Wood chips ricocheted against the support lath, hit the back of her neck, stung her bare arms until she cried out. She buried her chin in her chest and crooked her arms over her head. With each precious gulp of air, she spewed out sawdust.

She lunged at the plywood door. It wouldn't budge. She rattled it, rammed it with her knees, slapped it with the heels of her hands until they bruised.

The silk blouse she'd so meticulously ironed that afternoon inched up her back, exposing bare skin. She pulled the hem over her head, held the shirttail in front of her nose, and crawled with one hand to the corner, away from the thrust of the blower.

She tried to swallow, but couldn't manufacture any spit. Wads of damp sawdust stuck to her teeth and gums. Patches of pulp clung to the back of her tongue like ground cornmeal. She put her head down and crawled along the perimeter of the enclosure. Her lucky buckeye banged against her chest. The blower's gale force wind lashed across her neck. Cold air rushed up her nose. What was left of the sawdust roiled up from the ground and caught in the twisting air.

She edged closer to the blower, grinding her knees into the rough plywood floor, then squeezed her hand between the bottom two laths. The raw edge skinned the back of her hand until it bled. She pressed her collarbone against the board and tried to reach the cord. She couldn't give up. As a dancer, she'd been trained to keep trying, to always do one more step, and do it better. One more good stretch and she could...it was no use. She fell back, panting.

The muscle below her injured hip cramped. She shifted her weight and held her foot at an angle to ease the strain. Her gaze fell on her black leather flats. She slid one off and pushed it toe first through the triangle-shaped opening until it reached the blower cord. She worked the cord toward her, then wrapped it around her hand and jerked.

The motor stopped abruptly. Giant fan blades spun in silence, slower and slower. She picked up a stray woodblock and scooted as far back into the corner as her hip would allow. Then she crouched in the shadows to wait.

For what, or whom, she didn't know. But she did know one thing—this was no accident. Someone had locked her in the enclosure and turned on the blower.

She closed her fingers around the block of wood and held it hidden at her side. If whoever did this came back, she wasn't completely helpless. She had enough upper body strength to do some serious damage. She could hurl it if she had to, or smash it against the most vulnerable body part she could reach.

The front door crashed open.

Her heart slammed against her ribs.

"Annabel? Are you in here? Annabel?"

Selena.

Annabel peered between the crosspieces. Selena stood in the middle of the aisle, clutching her purse to her chest.

"Annabel?" Selena said in a small, frightened voice. "Where the hell are you?"

"Over here!" Annabel cried. "Beneath the bandstand."

"What are you doing under there?"

"Aspirating sawdust. Just get me out, okay?"

Selena flipped the latch and pulled the door open.

Annabel ducked under the doorframe, her legs suddenly powered by rubber bands. "Did you see anybody leave?"

"I didn't see anybody except Gil. He was walking back from the parking lot and—" Selena's eyes widened. "Did someone lock you in there?"

"You catch on fast."

Selena pointed to the latch. "No, it's a spring lock, see? When it swings closed, it locks itself. You probably locked yourself in."

Selena was right. With enough force, it could have locked on its own.

"But I never touched the door," Annabel said. "It couldn't have swung shut by itself. Someone had to have pushed it."

Keisha strode into the carriage house and skidded to a stop. Her dark eyes scanned the room. "Damn, girl, it looks like a bomb went off in here. Mr. Trent isn't gonna like it."

Annabel dropped onto the first folding chair her wobbly knees could reach.

"You just sit there, honey," Selena said. "You're shaking." She grabbed a jacket Ham had left draped over a sawhorse. "Here. Put this on."

Annabel slid her arms into the huge denim coat. The quilted lining smelled of wood smoke and axle grease. She tried to speak, but a skin of dryness had wrapped around her larynx like gauze.

Selena handed her a tissue. "You have sawdust on your chin."

"And up my nose," she croaked. "And in my bra."

"At least it didn't go in your eyes," Selena said.

"Someone did this on purpose," Annabel said to Keisha. "The lights dimmed just before the blower started up. My music and dance graphs were spread all over the floor. That's why I crawled under the bandstand—to pick them up. It all happened so fast, I'm not sure if the blower turned on first or the door closed."

Keisha and Selena exchanged looks.

"I'll check the building," Keisha said. "If somebody's hiding down here, I'll find them." She held her silver flashlight out in front of her and disappeared through the back alcove.

"Will she be all right?" Annabel asked.

"Are you kidding? That girl's biceps are bigger than my thighs. Trent pays for her gym membership because it's cheaper than hiring a security guard."

Annabel clasped her hands to keep them from trembling.

A few minutes later, Keisha came through the front. "I didn't see anything."

"You weren't out there very long," Selena said. "Did you even look?"

Keisha glared at her. "I'll tell you the same thing I told your dead sister. Your last name ain't Sheffield yet, so stop giving me crap about how I do my job."

A crimson flush settled across Selena's cheeks. "You've been abrasive with me before, Keisha Releford, but this time I'm reporting it to Trent."

Keisha threw back her head and laughed. A short hysterical laugh. The kind Japanese Ninja unleash right before they karate-chop their way through an enemy's spleen.

"You're crazy," Selena said.

Keisha pulled out her cell phone. She thumbed a quick text then turned to Annabel. "Come on, lady. Let's see if you can walk or if I need to carry you." She glanced back at Selena. "You can ride your broomstick."

****

Byron picked up his glass and tossed back the remaining whisky like a cowboy leaving the Longbranch. Trent wished he'd ordered one for himself.

"So, about Rachel," Byron said. "You do know where she's been, don't you?"

"Yes."

"Well, thank God for that. The name of the rehab center is Seabrook House. I'm telling you this, so when she falls off the wagon—and believe me, she will—you'll know where to ship her."

"You don't seem to have much faith in her recovery." Trent had had the same reaction, but for some reason, it sounded weaselly and heartless coming from Byron.

"When the drugs took over her life, I tried to help her. But I finally just had to stop and face reality. I mean, you can intervene until you're blue in the face, but unless someone wants to change, it'll never happen, right?"

"That's what they say."

Keisha walked into the lobby, followed by Annabel and Selena. Keisha's steely gaze searched the room until she spotted Trent in the bar. She looked distraught, which unnerved him because the woman was a piece of granite.

Keisha nodded toward Annabel, standing beside the courtesy desk with her shoulders hunched over as if something had crushed her.

Trent's chest tightened. He jumped to his feet, knocking the wine list into Byron's lap, and tore across the lobby.

"Annie, what's wrong?"

Annabel turned around. The pain in her soft gray eyes startled him.

What in Christ's name had happened to her?

"I'm all right," Annabel said.

Keisha was suddenly beside him. "We need to talk. I need to know how you want me to proceed." He couldn't tear his gaze away from Annabel. Not until he figured out what was wrong and how he could fix it.

"I think we should call the police first," Keisha said.

"The *what?*" For the first time, Trent noticed Annabel's clothes were ripped and filthy. Sawdust clung to her hair and arms. Streaks of dirt smeared across her forehead. The backs of her long graceful hands had been scratched raw. "Just tell me," he said hoarsely. "What happened to you?"

"I'm fine," Annabel said, not looking at him. "Someone tried to scare me."

"Annabel!" Byron's voice trilled from across the room.

Annabel let out a strangled cry. She pulled away from Selena and ran past Trent. She threw her arms around Byron's neck and buried her face in his coat. He rocked her back and forth.

Like a lover, Trent thought, fending off a wave of jealousy.

"What's *he* doing here?" Selena hissed to Trent.

"Byron Patrick? You know him?"

"That man—and I use the term loosely—made Quinn's life a living hell. He's a horrible old gossip. He blabbed every secret Quinn had, then made some up. He makes me sick. Quinn loathed him. Someday that miserable creep will get what's coming to him."

Trent stared at Selena. She had always been the cool, rational one, the one who could keep her head in the midst of the chaos that masqueraded as her family. She was the first person he sought when he needed a comforting shot of peace and tranquility. But seeing her reaction to Byron had been a revelation. Who knew Quinn's meek little sister owned a voice that could drip with ice? Or a pair of eyes that could shoot daggers with the best of them? Even sweet, gentle Selena, his trusted island of calm, had a boiling point like everybody else.

But the most disturbing part, the part he would probably have nightmares about, was that for one freaky, terrifying moment, Selena had looked exactly like her mother.

Chapter 9

Annabel's suitcase sat on the wobbly luggage rack in the center of the room, bulging with her belongings. She was doing the right thing by leaving. Every instinct told her it was time to bail. If she'd been a braver person, someone with passion and pluck, it would be different. But she wasn't. She knew her limitations where heart pounding courage was concerned, and it was better to stop the charade before someone stopped it for her.

Quinn would understand; she was a master at self-preservation. Quinn always looked out for Number One, and expected the rest of the world to do the same. As soon as Annabel got to wherever she was going, she would call Ruth Donovan and tell her everything, let her hire a private investigator to look into her niece's death. She should have done that months ago. It had been foolish to think she could handle this on her own.

She opened the cabin door, careful to check the lock on the screen, and peered outside. Wind rustled the feathery tops of two Carolina pines, then swooped down to scatter a pile of dead leaves beside the road. A sharp gust blew the silver loop earrings against her neck, stung the fresh scratches on her wrists and hands. She choked back a wave of betrayal. Selena, who had been so sympathetic at the carriage house, had convinced Trent and Keisha to investigate the incident on their own without bringing the police into it. Only Byron seemed to believe Annabel had been in any real danger.

Trent had made sure Annabel was all right, then barely looked her in the eye. Clearly, he wanted her out of there as much as she wanted to go. And that hurt more than anything.

She leaned her back against the screen door. She would miss the cabin. She'd only lived in it for two days, but she loved it there. The atmosphere was more her style; faded quilts, decorative oil lamps, chintz-covered chairs. It reminded her of Aunt Lou's old clapboard house on Chestnut Lane. That's where she longed to go. But if she went back home, what would she do? What kind of job could she get? Waiting tables? Driving a tractor? She could teach dance, but she'd have to commute to a larger city, South Bend or Fort Wayne, in order to find a studio that paid more than minimum wage.

Her old best friend Nikki still lived near Laotta. They'd been inseparable in high school, taken dance class together, shared the same shimmering dream of making their marks on the Great White Way. Nikki was a dentist now with three cats, one daughter, and two ex-husbands. But that was the way life worked. Things never stayed the same or turned out like you expected them to. Some people grew up and acquired comfort zones, casually putting down roots that turned into cast-iron. Others were destined to thrash their way through the world one city at a time, making deals with the devil in order to survive.

If she wanted to, she could be in Marshall Hill by dinnertime the next night, riding up the highway in George Hutton's beat-up cab, bumping along the two-lane dirt road behind her daddy's soybean field. Aunt Lou's kitchen would envelop her with love: the comforting aroma of beef stew and cornbread, the table lamp spreading a golden circle of warmth, the blue calico sofa where her mother spent the last month of her life when the chemo stopped working. Annabel could close her eyes and see it all.

"Annabel?"

She spun around. "*Selena!* You scared me!"

Selena stepped closer. The amber porch light spilled across her white jacket like shards of yellow glass. "Come out here. I brought you something."

"A defibrillator?"

"Sorry." She held up a bottle of wine. "We never got to have our drink."

"Let me get some glasses—oh, wait. I don't have any." She unlocked the screen and pushed it open. "Come on in."

Selena stared at Annabel's suitcase. "Oh, my God," she whispered. "Are you packing? Are you leaving?" Panic washed over her face. "No! You can't leave! What about the supper club? Gil is counting on you. If you leave, who'll do the choreography? Will there even be a show?"

"The show will go on, Selena. It'll just go on without me. A friend of mine from New York has agreed to replace me."

"Who? Rachel Finley? Gil said she was here. Quinn hated her."

"I'm beginning to realize that Quinn hated just about everybody."

"Please, Annabel. Don't go. I don't trust Rachel. Quinn didn't trust her either. But she respected you. She thought you were the best."

"I need some air." Annabel went outside and leaned against the porch railing. Selena followed her. "You know, Selena, if you hadn't talked Keisha out of calling the police so the inn wouldn't have to weather any negative publicity, I might feel better about hanging around here."

"I had to do it. If word gets out there's a crackpot on the loose, this place could go under in a matter of days. The inn is everything to Trent. If this stupid supper club idea of Gil's fails, then Trent will be the one who will lose everything he loves." Her voice broke. "And I don't think I could bear that. Just stay until it gets off the ground. *Please.*"

"You think there's a sadistic crackpot on the loose? And you still won't call the police?"

"If I thought you were in any real danger, I would."

"What makes you so sure I'm not?"

"Because what happened at the carriage house wasn't directed at you. Someone wants to close the inn."

"Who?"

"The competition. The Trillium Inn near the Parkway or Hawley's Blue Ridge Lodge. Marissa Hawley's had it in for Gil ever since he cut a better deal with her baker to provide homemade breads and desserts. She had to scramble to find someone else. Look, up here, the restaurant businesses are a close-knit group. They all know the inn is opening a supper club. They're probably worried it will be successful. And it will be. If I have anything to do with it."

Selena's determined face made Annabel shudder. Did Trent have any idea how much this woman loved him? She would do anything for him. Even throw Annabel to the wolves, if that's what it took.

Annabel cracked open the screw top cap on the wine. She might look like she had the word *gullible* stamped on her forehead, but she was no fool. Things were beginning to get nasty. Someone wanted her out of there. She knew it. Byron knew it. And Trent knew it. He had seen the note in the Curenol bottle. Didn't he care?

She took a swig of the acidic white wine—palomino pony piss, Drew used to call it—and glanced at the top of the hill. Lights from the inn flickered through a thick copse of Fraser firs.

"Selena, I can't stay," Annabel said gently. "I should never have come, but Quinn wanted me to, and—"

"Oh, *please.* Don't tell me what Quinn wanted. I don't *care* what Quinn wanted." She whirled around. Her long denim skirt ballooned in the air. "But you can bet your sweet ass that if Quinn wanted it, she got it. Do you know what it's like to have someone steal your dreams? Quinn took everything I ever wanted, including Trent. She came home one weekend, took one look at him, and decided he would be perfect for her. She talked him into going to graduate school in New York, talked Aunt Ruth into finding a job for him. In three weeks, she had systematically taken everything I wanted and turned me into woodwork." Rage shone in her eyes. "If the inn goes under, Trent will move away, and I'll lose him again. Do you understand? *I'll lose him.*

"That's what I wanted to show you tonight at the carriage house. I've been secretly taking dance lessons, and I wanted to show you what I could do, audition for the floorshow. But I've had second thoughts. I'm not a dancer. Never was, never will be. I just wanted Trent to see me onstage and look at me the way he looked at Quinn."

Annabel's heart went out to her. How long ago had all this happened? How many years had Selena been carrying a torch for Trent with no hope of ever extinguishing it? Annabel knew other women who hadn't been able to move on after their men had left them. Heartbreak didn't include a statute of limitations, especially when the man you loved dumped you for your sister. Although she imagined that would speed things along for most people.

"Don't worry," Annabel said. "Rachel has a lot more experience than I do. She'll be fine."

"No, she won't." Selena's soft brown eyes turned

to steel. "I'm through begging. Do you know what I do for a living?"

"Trent said you worked in a bank."

"That's right. I'm a seasoned senior loan officer. I supervise corporate loans in the southeastern quadrant, but my contacts stretch from here to the west coast. For the last ten years I've worked my butt off covering other people's mistakes. Big mistakes. Career destroying mistakes. I've racked up more IOUs than the Gambini family."

"What does that have to do with me?"

"One phone call—well, four, actually—and I obtained access to your family's credit history. I know what your father's last three mortgage payments were, the amount of the lien on the new barn, a bank loan applied for by your brother without sufficient collateral. Seems times are just as tough in Marshall Hill, Indiana, as they are here."

"What are you saying?"

Selena laughed. "Don't look so shocked, Annabel. You're a farm girl. You know how unpredictable crops and weather can be. And when things start wearing out, and the medical bills start piling up, it's all over but the bankruptcy hearing."

Annabel's pulse roared in her ears. "What medical bills?"

"The bills for your sister-in-law's toxemia. The MRI for your father's deteriorated hip. If you stay and get the supper club up and running, I'll make sure your brother's loan goes through. I can get an extension until your father is on his feet again. I can keep your family from losing everything."

Annabel reached out and grabbed Selena's arm, encircling it with fingers that had spent years grasping a ballet barre. "What kind of a person are you?"

"You're hurting me," Selena whimpered. Annabel let go abruptly. Selena rubbed her arm. "It's simple. Just say you'll stay, and I'll call your father's bank."

Was Selena telling the truth? She had to be. She knew too much. People didn't make threats like that without the facts to back them up. Selena had done her research. She'd played her one and only card. But that was the only card she'd needed.

Cold clutched the back of Annabel's neck. It seeped into every nerve ending until she began to shake. She couldn't answer Selena. Even though they both knew what the answer was going to be. Instead, she turned and went inside. She shut the door in Selena's face and turned out the porch light.

If Selena had no qualms about threatening a houseful of innocent people with the loss of their home, how hard would it be for her to slip a sister a nice fat hit of codeine to prevent her from stealing anymore dreams?

Guilt flooded her heart, stung until it hurt to breathe. She leaned against the door and covered her face with her hands. Her family was in trouble. Big trouble. Why hadn't Aunt Lou told her what was going on? Had her father forbidden it? Was keeping her out of the loop his way of punishing her? In his eyes, she'd committed the unforgivable—left home and turned her back on her family. He'd cashed the checks, though. Every month, as disgraceful as he thought she was, Henry Maitland endorsed the check his daughter sent in thick blue ink, with the same square, tilted script he'd used to sign her report cards. And now the old man was in a jam. But no matter how desperate things got, he would never ask for help.

Annabel moved an oil lamp to the table beside the front window. She lifted the glass globe, lit a match, and held it to the frayed wick. The smell of sulphur and burning cinnamon streamed into her nose. A white-yellow flame rose up and wavered in front of her eyes.

Father and daughter. Two people so stubborn, they wouldn't give an inch if their life depended on it. Wasn't that what her mother always said about them? She'd also said that forgiveness was a gift you gave yourself. You could whine and feel resentful and assign all the blame you wanted. But in the end, if you were alone, it was nobody's fault but your own.

Annabel reached for the phone and listened to the steady b-flat hum of the dial tone. Then, with a slow, trembling hand, she dialed her father's number.

****

Trent had waited in the shadows for Selena to leave Annabel's cabin. She'd stood on the porch in the dark, staring at the door, like a dog that's been left in the cold for too long. What the hell was she doing? Why didn't she leave, for Christ's sake? He wanted to make sure Annabel was all right and let her know he'd told Keisha to call the police. And he wanted to do it without Selena Wolcott breathing down his neck.

He liked Selena. She'd been a good friend to him, especially after he and Quinn parted ways. But he couldn't get his breath when she was around. She was always smiling at him, searching his eyes, expecting something they both knew he'd never be able to give her. There was no spark between them. And there never would be.

He'd have to deal with it. Tell Selena straight out their friendship was destined to stay just that—a friendship. There was no easy way to do it without hurting her, but he knew he couldn't wait much longer. He'd put off telling her until the shock of Quinn's death had diminished. At least, that's what he told himself. Jesus. He was a great one for telling other people to get things done, but when it came to sorting out his own personal life, he procrastinated like a kid leaving school with the class bully waiting outside.

Soon. He would do it soon. But not tonight. Tonight he was lurking behind a Fraser fir like a common stalker, holding a pink plastic laundry basket under his arm.

He glanced down at the ruined sheet music: Rosemary Clooney's streaked face, Tony Bennett's missing mouth. That damned rental blower had really done a job on them. The sheets of music that were covered in protective jackets had survived intact, but the rest of them were ripped and wrinkled, smeared with sawdust and dirt. Keisha had helped him wipe them off, but it hadn't helped much.

Something stirred on the porch. Was Selena finally going? He peered through the dense branches and watched Selena walk through the yard to the path. Her thick leather heels clicked sharply against the black-top pavement. Why did she always wear such big ugly shoes? They reminded him of the brown lace-ups Aunt Margaret wore in winter when her bunions throbbed.

He waited until Selena was out of sight, then pushed through the branches and stepped into the clearing.

Annabel appeared at the window, and his heart lurched.

She stood beside the soft glow of a flickering oil lamp. Streaks of gold played across her hair, shaped the elongated line of her throat, drenched her face in incandescent light. Had she seen him? Did she know he was there? The last thing he wanted to do was frighten her.

He shifted the heavy laundry basket to the other arm and waved. "Annabel!"

She hadn't heard him. She stood in the center of the narrow window, staring into the night. He opened his mouth to call to her again, but before he could utter a sound, she lifted her hand, that graceful, slender swan-of-a-hand, and wiped away tears. Then she pounded the windowpane with her fist. Over and over. Until he was sure the rippled glass would shatter and break.

Helplessness engulfed him.

He wanted to go to her, take her in his arms, make the bad stuff go away. He wanted to hold her and stroke her hair and feel the soft breath escape from her lips as they brushed against his. But he couldn't.

But he wanted to.

He didn't know what to do. And not knowing what to do was the one thing that made him categorically insane.

He left the path and charged through the woods, tripping over rocks, flattening new undergrowth, crashing through a low tangle of forsythia like a wounded boar. He didn't look back. He didn't have to. The image of her beautiful, sad face had branded itself inside his head. Inside his heart.

When he reached the top of the hill, he stopped beside the fire hydrant to catch his breath.

Why was he running away from her? Annabel wasn't Quinn. She would never hurt anyone on purpose. If her being at the inn forced some truths about Quinn into the light, then maybe that was what was meant to happen. God knows, he'd hidden some of those truths from Gil for too long.

He stood looking at Annabel's cabin. He didn't care what Selena said, what had happened in the carriage house was no accident, and as long as he had a breath left in him, he'd find out who was behind it. He'd told Keisha that, and she'd flipped out her cell phone and called the cops. No questions asked. God, he loved that woman. She was the big brother he'd always wanted.

Keisha had pointed out that air from the blower couldn't have scattered the sheet music beneath the bandstand; it had to have been planted there to lure Annabel in. Keisha had made him realize what a damned close call Annabel had had. She could have been blinded or suffocated. Or worse. When he'd seen her standing in the lobby, and realized she'd been hurt, white-hot fear had paralyzed him. He hadn't felt white-hot fear for anyone. Ever.

He started walking back down the hill. If Annabel was crying because she thought no one believed her, then he could fix that. Because, God help him, he believed every word she'd ever said to him. With all his heart.

The sharp crunch of broken twigs cut through the night.

Trent turned around, expecting to see Selena. The girl had built-in radar when it came to tracking him down. His eye caught a movement. Something sudden and dark. Just before it slammed into his skull.

A spray of white sparks exploded behind his eyes. He fell to his knees. The music flew out of his arms. He grabbed the back of his neck and blinked.

The last thing he saw before the clanging in his brain took over, and the encroaching waves of blackness obliterated his sight, was the pink plastic laundry basket, sliding down the hill like a runaway sled.

Chapter 10

The car careened around another sharp hairpin turn.

"*Byron!*" Annabel cried.

"The trick to navigating mountain roads is only use the brake when it's absolutely necessary. If you don't, it disturbs the flow."

"I'm about to disturb *your* flow." She grabbed the armrest. "Slow *down.*"

"Okay. Stop yelling at me." Byron tapped the brakes. "This is a nice little sedan. I'll have to give Craig something special for loaning it to me."

Annabel glanced at him sideways. "He's just a kid, Byron. I know he thinks you can dance across water, but—"

"Craig is twenty-one. And in my book, that makes him fair game for anything. I might even consider mentoring him."

"Is that what they're calling it these days?"

Byron laughed. "That's one thing. Let me figure out where to park, and I'll let you out."

Annabel held on to the overnight bag Gil had packed for Trent. She took a breath and closed her eyes. The memory of the last few hours kept playing over and over in her head like a bad movie trailer.

It had all happened so fast. Rachel's screams, the 911 call, sirens echoing up the mountain. Trent lying on the black pavement, blood streaming down his neck into his shirt collar. Annabel had held his head on her lap and kept stroking his face to make sure he was still breathing. She stayed with him until the EMS truck slammed its doors and roared into the night, leaving her standing in the middle of the road with her heart still lodged in her throat.

Byron pulled into a reserved space beside the hospital entrance. “So, you’ve definitely decided to stay at the inn? I can’t change your mind?”

“I don’t have a choice. I told you what Selena said, and she was telling the truth. My father’s in bad shape. I’ve never heard him sound so despondent.”

“Then screw Selena,” he said gently. “Screw them all. You’ve only been here a week. You don’t owe these cretins anything. I think you ought to contact Selena’s bank and tell them she’s blackmailing you.”

“But I don’t have any proof that’s what she’s planning to do. It would just be my word against hers.”

Byron parked the car and turned to her. “I’m worried about you, sweet girl. These people are awful—worse than any I’ve ever met in theater. No one cares if you’re safe here or not.”

“I know. But it’s not like I don’t want to leave. I *do*. But I can’t. If I don’t see this through, my family will lose everything. For the first time in my life, my father needs me. He may never admit it. But he does.”

“Then I’m staying too. For a few more days, anyway. We’ll get the damned floorshow finished, appease Selena, and get you the hell out of here.”

“Appease Selena? It sounds like she’s sitting on a skull throne, waiting for the natives to toss the next human sacrifice into the volcano.”

“Just like her sister. Family trait, I guess.”

Annabel gathered up her jacket. “I’m sorry about the music. I know Gil said the inn’s insurance will cover it, but I wish I could get it back for you.”

"I'm sorry your guy got whacked on the head when someone stole it from him."

"He's not my guy."

"Uh, huh. And that's why you're staying at the hospital with him tonight. Because he's not your guy."

Annabel took a deep breath. She couldn't tell Byron that Trent would never be her guy. He'd sampled the goods—at least the first-base goods—and decided that anything physical between them was a mistake he couldn't afford to repeat. Which was something she would have to get over. But he'd gotten his head bashed in returning Byron's music to her, and even though he had added her name to the "last woman in the world" list, she wasn't going to turn her back on him.

"I'm staying with Trent because I've spent a lot of time in hospitals. Most of them have tremendous nursing shortages, and if you're sick, you need someone to watch out for you. My mother almost aspirated melted green Jell-O once because the night nurse was too busy to answer her call."

"Point taken," Byron said. Annabel swung Trent's bag over her shoulder. "Just be careful."

"When I get back to the inn?"

"No, when you see Trent. You've spent the last four years around male dancers and chorus boys. You're not used to dealing with a man whose testosterone is at full throttle."

Annabel laughed, thinking of the easy heat Trent Sheffield could generate just by looking at her. "You make him sound like a racecar."

"I know." Byron kissed her on the cheek. "Vroom, vroom, darling."

****

Trent opened his eyes and gazed across the room. Annabel was still there, leaning against the windowsill. He thought he'd dreamed it.

He tried to sit up, but the ton of scrap metal pressing against his head hammered into his skull. He groaned.

Annabel's head whipped around. "Are you awake again?"

"I think. Was I before?"

Suddenly, she was at his bedside, holding onto the aluminum railing, blinking those huge gray blue eyes at him. "Every twenty minutes or so."

"How'd you do that?"

"What?"

"Float across the room like that?"

"Good to know the pain medicine has finally kicked in."

He leaned forward and winced. "I wish it would kick me some more. This time where it counts."

"You're still hurting. I'll get the nurse."

"No, I'm fine." He managed a weak smile. "Please. She'll just knock me out again. I want to stay awake."

"All right." She punched up his pillow and helped him lie back, then picked up a Styrofoam cup and held it to his lips. "This could be fun. When's the last time you used a bendy straw?"

"You act like you've done this before."

"I took care of my mother for a while when she was sick."

"How long?"

"Two years."

"What was wrong with her?"

"Ovarian cancer."

"That's terrible. How is she now?"

"Dead."

He reached out and grabbed her hand. "Oh, Christ, Annabel, I'm so sorry. I didn't know." He slid his hand across hers, palms touching, smooth as polished jade. A stream of warmth traveled the length of his arm, erupted into a fleeting burst of heat.

"She's been gone a long time. Over five years." She maneuvered herself around the IV trolley, but didn't extract her hand from his. "Gil and Rachel were here earlier. Do you remember?"

"Not really." He closed his eyes. He remembered a long gray hallway with squares of fluorescent lights flying by overhead. He remembered riding on something that sounded like a Wal-Mart basket, and some smartass technician who reeked of cigarette smoke making him stay awake through the CT scan. "I was coming to see you. I was bringing the sheet music."

"I know. They found some of them behind a bush. Rachel found you when she was walking back."

He tried to focus on her face, tried to pretend something sharp wasn't stabbing sideways into his brain. "That's why I got hit, wasn't it?" He winced again and moaned. "So someone could steal the music?"

"I'm calling the nurse." She pushed the call button before he could protest, and in a matter of minutes an RN was at his side, shooting a hypodermic into his IV. The pain drifted upward and out the top of his head like mist evaporating off a hot sidewalk. Annabel leaned close. He could see the reflection of his bandaged head in her glasses.

"I look like a swami, don't I?"

"Yes. And what a shame I sent my crystal ball out to be polished."

"Do you have it waxed too?" His grin felt lopsided. "Do you have other things waxed?"

"I was a dancer in an off-Broadway show. I've had everything waxed. Many times."

He laughed, then pressed his fingers against his head to keep it from throbbing.

"You should rest," she said. "Lie back and try

not to talk so much."

"But I want to talk. With you, it feels more like a game. Like a great tennis match without the stupid clothes."

She pulled the chair close to the bed and crossed her legs, wrapping the top one around the other until her toe hooked behind her ankle.

"Doesn't that hurt your hip?" he asked.

"Everything hurts my hip." She leaned up in the chair and rested her chin on her hand.

Trent wished he still had hold of that hand. His felt empty and cold without it. He looked into her eyes. He could tell she didn't trust him. Or maybe she wanted to trust him, but just couldn't give in to it. Whatever the nurse had shot into his IV had rendered his judgment more or less a crapshoot.

"I want to ask you something and tell you something," he said. He tried to push himself up.

"Okay. But keep your head on the pillow."

"Question first." He waited for her to look into his eyes. Waited for his heart to squeeze in his chest when her gaze met his. "Why were you crying at the window?"

Embarrassment flushed across her face. "You saw me?"

"I was halfway down the hill on my way to your cabin. It was the last thing I saw before the lights went out. Maybe that's why I can't get it out of my head."

She extended her back and leaned to the side, then stretched forward again. The chair was uncomfortable for her. He knew he was being selfish, but he wanted her near.

"I had just talked to my father for the first time in four years," she said. "And it didn't go well. He and my sister-in-law are having some health problems, and he kept pretending everything was fine, like he had everything under control. Which is how he copes."

"Do you need to go home? Why don't you go visit him?"

"I will in a couple of weeks, after I get the floorshow ready."

"Forget the floorshow. I mean it. If you need to be with your family, then go."

"It's complicated."

"Hell, Annie, everything's complicated. People can't back off from things just because they're complicated. If they did, no one would ever connect with anybody."

"Is that what you do?" She raised her eyebrows. "Is it?"

"No. I haven't seen my own father in four years too. Not since the day he showed up at Gil's graduation with one too many scotch and sodas under his belt."

"What happened?"

"After he dove headfirst into the buffet table? Or after he decided to tell Gil he wasn't Gil's real father?"

"You're kidding. That's some graduation present."

"Yeah," he said bitterly. "Now I have to find him and beg him to sign off on the lots we own jointly. I want to sell them to pay off our debts."

"And you have no idea where he is?"

"No. I've searched for months. In person, on the phone, on the Internet. I tracked him to Brooklyn, then to a little town in north Jersey. He worked in a bakery there. Between acting jobs, he's always been able to find work in a bakery."

"He was an actor, too?"

"Still is. I keep thinking some theater will offer him a part he can't turn down, and I'll locate him."

"Are you sure he doesn't want to be found?"

"I think he just drifted away. Like he always did

when things got sticky. Like Gil does now. When our mother went to New York to try to get work in the theater, he dumped us with his sister, Margaret. Margaret wasn't exactly the motherly type, and survived our being there by pretending we didn't exist. Gil's been my responsibility since I was thirteen. Which is why I'm overprotective of him. I've taken care of him for a long time, longer than I probably should have, but I didn't have a choice."

He closed his eyes and swallowed. The pain meds were making him more emotional than he allowed himself to be. He had to be careful when talking about the past. Some memories wielded their power over him without mercy, leaving him weak with anger and regret, pricking a raw spot inside his heart that would never heal.

He pushed himself up in bed. "My father isn't part of my life anymore. Once he signs the sales agreement, he can rot in New York, or New Jersey, or hell, for all I care."

"I don't believe you," she said softly. "I think you care a lot." She stood and walked to the window. Air from the heating vent ruffled the hem of her light blue blouse. "Last night, at the window, talking to my father wasn't the only reason I was crying."

"Tell me."

She turned and faced him. Christ, he could drown in those eyes. Short dark blond curls blew around her face, flicked against the soft slope of her jaw. "I was wondering what might have been."

"You mean if Quinn hadn't died?"

"No. A long time ago, back home, I taught a theater class for underprivileged kids. Most of my students were itinerant farm children. I don't even think they'd seen a real play before. They worked all day in the fields, then came to class with blistered hands and feet, so tired they could barely keep their eyes open. But they loved it. Pretending they were someone else for two hours helped them forget the harsh reality of their lives. It transformed them. It transformed *me*."

"That's wonderful," he said, slurring his words.

"I haven't thought of those kids in years. I finally got the courage to leave home, so I cancelled the program, set out for New York to follow my Big Dream, and never looked back. By now, some of those children have families of their own. God knows what they're doing in this economy. Probably still moving from town to town, harvesting other people's produce, trying to survive."

"Why did that make you cry?"

"I just wondered how selfish I would seem to them now, or if they'd even recognize me as the same girl who was part of their lives one summer in the basement of an Indiana church."

"I'm sure they've never forgotten you. How could they?"

She shoved her hands in her jean pockets and leaned against the window sill. "You know, the thing is I liked that girl—the one who tried to make a difference in other people's lives. And I was crying because I don't know where that girl went. Or why I haven't missed her before now."

"She's still there. You haven't lost her."

"That girl was part of the package I left behind in New York when I had to stop dancing." She laughed softly. "See, I told you it was selfish."

"If it still tugs at your heart that much, maybe that's what you were meant to do."

"Maybe." She walked back to the bed and stood with her hands on the railing, looking down at him. "You've asked your question. Now, what did you want to tell me?"

He held out his hand to her, and after a few moments, she took it. He knew he wasn't firing on all cylinders, but the heat from her hand felt like it was shooting up his arm, healing him. He looked into her eyes and fought the urge to pull her toward him.

"I just want to tell you that...you scare the hell out of me. You know that, don't you?"

"I..." She took a deep, ragged breath. "Yes."

"And those things I said about never wanting to kiss you again were stupid and spineless, and I didn't mean any of them. I was pushing you away because—"

"Because you think I'm like Quinn, and that scares the hell out of you."

He turned her small hand over and pressed his lips to her bandaged palm. And then he grinned up at her, because he didn't know what else to do. "Yeah. But I can't tell you how brave you're starting to make me feel."

Someone knocked on the door. A stocky, uniformed policeman breezed into the room. "Officer Robert Vance." He shook Trent's hand. "I know it's late, but they never let you sleep in hospitals anyway." He squinted toward the window. "Starting to rain out there. We've been going over both assault sites, trying to gather evidence before the weather turns it to mush."

"Both?" Annabel said.

"Yes," Vance said. "Yours and his. You are Annabel Maitland, aren't you?"

Annabel nodded then looked at Trent. "You called the police?"

"Keisha called them. I was coming to tell you that when I got hit on the head."

Vance pulled a spiral notebook from his pocket and flipped it open. "On the surface, it looks like a simple robbery—clunk someone over the head, grab the goodies, and go. We've talked to...uh..." He glanced at his notes. "Mr. Byron Patrick. He's the owner of the sheet music, right?"

"Yes," Annabel said. "He loaned it to me."

"I can't believe those old things are worth that much," Vance said. "But I guess there's a market for it." He turned to Trent. "Now, let's see. You were carrying them down the hill in a pink laundry basket. Did you know they were valuable?"

"A pink laundry basket?" Annabel asked. Her lips twitched, suppressing a smile. "Was it yours?"

"It matches my bathrobe," Trent said. "I hadn't really thought about their value. I was just returning them when—"

"—someone stopped you," Vance finished. "We've already questioned the hotel staff. Do you think anyone else might have heard what happened to Miss Maitland tonight and realized their street value? A guest, maybe?"

"Maybe," Trent said.

Vance chewed the end of his pen. "Exactly what *did* happen to you, Miss Maitland?"

Annabel gave Vance a little background about Quinn's death, then recounted her ordeal at the supper club. When she was through, Vance snapped his notebook closed and clasped both hands over his large paunch. "Looks like someone's playing a game with the two of you, someone who isn't too keen on you poking into the death of this friend of yours. I can talk to the NYPD, if you want, see if any of this warrants reopening the case. But until then, my best advice is to stay alert and be careful."

"Oh, thanks," Trent said. His head had begun to throb again. "We never would have thought of that on our own."

Vance tucked his pen in his pocket. "Okay, kids. You know where to find me. I'll call when we have something."

After Vance had gone, Annabel said, "Why didn't you say something about the gunshots in the woods?"

"Because we know it was Eli."

"Do you think he—"

"No. Eli wouldn't sneak into the carriage house and try to sabotage you. He doesn't even know you. And frankly, he's not that smart." He pressed his head with this hand. "We should make a list of suspects, starting with Rachel."

"Why Rachel?"

"Because she showed up here out of the blue."

"Are you sure you feel up to this?"

"Sit down," he said. "It'll take my mind off the pain. And I get to look at you."

Annabel shook some crushed ice into a clean cup and sat on the chair beside the bed. "Rachel and I had a falling out back in New York when she was using drugs."

"Then why did you hire her to work here?"

"Because I felt guilty. When she was in trouble, I should have treated her with more compassion. I dropped her as a friend because I didn't want to hang around with someone who was considered toxic by—"

"Quinn?"

Annabel crunched down on a chunk of ice. "Yes, but it wasn't just Quinn. It was everyone. What Rachel was doing was dangerous."

"Taking drugs?"

"Taking drugs and dancing on a twelve-foot platform. She could have fallen and killed herself, not to mention the dancers on the floor beneath her. I felt bad she got booted back to chorus, but I truly believe it saved her life." Annabel sighed. "I know Rachel and I have a history together, and I know she resented Quinn. But Rachel is a gentle soul. I don't think she's capable of hurting anyone, other than herself."

"What about Byron?"

"That's ridiculous. Besides the fact that he's the

dearest friend I have, he wasn't even here. He was either still in the air or on his way in from the airport."

"No, he was here. He showed up in the Laurel Room while you were in the carriage house eating sawdust. We had a drink together in the bar."

"Oh," she said. "When I saw him in the lobby, I thought he'd just arrived."

"Did Byron and Craig know each other before? I saw them talking on my way down to your cabin, and they seem awfully friendly for two people who just met."

"Craig's a huge fan of Byron's, and Byron just eats it up."

"To put it figuratively."

"Right."

"Donald barely knew Quinn, and I can vouch for Keisha. Mrs. Rosetti isn't exactly suspect. If she'd wanted me gone, she could've put arsenic in my calzone months ago, not walloped me on the head with a river rock."

"What about that innkeeper? The one who had it in for Gil?"

"Marissa Hawley? That's old news. She hired some displaced bakery chef from New Orleans, and has more business than she can handle. Last month, they were both featured in *Southern Living* magazine."

"Some people like to tie up loose ends revenge-wise."

"I guess. People can be crazy. Even the sane ones."

"Especially the sane ones."

He pulled the white thermal blanket up around his shoulders. She was on her feet instantly, smoothing out the lumps, fluffing the flat pillow behind his head.

"What about Selena and her mother?" she

asked.

Trent tried to keep his eyes open. He fought off the urge to pee. He would deal with that later, send her out to find him a newspaper or something. Right now, all he wanted was to keep her near and try to figure things out.

"Selena's like a sister to us," he said. "She wants the inn to succeed as much as we do."

"But she and Mrs. Wolcott were at *Moondance* the night Quinn died."

"And so were you, and Byron, and Rachel."

The heating unit in the wall switched on. Warm air swirled around them. He wanted to gulp it in until it hurt. He wanted Annabel to smile at him. Just once more. Because after he said what he needed to say, that might not happen for a very long time.

"There are two more suspects to add to the list," he said quietly.

"Who?"

"Gil was in New York the night Quinn died. And so was I."

Chapter 11

Annabel was still fumbling for her seatbelt when Rachel gunned the motor. The car swerved sharply to the right then sped toward the hospital parking lot exit.

"Sorry," Rachel said. "It's been a while since I've driven a car."

"I think I've finally found something you and Byron have in common—your driving."

"Let's not get snippy." Rachel grinned. "Get much sleep last night?"

Annabel looked at her sideways. "Enough."

She and Trent had talked on and off until the wee hours. He'd struggled to stay awake, but refused to give in. After a nurse had helped him to the bathroom and back, he finally fell into a deep sleep. Annabel sat in the soft glow of his nightlight, watching him. She wondered what it would feel like to climb in and curl up beside him, close her burning eyes, rest her head on the gentle rise and fall of his chest while the rest of the world melted away. She'd listened to his heartbeat once before, in the tall grass, when he'd held her so tightly she'd forgotten how to breathe. She finally stretched out on the hospital sleeper chair next to his bed and relived those moments, playing them over and over in her head until she finally drifted off.

Rachel bumped over the curb and flattened a small shrub. "Last night Byron said he was picking you up. He said to call him by ten to make sure he was awake, then the scumbag wouldn't answer his phone. Just his little way of controlling the universe, I guess. At least his new boyfriend didn't mind loaning me his car."

"Come on, Rach. Byron is Byron. You have to take him or leave him."

"Then I'll leave him, thank you very much. You want to know why I can't stand Byron? Because he doesn't care whose life he destroys. He told a story once about this guy he had the hots for in college. The only trouble was the guy was straight, and at school on a basketball scholarship. Byron stalked him for weeks. He sent leopard skin jockstraps to his dorm, left little love notes in his gym locker. The poor guy couldn't take it. He quit school before the semester was over—just gave up his scholarship and fled. And Byron laughed about it. Byron ruined a huge chunk of a man's life, and he uses it as an anecdote to tell at cocktail parties."

"I can't believe Byron would be that coldhearted."

Rachel sighed. "I love you, Annabel. You always look for the good in people, but you ignore the obvious. You believe the assholes of the world all have redeeming qualities. Well, they don't." She swerved, barely missing a parked furniture truck, then wound the car through the narrow streets of Asheville.

"How's Mrs. Richmond's ankle?"

"It was only a sprain. But damn, that woman is a pill. A sad and lonely pill."

"You'd think her money would take the edge off some of that loneliness."

"That's just it. Keisha doesn't think she's rich at all."

"You talked to Keisha?"

"Last night, when Gil and I got back from the hospital. She said Gil and Trent let people walk all over them. Did you know Trent lets Mrs. Richmond stay at the inn for free because she's got nowhere else to go? She looks rich, with her diamond bracelets and that vile little dog she carries under her arm, but she can't pay her bill. She keeps saying her daughter's gonna come and take her back home. Keisha wonders if she even has a daughter."

"What else does Keisha say?"

"She said Trent can't stand to see anyone down on their luck. A nice quality if you're handing out cheese sandwiches at a soup kitchen, but even I know you can't run a hotel like that and turn a profit."

So. On the inside, Trent Sheffield was a quivering glob of pudding.

"Let's take the Black Mountain exit," Annabel said.

"Where are we going?"

"To see Mrs. Wolcott. I've got an address and a map."

"We're going to ask questions about Quinn's death, aren't we?"

"I am. You're going to watch my back and keep your mouth shut." She started to protest. "I'm serious, Rach. The woman owns a gun. I don't want to upset her."

"Won't Selena be there?"

"She's supposed to be out of the house on Sundays. I'm not sure about the nephew, Eli. If he's there, we'll just have to deal with it."

"This map says the Reverend Billy Graham is from Black Mountain." Rachel laughed. "That would explain it, then."

"Explain what?"

"Gil and Trent's accents. They sound just like him."

"They were there, you know. In New York the night Quinn died—both of them."

"This requires nicotine. There's a place to pull off up ahead. I'm stopping."

They got out of the car and stood beside a low rock wall. The Blue Ridge Mountains spread across the foggy horizon like a smudged watercolor. The air smelled loamy and damp.

Rachel lit a cigarette. "I like Gil. A lot. I know I just met him, but I can't help it. I think he feels the same spark too. And yes, I know we're the walking wounded, and will have to take it slow. I don't completely trust him, but I'd sure hate to find out that the first guy I've been attracted to in years murdered his ex-fiancée." Panic crossed her face. "Oh, God, you don't think Gil could have—"

"No," Annabel said gently. "I do not. He loved Quinn with all his heart. You can see it in his eyes every time he says her name."

"Wasn't that what the defense said at the O. J. Simpson trial?"

"Gil is the one person at the inn I haven't really talked to about Quinn's death. He seems so torn up about it, I haven't been able to bring myself to dredge it up again for him."

"I'll see what I can find out. Gil's pretty forthcoming if you ask the right questions. But just so we're clear, I'm doing this for you and me. Not for Quinn."

"One more person who hated Quinn," Annabel said wearily. "Have you thought of organizing a support group?"

"Quinn treated me like dirt. She was after my part from Day One. She knew how vulnerable I was and she still loaned me drug money. If she hadn't, I might never have sunk back to the bottom of the cesspool."

"You have a lot of nerve blaming Quinn for that."

"Okay. I take full responsibility for every self-destructive thing I did. I'm only saying that Quinn was a rotten person, and everyone knew it but you. And Gil."

Annabel gazed across the meadow. "I knew what she was like. I just didn't want to believe it. Quinn had her faults—we all do—but she was a good friend to me."

"Whatever." Rachel took a deep drag on her cigarette. "Maybe you just bring out the best in people. Or maybe you're an angel. Or delusional. Or both. But if Quinn was a good friend to you, then you, my dear, were the only one."

****

Mrs. Wolcott's house sat off to the side of the road. A tangle of overgrown branches swept across the yard, blotting out all available sunlight. Rachel pointed to an old Chevrolet propped up on cinderblocks. "Look at that bumper sticker. *I Brake for the Rapture.* What a hoot! At least she has a sense of humor."

"I don't think she means it as joke."

Annabel rang the doorbell. Mrs. Wolcott opened the door and peered through the screen. Long strings of reddish gray hair framed her face like a worn-out mop. "What are you doin' here on the Lord's Day?"

"I came to ask you a few questions, Mrs. Wolcott. I'd like to find out why you were at the Park Square Theater the night Quinn died."

At the mention of Quinn's name, Mrs. Wolcott's face crumpled into a mass of loose wrinkles. Her bulging green eyes filled with tears. She opened the screen door and took an unsteady step back, then motioned for Annabel to come inside.

"Good luck," Rachel whispered. "I'm gonna stay out here and poke around a little."

Mrs. Wolcott leaned heavily on her cane while she hobbled across the floor, then lowered herself into a platform rocker. An oil painting of Christ praying in the garden of Gethsemane hung above the brick fireplace. A framed photograph of Quinn with long brown hair sat on the TV. Two white votive candles flickered on either side of it.

"My Quinn looked beautiful then," Mrs. Wolcott said. She pulled out a tissue and dabbed at the puffy bags beneath her eyes. "She was a good girl until those sinners got a hold of her. We prayed every night for her soul to be released. And our church prayed for her every Sunday."

"What church do you attend, Mrs. Wolcott? Is it near here? The church I went to growing up in Indiana was almost forty miles away."

Mrs. Wolcott's head shot up. "You went to church?"

"Oh, yes, ma'am. Every Sunday. My father insisted." Annabel didn't mention the heated arguments they'd had the year she turned fifteen, when Annabel refused to go. Her mother had cajoled; her father had demanded. But by then it had become a power struggle for her independence, and Annabel wouldn't give in.

"Honor thy father."

"Mrs. Wolcott, why did you go to see *Moondance*? I thought you hated Quinn's dancing."

Mrs. Wolcott closed her eyes. "I went to tell Quinn I forgave her. To save her precious soul."

"Did Quinn know you and Selena were coming?"

"No. Selena said it would upset her." She looked at Annabel, bewildered. "Why are you asking me these things?"

"I promised Quinn I would help her find peace. You want that too, don't you, Mrs. Wolcott? You don't want Quinn to be sad while she's in heaven."

"I...I didn't think you could be sad there."

"Did Quinn ever say she was afraid someone might want to hurt her?"

"Hurt Quinn? Who would want to hurt my Quinn?"

"Theaters are full of evil people." Mrs. Wolcott nodded solemnly. "If someone knew Quinn was allergic to something, they could use that information to harm her."

"They could," Mrs. Wolcott whispered.

"Something like codeine."

"That's what she took. I never knew it was on her allergy list. None of us did. Quinn was allergic to so many things, I couldn't keep track—dust mites, cat fur, shellfish. But codeine...I didn't know about that. Selena said you thought you were giving her Curenol."

"Did the coroner say she died of a codeine overdose? Or was something else in her system? There were paint fumes in the dressing rooms. Some of the dancers felt quite ill."

Mrs. Wolcott got up and limped to a drop-leaf desk. She lifted a stapled packet of papers from the bottom drawer and pushed it at Annabel. "Here."

Annabel scanned the autopsy report. *Cause of death—anaphylaxis. Caused by severe allergic reaction, most likely to codeine. 240 mg of codeine present at time of death, resulting in acute respiratory distress followed by a grand mal seizure.*

The memory of that night flashed behind Annabel's eyes—an amber spotlight shimmering across Quinn's face, her mouth gasping for air, her pale green eyes twitching and rolling behind half-closed lids.

Annabel read the last paragraph. *Other anatomic findings include an intrauterine pregnancy. Fetus approximately 8 weeks.* She looked at Mrs. Wolcott. "Quinn was pregnant. Did you know that?"

Mrs. Wolcott began to cry. "Selena told me. I begged Quinn to ask the Lord's forgiveness."

"Did you tell anyone else?"

"*No!* We live in a town where Christian values still mean something. I couldn't let the church know my daughter had strayed. How could I explain that to Pastor Simcox?"

"But Gil knew, right? Surely she told the father of her baby."

"Don't know." Mrs. Wolcott slumped over her cane. The anger seemed to drain out of her. All that was left was the empty shell of a despondent, grieving old woman.

Had Gil known about the pregnancy? Was it even Gil's child? Quinn cut a wide swath where men were concerned. Was that why she had broken off her engagement to him? Because she was having another man's child?

Mrs. Wolcott's gaze drifted upward to the painting of Jesus. "Quinn's living in the Father's house now." She turned to Annabel and harrumphed. "Just like you're living in the inn." Her eyes burned into Annabel's. "Won't do you no good, though. That man will never love you. Not like he loved my Quinn."

"What man are you talking about, Mrs. Wolcott?"

Mrs. Wolcott smiled. "Why, Trent Sheffield," she said. "Who did you think?"

****

Rachel slammed the car door. "Quinn was pregnant? Good God."

"Do you think 240 milligrams of codeine could cause a miscarriage?"

"Oh, Jeez, Annabel. Do you think Quinn took it on purpose to lose the baby? I mean, I couldn't really see her having the thing, could you? She thought she was up for the lead in Freeman's dance piece along with you and Byron. There was a chance *Moondance* might move to Broadway. A baby would have brought everything to a screeching halt."

"Someone made sure of that."

"I know this sounds callous, but in this day and age, why didn't she just go to a clinic and have an abortion? I didn't think she was that religious."

"No, but her mother is." Annabel held onto the seatbelt while Rachel barreled onto the highway. "Did you find anything interesting when you were poking around the yard?"

"More like strange-as-hell. I found a cage of poisonous snakes in one of those old outbuildings behind the garage."

"Are you serious?"

"Oh, yes. Must have been ten or twelve of them. Totally freaked me out."

"Maybe they belong to Eli. Maybe they're pets. You know, a school project or something."

"What? Like Eddie Munster?"

"Are you sure the snakes were poisonous?"

Rachel reached in her bag for a cigarette. "Honey, you're talking to a gal from the islands of south Georgia. I may not know much, but I know a Florida cottonmouth when I see one."

Annabel rolled down her window and sucked in a last breath of fresh air. "Very weird."

"Me or the Wolcott's?"

"Both."

Rachel laughed. "I've missed you, Annabel. And for the record, I heard what the old bat said before we left. About Trent never loving you the way he loved Quinn."

"She was upset "

"Maybe. But she hasn't seen the way he looks at you."

"Like I've got spinach stuck in my teeth?"

"No, baby. Like you're the Second Coming."

Chapter 12

Annabel stood on the tiny stage and looked around the carriage house. Someone had removed the blower machine and vacuumed up the sawdust. The bandstand door had been nailed open. The night before felt as though it had happened to someone else. But it hadn't. And if she wanted proof, all she had to do was look at the deep scratches on her wrists and legs.

She glanced at her watch. She had time to stretch; rehearsal wouldn't start for another thirty minutes. Rachel had found the third dancer, a twenty-two-year-old African American girl from Asheville named Marva, who looked like Bernadette Peters with black hair and sang like Whitney Houston. Or at least thought she did. Which did liven up the place.

Annabel had wired the last of her savings to Drew that morning, hoping it would buy him some time with the bank. Until she could get back to New York and sell some of her belongings, it was the best she could do.

She turned on the CD player and popped in one of the CD's she'd borrowed from the Laurel Room. They had a nice little collection they played on the nights the band wasn't there. Old stuff, mostly, but classic. The swoony strains of violin music filled the room.

She turned and positioned her arms. By the time Andy Williams crooned the first lines of "Moon

River," she had stretched her left leg behind her and rippled her back into a shoulder roll. She spun slowly, testing the waters, relieved she could feel the core strength in her hip. She knew it wouldn't last, but before it vanished, it was a gift she planned to enjoy. She dipped and twirled, then segued into a progression of rapid waltz steps, gliding effortlessly across the floor.

The music propelled her from one side of the stage to the other, pushing her up, drawing her back, spiraling her into a low, sensuous layout at the end of each turn. The music soared beneath her like a ribbon of Novocain. Dancing had always been that way for her. As long as she was dancing, it all fell away: Quinn's death, the danger she was in, her father's illness, Selena's threats, the sickening fear that the doctors were right, and she might never dance again. For a few precious moments, nothing existed except the cool air swirling against her face and the beat of the music pulsing in her ears.

The last, lingering notes pulled her to center stage. She stood with her arms outstretched, then closed her eyes and leaned back. Energy zinged through her as if she'd been flying.

"Annabel." Trent's deep baritone echoed through the empty room. "Damn, you're good."

She opened her eyes. Trent was walking down the side aisle toward her, smiling. Her heart pounded even harder at the sight of him. She lowered her arms and floundered for a second, watching his face. "How long have you been back there?"

"Long enough." His smile slid into a heart-stopping grin, deepening the dimples that slashed the sides of his cheeks. "So this is how you look when you're happy."

She gave a little shrug. "Dancing makes the world go away."

"Wish I had something to make the world go away. Besides a bottle of Johnnie Walker Red." He held out his hand and helped her off the stage. The heat from his touch flooded through her. "How's the hip? It looked pretty good up there."

"It's stronger, but deceptive. A few hours from now, when it stiffens up, I'll be hobbling down the path like Quasimodo." She looked into his eyes and tried to remember how to breathe. "Shouldn't I be asking how you are? You're the one with the big goose egg on your head."

Trent patted the large Band-Aid covering the square, shaved patch and the neat row of stitches. "Much better. Thanks to an angel who slept on a cot beside my bed last night. Not sure how I'm going to thank her."

"I don't think she expects you to."

"We'll see about that." He brushed the back of her bruised hand with his knuckles. "Rachel sent me to tell you she's moved rehearsal to the Laurel Room. She thought it might upset you to be in here after what happened."

"I'm fine. But I should have warned you. Rachel can be very bossy, especially when she's sober."

"As long as she stays sober, I can deal with bossy." He glanced around the room. "You know, this is nice. Fred and Ginger's is really coming together, isn't it?"

"I thought you hated it."

"I did. But I have to admit, it's growing on me." His eyes caught the light as his gaze met hers. "A lot of things are growing on me. You, for example."

"Like a fungus?"

"More like soft Irish moss."

He laughed then, crinkling the fine chiseled lines around his eyes. She had the sudden impulse to reach out and touch the contours of his face, feel his breath slide across the inside of her wrist. The memory of his lips trailing soft kisses down her throat sent a flush of crimson spreading across her cheeks.

"Hey, Annie, can you sit for a minute?" He slid onto the edge of the stage. "I want to tell you something."

She sat beside him and winced. "See, I told you it wouldn't last. It's awful to have a body part you can't trust."

"I know what you mean." He waggled his eyebrows so discreetly, she wasn't even sure he'd done it until she noticed the twinkle in his eyes.

"That's a guy thing, isn't it?"

"Oh, yes, ma'am." His sweet, lopsided grin tugged at her heart. His soft Western Carolina drawl slurred each vowel with a honeyed sexiness she found irresistible.

The irresistible ones were always a gamble. Men who exuded that quiet sexiness and stayed just a little bit guarded and lost. To some women, they were like magic elixirs, the kind the crew of *Star Trek* were always stumbling upon. The kind that, once tasted, were as addictive as chocolate or air.

Annabel didn't have the skills to deflect that kind of magic. Being on the receiving end of a magnet was new to her. She'd never felt an overpowering attraction to anyone, not even in the backseat of Jimmy Doran's metallic green Mustang. Maybe she was too picky, but every man she'd ever dated had disappointed her in some way. Jimmy had joked about her flat chest then left sweaty, slow-dance handprints on the back of her blue velvet dress. Eric's lips felt like a couple of wet marshmallows. Ryan pushed food onto his fork with his thumb. Pierre rarely bathed. And after a couple of less than stellar tumbles on her new Ralph Lauren sheets, Rick decided he had the hots for a lacrosse player named Hank.

Trent rubbed the back of her hand with his thumb, sending little shivers rocketing along her skin. Oh, God, she was toast. Unsalvageable, burnt-to-a-crisp, toss-in-the-trash toast. And she had the sneaking suspicion he knew it too.

"Selena said you were packed and ready to walk out last night."

"Did she?"

"After everything that's happened, I can't say I blame you. But I'm glad she talked you into staying. For Gil's sake. For the inn's sake." He reached up and slid an errant curl back from her forehead. A current jumped from his fingertips onto her skin. "For my sake," he added huskily. "I hope you know that if I thought you were in any real danger, I would send you away in a heartbeat."

"What about the seven stitches in your scalp?"

"I think someone realized how valuable that old sheet music was and decided to take it."

"But who? Who even knew it was there?"

"Gil said the wait staff has been in and out. We've had lumber and supplies delivered there. The blower took four men to move. It could have been anybody. A guest, even."

"Mrs. Richmond?"

"She could have whacked me on the head with her cane." He laughed and moved closer. The barest hint of his spicy sweet aftershave drifted toward her. Sandalwood and musk? Sandalwood and vanilla? Whatever it was, she couldn't get enough of it. She had visions of her trailing behind him, drooling like a dog after a Big Mac.

"I also wanted to tell you—" He stopped.

"Yes?"

"How much I regret all the horrible things I said to you."

"What horrible things?"

"Comparing you to Quinn. Questioning your

motives for coming here. Telling you I never wanted to get...close to you again." He slid his arm around her shoulders. "I know I spent a good portion of last night in a drug-induced haze, but at some point—around three in the morning, when I opened my eyes and saw you sleeping in that God-awful chair—I realized that getting close to you was *exactly* what I wanted. And I vowed that if I ever had the chance again, I sure as hell wouldn't throw it away."

"Those were some drugs they shot in your IV."

He pulled her toward him. "You're changing me, you know that?"

"From a frog to a prince?"

"No, I'll always be a frog." He chuckled softly. "From a non-believer to a believer."

"And what do you believe in? Now that I've changed you?"

"You. Destiny." He nuzzled his soft beard stubble against the hollow of her neck. "Have dinner with me tonight."

"Only if you promise to wear a hat. I don't want people to think I whacked you on the head with a two-by-four."

He grinned again—that sweet, sexy, half-crooked grin—and she caught her breath. What lengths would the average woman go to in order to generate that grin? Dear God, it was contagious. Trent Sheffield was carrying around a secret weapon he didn't even know he had. Men were so clueless. The straight ones, anyway.

Trent pulled her to her feet. "You're different," he murmured. "Tell me you're different."

"Different from what?"

"From the other women I've known."

"Well." She laughed nervously. "My ears are upside down, and my knees don't quite match, and I've got this funny-looking mole on the bottom of my—"

"You always have an answer, don't you?"

"That depends on the question."

Trent's mouth moved toward hers. He shifted his head to graze the hypersensitive column of her neck, then traced a line from the tender spot behind her ear to the base of her throat. A blaze of heat surged through her like a double shot of tequila. Her head tilted back. A soft moan escaped her lips. If he didn't kiss her soon, she was going to melt into a puddle on the floor.

"Annabel?" Ham lumbered down the aisle and came to a screeching halt. "*Oh, Jeez.*"

Annabel and Trent sprang apart.

"Oh, Jeez, I'm—I'm sorry." Ham set a cardboard box on the floor. "I picked up the bulbs for the lighting grid. You said you wanted to start testing them this afternoon. Oh, Jeez, Annabel. I'm really sorry about this."

"It's okay," Annabel said. "You're not interrupting anything."

"Like hell," Trent said under his breath.

Ham stumbled over a folding chair. "There it is! Right where Leon said he left it." He climbed onto the stage. His face had turned as red as the Crimson Tide jersey pulled tight across his large belly. He pointed to the tall stepladder standing beside the back wall. "My battery-powered screwdriver's up there. Can't forget that. Leon and I have another job this afternoon."

"I'll get it," Annabel said.

"No, no," Ham said. "I can climb that far. You go on back to what you were—I mean, don't let me—oh, Jeez, I'm sorry."

"It's all right." Annabel laughed softly. "Mr. Sheffield was just...I'm not sure what he was doing, exactly." She turned to Trent. "So, Mr. Sheffield. What were you doing...exactly?"

"Shit!" Ham cried.

Annabel spun around.

Ham's foot crashed through another rung. His strangled yell ricocheted through the room. The wooden ladder teetered for a moment then slipped out of his grasp and hurtled to the floor. Ham's crumpled body slammed into the bandstand.

"*Ham!*" Annabel screamed.

Trent leapt onto the stage. He dropped to his knees beside him.

"Is he okay?" Annabel cried. "*Trent!* Is he—"

"He's breathing," Trent said. "We need blankets. He's going into shock. Call 911. Tell them he's broken his arm. Don't come up here, Annie. The bone is sticking through his shirt."

****

Annabel stood in the middle of the road and watched an ambulance pull away for the second time in two days. She wrapped her arms around her waist to stop them from shaking. Her hands still ached. Ham had held onto them until Trent could get the back doors open to let the paramedics wheel in the stretcher. She had knelt beside him, forcing him to focus on her face and not the bloody tourniquet Trent had tied around his forearm. She filled the endless minutes crooning to him, repetitive, inane words of hope that kept him from screaming out in pain.

She shuddered and glanced up. The sun shone above her, relentless and bright, but she couldn't feel it. She couldn't feel anything except a thin blanket of cold encasing her skin like a shell. "I can't believe someone would do this," she said for the tenth time. "I just can't."

"Trent said he'd call from the ER as soon as he knew anything." Keisha flicked a loop of tightly wound braids over her shoulder and checked her watch. "Where are the police? I called them twenty minutes ago." She squinted at Annabel. "I think

Quinn's behind this."

"Well, that would be good trick. Quinn is dead."

"That girl was a piece of work, you know what I'm sayin'? You think she'd let a little thing like death keep her from hurting somebody she hated?"

"I'm the one who should have fallen through the ladder, not Ham."

"Or me. That's the ladder I always use to change the porch lights. No one but us has the guts to climb that rickety thing." She started walking up the path. "And Quinn hated me."

"Why?" Annabel struggled to keep up.

"Because she knew I had her number. She knew I wouldn't put up with her crap."

"Were you in New York the night she died? Everyone else seems to have been."

Keisha stopped beside the makeshift railing. "I wondered when you were gonna get around to asking me for an alibi."

"I'm asking you now."

"I was here at the inn working my butt off covering for Trent and Gil. And I can prove it."

"Do you know why Quinn and Gil broke up?"

"Sure. She was tired of him, but she wasn't decent enough to let him go. That bitch didn't have a heart. When the poor guy got on his knees and begged her to stay, she just laughed at him, said he was too immature, said she needed someone who could satisfy her in the sack." Keisha's dark eyes burned with hatred. "I wanted to kill her that day." She paused. "But I didn't."

"How long had they been together?"

"Not long. She only used him to make Trent jealous. Trent was the one she was wild about. When she stayed here last December, in the afternoon, while Gil was out picking up supplies, she went up Sourwood Hill. Every day. Like clockwork. She never tried to hide it."

"What was she was doing up there?"

"What or who?"

"Oh."

"Yeah. She had to be meeting someone. What else could it be?"

"Do you think she wanted to get caught?"

"No way. Gil loved her, but he was jealous, almost to the point of being obsessive. He's got a hell of a temper. I'm sure she didn't want to stir things up."

"What about Trent? Do you think she could have been meeting him?"

Keisha shook her head. "I don't think so. Not after what she did to him."

"What? What did she do?"

Keisha started up the hill. "Can't say. It was told to me in confidence. But I can tell you one thing. She destroyed Trent Sheffield. He hasn't let another woman in his life since."

Annabel didn't push for details. She was learning that no one pushed Keisha too far without pulling back a stump. "How do you get to Sourwood Hill? Is there a path?"

"Just walk across the road from the inn, and you'll run into it. Sourwood is the back part of Peg Leg Mountain. It's all connected."

When they reached the top, Officer Vance was waiting for them.

"I hear you ladies ran into some more trouble."

Keisha grunted. "Like I said on the phone, Vance, the ladder rungs have definitely been tampered with. I cordoned off the stage area. Nothing's been touched."

Vance's gaze lingered appreciatively on Keisha's muscular arms. "You want me to get someone in here to dust for prints?"

"Uh...*yeah*." Keisha laughed. "Hell, Vance, I might have to join the force just so I can come down there and whip you girls into shape."

Officer Vance chuckled. "Is that a promise, Miss Releford? I'd like to see that."

Annabel started toward the inn. When she passed the hedgerow of boxwoods she saw Byron standing at the end of the clearing with his hands on his hips, a mother-hen stance she had come to dread.

"I heard what happened," Byron said. "And if you don't get your boney butt on a plane today, I'm never going to speak to you again."

"Oh, come on."

"This isn't a game, Annabel. Somebody wants you out of here. Maybe they think you know something about Quinn's death."

"I don't know anything."

"Well, *they* don't know that. If you stay, you're going to get hurt. You're too careless. You trust the wrong people."

"I do not."

"Yes, you do. What about that big bruiser, Keisha? Have you seen her hands? She could flatten you without breaking a sweat. And what about Trent?"

"What about him?"

"Okay. I'll admit he's one good-looking guy, but if you're staying here because you have an itch for him, then you're as dense as that idiot carpenter."

"Don't make fun of Leon."

"Trent had a history with Quinn. I saw him at a *Moondance* rehearsal arguing with her, remember?"

"They had a thing going a long time ago."

He pushed his hat back from his forehead. "Well, it didn't look like a thing. It looked like he wanted to strangle her."

"Stop worrying about me. I'll be fine."

"Famous last words." His expression softened. "Seriously, sweet girl, I'd do anything for you. You know that."

She nodded, then turned to face him. "Okay. Here's something you can do. Are you still friends with that detective in the NYPD?"

"Yes, but he's been laying low. I haven't seen him since the DA ran into him at Duke's Leather Bar."

"Would you ask him to locate someone for me? Trent's father, Nolan Sheffield. I think he's from North Carolina, but he could be a baker or an actor, last seen in New York or Jersey. I know that's not much to go on, but Trent can't afford a private detective, and I really want to do this for him."

"Okay." Byron squeezed her hand. "I'll do what I can, *if* you promise you'll think about getting out of this hellhole. I can rent a car. We could leave today. We could be on the road by nightfall."

"I'll think about it. But right now, I've got to rest my hip. I'm going back to my cabin and lie down. Tell Rachel to start working with Craig on the "Carolina Moon" number."

Annabel walked back to the inn. She took her time, even limped a little in case Byron was still watching. One perk—maybe the only perk—of having a bad hip was being able to use it for an excuse when you wanted to be left alone.

She went to the courtesy phone in the hallway beside the lobby and rifled through the Yellow Pages until she found the name of the high school in Black Mountain. When the secretary answered she said, "This is Selena Wolcott, Eli's aunt. I just wanted to make sure he made it to school today."

"Oh, he's here, all right," the secretary said. "I just saw him in the hall."

"Thanks. That's a relief." Annabel wondered if her impromptu southern accent—a cross between Scarlett O'Hara and Dolly Parton—sounded as fake as she thought it did. But at least she knew Eli was in school, and not prowling through the woods firing his grandmother's gun.

She slipped out the side door, just like Quinn had done on her way to Sourwood Hill under the watchful eye of Keisha. When she got to her cabin, she dragged her backpack from under the bed, the one she'd worn on the streets of Manhattan like a second skin. Out of habit, she stuffed her billfold in the zippered side pocket and threw in a bottle of water. Then she circled the cabins and took the side path through the garden behind the gazebo.

The further she got from the inn, the clearer her head became. Why had it taken so long to realize what she needed most, besides a new career and twenty-four hour police protection, was time alone to think? She'd always gone off by herself to figure things out. In New York, she hopped on the Fifth Avenue bus and went to the Metropolitan Museum of Art. In Indiana, she ran behind the barn, skirted the perimeter of her daddy's cornfield, and hid in the woods near the creek. It was the place she'd sneaked her first cigarette, where she'd gone to weep after her mother's death.

She hiked to the top of Sourwood Hill and gazed at the Sheffield Inn. Seeing it from above gave her a different perspective. It was larger than she'd imagined, sprawled across the top of a grassy plateau. She pushed her sunglasses on her head, knocked back a few swigs of water, and started walking. Sunlight filtered through the tall trees, spreading random patches of diffused gold across the ground. The air smelled loamy and damp.

You're looking in the wrong place.

Where was she supposed to look? Here? In the woods? Or somewhere back in New York?

She wasn't sure what she thought she could find on Sourwood Hill. If Quinn had trudged down the same path five months before, what evidence would still be around to explain why she'd gone there, or who she'd met? If Quinn had been meeting someone secretly, why would she hike to Sourwood Hill in full view of Keisha? That kind of reckless behavior seemed a little dicey, even for Quinn.

But then, Quinn thrived on taking chances. It made her exciting to be around. And dangerous if you were the kind of person terrified of getting caught with your pants down. Quinn had been brave, fearless, and Annabel had admired her because of it. She'd often wondered where she would be without Quinn's lectures on bravery. Still dancing in the back row chorus of a bus and truck tour, too afraid to compete with dancers fifteen years younger than herself?

She'd met Quinn at auditions for *Moondance*. As usual, Annabel was the oldest dancer, and even though she'd made it past the first cut, she glanced around at the girls half her age and could see where it was going. She felt tired and worn-out and old. Something inside her came to a standstill, like a clock that stops ticking when the battery finally dies. All she could think was that she'd had enough rejection for one lifetime and it was time to swallow her pride and go home. Then she looked up and saw Quinn.

"I saw you dance," Quinn said. *"And I'm here to kick your ass."* She was leaning against the wall, watching Annabel stuff her dance shoes in her backpack. *"How old are you?"*

"Almost thirty-four."

"Then you're old enough to know better. So what if the director's looking for eighteen to twenty-year-olds? You don't have to be *a twenty-year-old; you just have to dance like one."*

Quinn had given her the hope and confidence to realize the dream she'd held in her heart for more years than she could remember. She owed Quinn everything. And no matter what anyone said, or thought, or felt about Quinn Wolcott, Annabel would always be grateful to her.

A sharp breeze cut through the trees, stirring up a mound of dead leaves. She untied the sweater from around her waist and slipped it on. Her hip had begun to throb. How far had she walked? One mile? Two?

She found a hickory log off the main path and sat down. She stretched her legs and took a long drink of water. Across the clearing, she noticed a sign that had been carved into the flat, smooth bark of a tree.

Quick Way
+o
The Sheffield →

Well, at least she wasn't lost, she thought. If she followed the arrow, she would probably end up on the far side of the inn, somewhere near the staff cabins.

Exhaustion seeped into her bones. She eased herself off the log to the ground and used her backpack for a pillow. She leaned back and yawned. Five—no, ten minutes. She'd rest for ten minutes before starting back. It had been stupid to trek so far on a whim. If Quinn had left a trail, it was long gone.

Her gaze drifted across the forest floor, from the woody brown canes of a budding rhododendron to the delicate sprinkling of white trillium nestled in the grass. The weeds beneath her shoulders smelled musty, like the stable hay she used to hide in from Drew. The woods on Sourwood Hill didn't seem like the kind of place Quinn would hang out. Especially in December. Quinn always said she was a country girl who hated the country. Why had Quinn climbed up here every day? Had someone been waiting for her? Someone besides Gil? And was that someone behind the recent "accidents" at the inn? Were they trying to frighten Annabel into leaving? Or did they want to permanently stop her from prying into Quinn's past?

And Ham. *Oh, God. Poor Ham.* She felt terrible he'd been hurt. It could have been her. It *should* have been her. Things were beginning to spin out of control. Innocent people were getting caught in the crossfire. If she didn't leave, who would be next? Rachel or Byron? Trent? He'd already survived one attack. The next time he might not be so lucky.

"I'm sorry, Quinn," she murmured. "I don't think I can do this."

Maybe she was trying too hard. If she could turn her brain into a blank slate, she might be able to think of something she hadn't thought of before, recognize some fact she'd overlooked. If she could let her mind drift slowly out to sea and back, maybe the answer would come swimming into view like the words on a Magic Eight Ball.

Annabel closed her eyes. But all she could see was Trent's face.

At the hospital, his gaze had followed her every move. The look of gratitude on his face every time she'd done even the smallest thing for him had touched her heart, made her wonder if anyone had ever done *anything* for him. How could Quinn have hurt him? How could anyone hurt him? At one time, he had trusted Quinn, probably loved her. Whatever Quinn had done to him had destroyed his faith in women and left him with a fierce determination to protect Gil from suffering the same fate. Did that include getting rid of Quinn?

Her eyes flew open. My God. What was she thinking?

Did she really believe Trent Sheffield was capable of killing anyone? Even to save his brother from the kind of heartache and disappointment he must have endured? No. She couldn't believe that for a second. Trent was not a fool. He was a sharp, well educated, cautious man who, by his own admission, never acted until he'd weighed the outcome against the risk. If he'd wanted Quinn gone, he would have begged her, or bribed her. He would have found some other way to rid their lives of her without resorting to murder.

She couldn't believe it.

She couldn't.

Because no matter what her heart believed, or wanted to believe, she was already falling in love with the man.

A tear slid out of the corner of her eye and slowly tracked its way across her nose and down her cheek. Her vision blurred, focused, then blurred again. Her eyelids fluttered, heavy with the promise of mind-numbing sleep.

Chapter 13

“What do you mean, you don’t know where she is?” Trent shouted. “I thought we promised someone would stay with her every minute?”

“It’s not my fault. She said she was going to lie down. She said her hip hurt.”

“Dammit, Byron. I had to go to the hospital with Ham. I thought you or Gil could pick up the slack.”

Gil came flying out of the Laurel Room and skidded to a halt in front of the reservation desk. “No one’s seen her.” He scowled at Byron. “I thought she was with you, man. Why didn’t you stay with her? What’d you do, dump her in the lobby and go have your nails done?”

“That’s enough,” Trent said. “Arguing won’t find her. It’s getting dark. We need to split up and look.”

“I’ll search the inn,” Byron said. “Rachel and Selena are looking in the gardens.”

“Be careful on the third floor,” Trent said. “There’s a stairwell missing.”

“I’ll take the cabins,” Gil said.

“Then I’ll do the carriage house,” Trent said. “Get some flashlights from the supply closet. If her hip gave out, she could have fallen. She could be—” His heart squeezed hard against his chest. He wasn’t going to think of Annie somewhere hurt and alone. He wouldn’t let himself.

He grabbed his jacket and a flashlight and ran across the veranda. He clattered down the porch steps, sprinted along the circular drive, then took the path leading down to the carriage house. When he reached the door, he fumbled in his pocket for the key.

"Annie!" he called. "Are you in here?"

He grappled in the dark for the lobby light. The smell of sawdust and paint thinner crept toward his sinuses. Where was the damn light switch? Why couldn't he find it? He hated theaters. Nothing was ever simple in them. He blew out a deep breath and directed the flashlight beam along the wall until he located the switch. Seconds later, the white glare of the house lights flooded the room. It had only been a few hours since he'd been there, but it startled him to see the carriage house transformed into a full-blown theater.

"*Annabel!*" His rumbling baritone hit the walls and bounced back at him, shattering the silence.

A chill rushed down his arms. He felt like an idiot getting spooked at his age, but he had a long history with empty theaters. He'd listened to their mournful creaks and moans, heard his mother's cast mates tell enough strange tales to substantiate his fears—props that would disappear then reappear across stage, sounds only the actors onstage could hear, the ghostly image of a face floating between stage lights while the actors took their bows. It was enough to make a young boy's imagination run wild, sending him clambering out the first unlocked door he could find with cold, sweaty palms.

Trent shook off the memory and concentrated on Annabel. When he was satisfied he'd checked every inch of the building, he went outside. *Where the hell was she?* It was almost pitch dark. Where had she gone?

"Trent!" Gil shouted. "Goddammit! Where are you?"

"Over here!" Trent reached the top of the hill and stopped to catch his breath. Gil ran along the driveway, waving his arms.

"*Hurry!* There's a fire! Annabel's cabin is on fire!"

Trent's heart slammed into his throat.

He didn't remember when his slow, loping jog turned into a sprint, or when the oxygen he gulped refused to fill his lungs. "Have you found her?" was all he managed to get out.

"Not yet," Gil puffed, jogging alongside him. "The fire department is on its way. The wait staff is hosing down the other cabins. Damn these mountains. I tried calling your cell but couldn't get a signal."

They cut across the south lawn and ran through the parking lot. As their feet hit the graveled path, Trent's shoes made an even, crunching sound. One foot, then the next, their syncopated rhythm pounding out her name in his head. When he turned the corner, the pungent smell of smoke ripped through his nose, filled his lungs until he had to stop and cough it out.

"Stand over here," Gil yelled. "The wind's blowing toward the parking lot. I hear sirens."

Trent circled Annabel's cabin like a caged leopard. The pitched shingled roof was still intact. Orange flames shot out the windows. They licked at the broken panes, spit wispy, glowing bits of tissue paper into the air.

Craig and Dave held garden hoses. They directed streams of water toward the bushes and trees, wetting them as soon as they released thin, curling trails of smoke. A harsh, radiant light exploded against the sky. Firemen appeared, running toward the cabin in stiff brown coats, shouting gruffly for people to stay back.

Gil put his hand on Trent's shoulder. "She wasn't inside. Craig said he managed to look through the windows just before the glass blew."

"Then where is she?"

A police car roared into view. Dizzy red and blue lights cut across the sky like out-of-sync lasers.

"I can't stay here," Trent said. "I've got to find her."

Gil nodded. "I'm right behind you."

They ran up the hill and tore across the parking lot.

"When this is over," Gil panted. "Remind me to join Keisha's gym. Jogging every other day just ain't cutting it."

Keisha met them at the lobby door. "Sweet Jesus, is it true? Everything I own is down there. Donald won't let any of us leave the inn."

"It's okay." Trent struggled to catch his breath. "Annabel's cabin is the only one burning. The firemen are getting it under control."

"We still can't find her," Gil said.

"Oh, Lord," Keisha said. "You mean she isn't back yet?"

Trent grabbed Keisha's shoulders. "Back from where? Where did she go?"

"I think she hiked up Sourwood Hill." She glanced at Gil. "We were talking about Quinn going up there, and she asked for directions, and—"

Trent ducked behind the counter. He swung open the supply cabinet and rifled through the drawer until he found two fresh flashlight batteries. His hands were shaking.

"She's all right," Gil said. "She probably veered off the path and lost her way. Everyone does it. We'll find her."

"We'd better find her."

"I'll take the front side of Sourwood," Gil said. "You take the back, along the azalea path. If she made it to the top, even if she's lost, she'll be on her way down by now."

Keisha stood behind Gil, her dark eyes wide.

"What do I tell them?"

"Who?" Trent asked.

"Them." Keisha pointed to the elevator.

"There he is!" Mrs. Richmond limped across the lobby, brandishing her cane, carrying the squirming, yapping Pekingese under her arm. A group of elderly guests trailed behind her. "You listen to me, Trent Sheffield. I want to know what is going on." She glanced at her followers. "We are paying customers, and we have a right to know what kind of danger we're in!"

"I'll handle this," Gil said. "You go."

Trent didn't hesitate.

He turned away from Mrs. Richmond and raced across the lobby. Then headed for Sourwood Hill.

****

Annabel stared into the darkness.

Her left side was numb, her fingers so cold they couldn't make a fist. Adrenaline pulsed through her veins like ice water. She scrambled to her feet.

"Hello!" she called. "Is anybody there? *Anybody?*"

How could she have been so careless, so damned irresponsible? How could she have slept for—what? She pushed the button on the side of her watch. *Three hours?*

She pulled her sweater tighter around her and waited for her eyes to adjust to the dark. She had good night vision, enhanced from years of exiting offstage during blackouts. She forced herself to take deep, calming breaths. The last thing she needed to do was freak out.

Gradually, the dark began to turn a seeable shade of charcoal gray. She could make out a few things. The tall cylindrical shapes were trees; the short blobby shapes were bushes. Everything in between was too scary to think about. Once the moon came up—if there was a moon—she might be able to see well enough to make it down the mountain. She wasn't putting any money on it, though.

For an ex-girl scout, she was abysmally unprepared. She hadn't brought a flashlight or matches, and it was her own damn fault she didn't have a cell phone. Although it probably wouldn't have done her much good. She'd heard complaints at the inn about the lack of reliable cell phone service so far up on the mountain.

And she really needed to use the bathroom.

Well, she wasn't going to do it in the dark. Not with snakes and spiders and God knew what else crawling around. Did snakes sleep? She couldn't remember. Her back teeth knocked together. She sat on the log and clapped her thighs together to speed up circulation. It was an old trick she'd learned to keep her leg muscles warm. Sometimes it worked. Sometimes it didn't.

The shuddering cry of an owl screeched behind her. She wrapped her arms around her waist and rocked back and forth. If someone was looking for her, she had a better chance of being found if she stayed put.

She looked around and wondered what people did at night in a forest when they were stranded and alone? Her camping buddies had wolfed down s'mores, smeared petroleum jelly in the troop leader's sleeping bag, and sung "Kumbaya."

It was worth a shot.

She began to sing a sweet, haunting ballad from *The Robber Bridegroom* called "Deeper in the Woods." She congratulated herself on choosing the most appropriate song for the occasion, and was relieved to discover that the louder she sang, the less she shook. Her voice soared through the trees, giving her lackluster alto the kind of ripe resonance she'd always longed for. She sang the last two verses at top volume, holding the final note for a full count of sixteen.

"Annie!" Trent shouted hoarsely. "Annie! Where are you?"

She jumped to her feet. "*Trent!* Over here! I'm over here!"

She heard him crashing along the path, cursing as he stumbled through a thicket of undergrowth. The arc of his flashlight swept across the trees like a beacon from the sea.

And suddenly he was there.

Holding her. Kissing her. Clasping her to him as if he would never let her go.

"Oh, God, Annie. I was so worried. We were all so worried. What happened?"

"I fell asleep, and—"

"You fell asleep? We thought you were lost."

"Maybe a little lost."

"You're cold." He rubbed her back with his hand to warm her, then pulled back and shone the flashlight near her face. He searched her eyes. "You're okay, right? Tell me you're okay. You look okay."

She reached out and touched his cheek. "Trent, I'm okay."

"Okay, then." And then he laughed. His low baritone cut through the night. "Just don't ever do this again. I don't think my heart could take it." He slung her backpack over his shoulder. "Honey, we need to get going. It's shorter to go down the other side. Just follow my lead. Let me know if you need to stop and rest."

"All right."

The path proved to be more treacherous than she'd expected. She walked with him, dropping back when it became overgrown and narrow, moving to his side when it opened into a trampled stretch of ground. He held her hand when the terrain became steep, softly calling out obstacles. “Two rocks coming up. Go around them. Brambles on your right.”

“Tell me about you and Quinn,” she said.

****

He tripped on a root and faltered. The flashlight scraped against a tree. “What do you want to know?”

Here it comes, he thought. The conversation he’d been dreading since the day he realized Annabel Maitland had managed to worm her way into the deepest recesses of his heart before he’d even known what hit him.

“Were you in love with her?”

He shuffled through a pile of dead leaves, glad, for once, that his face was hidden in the shadows. “I thought I was. But if that was love, I don’t ever want to run into it again.”

“Are you bitter? You sound bitter.”

“It was a long time ago.”

“Because if you’re bitter, you can give yourself an ulcer. And then you’ll have to drink milk the rest of your life.”

“I’ll remember that.”

As a rule, Trent tried not to think about the time he’d spent with Quinn because it filled him with more regret than he could bear. If he had only followed his instincts and left Quinn alone. But he hadn’t been that smart. He’d ignored his gut and followed something else. Something powered by hormones and desire. There was a time when just watching Quinn cross a room made the muscles in his thighs take on a life of their own, when being near her sent emotions he’d held in check his whole life spiraling off the chart. But that petrifying helplessness didn’t last. Quinn lost her power over him the day he discovered the promises she’d made were empty words she had no intention of keeping.

Their long distance love affair hadn’t been easy. But he was committed to her, and the world couldn’t hold his happiness. While he was in North Carolina, and she was in New York, the raw ache of loneliness began to wear him down. He missed the contentment that enfolded him in her arms at night, the joy that filled the dark corners of his life. Without her, he was lost and miserable. So miserable, he decided to pawn his grandfather's gold watch, buy the best engagement ring he could afford, and leave Gil putting up drywall in the lobby to fly back three days early to see her.

He let himself into the apartment, set his carry-on in the floor, and clutched the tiny ring box he had hidden in his jacket pocket with a loopy, hopeful smile on his face. Then he walked down the hall and stood frozen, listening to the grunts and groans coming from the back bedroom. His fiancée, his beloved Quinn, was having sex with someone. Loud, sweaty, electrifying sex. And from that moment on, he felt nothing.

He couldn't bring himself to reveal the truth about Quinn to Gil. Gil loved Quinn. Had always loved her. And what was the truth, really? That Quinn had advanced her stalled career the old-fashioned way by successfully negotiating a business arrangement with an important producer when her aunt refused to help? That she couldn't see what the big deal was, or understand why the sight of her straddling a strange man in their bed made him want to put his fist through a plate glass window?

Nothing made sense to him after that. Nothing. And for the past year, he'd lived like a monk. A very cranky monk. No woman on earth had even tempted him until the day Annabel Maitland climbed down that damn ladder and looked into his eyes.

"Stop!" Annabel cried. She grabbed his jacket sleeve. "I smell something. Is that smoke?"

Trent held the flashlight at an angle, out of her eyes. The scrub cedars behind her took on an eerie, one-dimensional façade. "I didn't want to tell you until we were over the rough part of Sourwood. I knew you'd want to run back, and your hip was—"

"Tell me what?"

"One of the cabins caught fire. Your cabin caught fire."

"*Oh, God,*" she whispered.

"We don't know what happened, faulty wiring or a short somewhere. We don't know. The firemen were putting it out when I came to find you. I—we were so worried." His voice broke. "You told Byron you were going to lie down. We thought you might have been in there."

"Was anyone h-hurt?"

"No, everyone's fine. Here, you're trembling." He took off his jacket and tried to wrap it around her shoulders.

She shook him off and stepped back. "How bad is it? How much of it burned?"

"All of it."

"And you're just now telling me?"

"I didn't want to upset you until I had to. I know your hip isn't—"

"Screw my hip."

"I thought it best to wait until—"

"Until *what?* Until we got back and I noticed a big fire truck sitting in front of the pile of rubble that used to be my house?"

"No. I mean, yes, I—"

"Listen, I'm not the kid brother you don't trust to wipe his own nose. I'm a grown woman. How dare you decide what's best for me!"

Trent took a step back as if she'd slapped him.

Didn't she know what it meant to have her safe? Didn't she realize how crazy scared he'd been, tearing through the woods searching for her with his heart pounding out of his chest? He'd come as near to praying as he ever had, hadn't taken a complete breath until he heard her voice slicing through the night. When he found her, and knew she was all right, he was so weak with relief he'd almost thrown himself on the ground. He couldn't stand to see her hurt or upset. It killed him. Why couldn't she understand that?

She glared at him. "We've been walking for damned near an hour and you never said a word. I never suspected anything was wrong. Not once. How can you be so loving and open one minute and so guarded the next? What—did you think I would fall apart? Is that why you didn't say anything?"

"I did what I thought was best. For you. I was only thinking of you."

"Mister, you have some serious control issues." She grabbed the flashlight and pulled her backpack off of his shoulder. "Thanks for rescuing me, Mr. Sheffield. But I think I can take it from here." She started down the hill.

"Annie, please."

"Just shut up, Trent."

They walked the last quarter mile in silence.

The stench of dank, smoldering wood filled the air. By the time they reached the clearing, Trent could hear the muffled, tinny squawk of a police radio. Unfamiliar voices shrieked to each other. The lights in the inn twinkled through the trees, as if the folks inside were having a party.

He took a deep breath and swallowed. He had to try and make her understand.

"Annie, stop for a minute. Let me talk to you." She kept walking toward the end of the veranda. "Annie, *please*." She stopped then, but didn't turn to look at him. "I know you're mad, and I'm sorry about that. But I thought I did the right thing. That's all any of us can do."

"I want to see the cabin."

"Okay. Just let me go inside and tell them you're

safe, then I'll go with you. Please, honey, I don't want you to go alone."

She turned and started walking, past the side entrance, past the low wall surrounding the patio, past the crumbling fountain at the edge of the sundial garden. Her thin back was straight, her shoulders squared. The amber light beneath the eaves cast a shadow behind her on the ground—tall and resolute and strong. Watching her tramp off alone to face the unknown made his heart twist with fear and admiration. He tried to swallow the ache in his throat.

"Annie, wait!" Christ, she was stubborn, almost as stubborn as he was. Unless they both learned to bend, life with her would be one long standoff.

"I see you found her." Selena stood on the stone landing beside the side door. "Doesn't look like she appreciated it much."

"Not now, Selena."

"You're pathetic. You always were a sucker for a nice ass and a pair of long legs." She walked down the steps until she stood eye to eye with him. "You may think this is your big chance to relive the past, but believe me, Annabel is not Quinn. She doesn't even come close." She laughed harshly. "I would've thought this time around you'd go for something with a soul."

"You're right. She's not Quinn. And I thank God every minute I'm with her she's not Quinn. I've got to go. Annie doesn't need to be alone right now." He started up the steps.

"Poor little Annie. *Poor* little Annie doesn't need to be alone right now." She whirled around. "What about me? Did you ever think I might not need to be alone? Do you ever think of me at all?"

Trent looked at Selena. Her face had crumpled into something he barely recognized, something desperate and miserable. He knew he needed to talk to her, straighten things out, try to explain in the gentlest way possible that he could never love her the way she wanted him to. But Annie needed him. Whether Annie realized it or not. “I’m sorry, Selena. I can’t do this now.”

“Please, Trent. I need your help. We can’t find Eli.”

“Eli’s missing?”

“He was at church tonight with Mama. Then he ducked out and took her car. One of the women in the congregation had to bring her home. I thought you might have seen him.”

“Where? Here? Why would he come here?”

“Where else would he go? My God, Trent, how can you be so blind? That kid looks up to you. You’re a role model for him. All he talks about is going fishing with you and Gil on Lake Lure. You promised him, remember? Why did you say you’d take him if you never meant to go?”

Okay. He didn’t know what game Selena was playing, but their warm, easygoing friendship had just turned into a minefield.

“Gil must have promised to take him,” he said carefully. “It wasn’t me. And I’m not sure why you’re exaggerating Eli’s regard for me. I’ve only talked to the boy a couple of times, and believe me, he could care less about going fishing. All he cares about are cars and guns and getting the hell away from Black Mountain.”

Selena put her hand on his arm. The soft brown eyes he’d always found so consoling had turned to stone. “Why don’t you like me anymore? Why won’t you look at me the way you look at Annabel? She’ll never understand you. Not the way I do.”

“Selena—”

“Let her go, Trent. She’ll break your heart just like Quinn did. Only this time, you might not recover.”

Trent shook off her hand and took the rest of the steps two at a time. He flung open the door, strode across the lobby, and stopped cold.

Ruth Donovan.

Was he hallucinating? Was Ruth Donovan really standing there, or had he blacked out on top of Sourwood Hill and fallen into the fourth circle of hell?

"Ruth?" His voice traveled across the room in slow motion. He could almost see the words fly through the air—gliding past the gilded wall mirror, taking a left at the Chinese urn, lining up their target for a direct hit.

Ruth's head whipped around.

"Hello, Ruth. As usual, your timing is impeccable."

****

The smoldering cabin assaulted Annabel's senses: the sharp stench of singed wood, the hiss of wet boards, the incomprehensible devastation. What was left of the structure remained encapsulated within the perimeter of the small lot, as if something had flown over and zapped it with a ray gun. The stove and refrigerator huddled together beneath a pair of smoking, splintered beams. Clouds of gray smoke hung suspended in the air, floating past the trees like lazy ghosts on the prowl.

The tears she'd been holding back streamed down her face, and she batted them away. What was she going to do? What *could* she do? Everything was gone.

Gil was suddenly beside her. He pulled her to him and turned her face away from the charred ruins. "Don't cry, Annabel."

"It's a lot worse than I thought it would be."

"I know. I'm sorry."

"How could this have happened? Did someone do it on purpose? Do you think—"

"We're not sure. We had the cabins rewired last fall. The inspector will be here in the morning. Let's not think the worst until we know something. Did you lose anything valuable? We have insurance."

"Oh, God, Gil. The account book for Fred and Ginger's was in there."

"I don't give a damn about the account book. I meant was there anything of yours that can't be replaced—mementos, family photographs, things like that."

"Not much. A picture of my mother. Some jewelry she'd given me. Her favorite book, *To Kill a Mockingbird*." A fresh surge of tears spilled onto her cheeks.

"Come on." He steered her to the path. "Let's get you back to the inn. You need a hot bath and a bed." He smiled at her with Trent's sweet, crooked smile, the one that never failed to melt her heart, and put his arm around her shoulders. "Don't look back, babe. Just keep looking ahead. We'll get you dry and settled, and I'll send you up a cup of amaretto decaf—heavy on the amaretto—and one of my cinnamon-walnut muffins. We'll figure things out."

She wiped her face with her hands. "That's what you want to do, isn't it? Cook? Be a chef?"

"Cooking's the one thing I seem to be good at."

"Are you going to culinary school? The Culinary Institute of America is near New York City, isn't it?"

"Yeah, I'm going. When I win the lottery, I'm going. That place costs an arm and a—" He stopped. "How did you know I wanted to study there?"

"Well, it's the best. And I thought that might have been the reason you and Trent went to New York—to check it out."

"You mean the day Quinn died?" He stopped walking and turned to her. "I know you're upset," he said softly. "But cut the crap, Annabel. If you want to know if I saw Quinn while we were there, then just ask me."

"Did you?"

"Yes. But I never went inside the theater. I called her apartment that morning and asked if I could see her. I...I just missed her, you know? I missed seeing her face, hearing her voice. At first, she said she couldn't see me because she wasn't feeling well. I thought she was having an allergy attack. She was *always* having an allergy attack. But then, she agreed to meet me in the alley next to the stage door, but only for a few minutes."

"Why there?"

"I don't know. I figured she didn't want anyone to see us. I thought she might have found someone new—someone in the cast or crew, maybe—and didn't want him to see us together."

"So, you met her at the stage door. What did you talk about?"

He ran his hand back through his hair. "The usual. I begged her to come back, and she listed the eighty-five reasons why she wouldn't."

"Did it make you angry?"

"Angry? Like mad-enough-to-kill-her angry?"

"It can't have been easy hearing her reject you again."

Gil hesitated a moment, then shoved his hands in his pockets and glanced up at the moon. "Actually, it didn't bother me. It was strange. But while I was standing in that filthy alley, freezing my ass off, watching Quinn not even pretend to care about me, something clicked. I finally realized it was over. Oh, I still loved her. I'll always love her. But I knew I was ready to move on. I'd never felt that before."

He raised his eyes to meet hers, and in that one second, she knew instinctively, from the deepest part of her soul, that he was lying.

She shoved the thought away. What was wrong with her? No one could blame her for being paranoid, but she was letting fear render her completely irrational. She was suspecting everybody, even the one person who had loved Quinn with all his heart. Who would be next? Mrs. Rosetti? Mrs. Richmond's dog?

She turned, and they started up the hill. "Where was Trent while you were at the theater?"

Gil shrugged. "We were staying with Keisha's brother in Queens. He could've been there, or out looking for his father. These days, it's his second job."

"Will the inn go under if he can't find him and sell the land?"

"Ah, hell, who knows? I hope it won't. I believe you and Rachel are gonna make Fred and Ginger's so spectacular, it will save the day." He grinned. "Like the cavalry, only better looking."

"I wish Trent believed in us. He's getting more used to the idea, but he's still a long way from being happy about it."

"Trent has a hard time putting his faith in anything he can't predict with a spreadsheet and a calculator. He's afraid to leave things to chance. He has to control the outcome."

"So I've noticed."

"Well, don't hold it against him. It's an old habit he can't break, like putting orange juice on his cereal or grinding his teeth."

Donald met them on the stone portico. "Here's your room key, Annabel—the Rose Room again. They're making it up for you. It ought to be ready in about ten minutes." He looked at Gil and swallowed hard. "Mr. Gil? Your brother wants to see you in the office."

"In a minute," Gil said.

Donald cleared his throat. "Gil, I think you should go now. Things are—I've never seen him like this."

Chapter 14

"Where's Annabel?" Trent asked.

"Outside on the porch," Donald said. "She wouldn't come in."

Trent's heart squeezed hard in his chest. "Call upstairs and tell them to hurry up with her room. The night air is cold. I don't want her sitting out there too long."

"Yes, sir."

"And Donald?"

"Yes, sir?"

"Let me know if she...if she needs something. Or if she looks upset. Or if she's..."

"I won't take my eyes off her, sir."

Trent sighed. "Thanks, friend."

Trent strode to the office and sat at his desk, steeling himself for the worst. When Ruth Donovan swooped in like a she-vulture in heat, the worst nightmare imaginable would pale in comparison.

Ruth's hawklike features had been nipped and tucked and stretched, leaving her face so petrified and slick, she resembled a store mannequin. Ruth and her sister didn't look very much alike, although they both had the same thick ankles—Phyllis's supported by sturdy crepe-heeled shoes, Ruth's stuffed into a pair of stilettos that cost more than the inn's January electric bill.

He rubbed his forehead. The bump on the back of his head was pounding.

Gil stood at the window with his back to Ruth. "I

should be down at the cabins. What's this all about? I feel like I've been hustled into the principal's office."

"Ask Ruth," Trent said. "She's the one who called this little meeting."

"What do you want, Ruth?" Gil asked impatiently. "We're kind of busy right now."

Ruth's scarlet fingernails tapped the armrest of her chair. "Then I'll get to the point before the whole place goes up in flames. Your mother was an actress—not a very good one, I'm told—but I'm sure she taught you how unpredictable the world of theater is." Ruth leveled her gaze at Gil. "Let me cut to the chase, kid. It looks like I'm going to need the money back I loaned you sooner than I thought."

"What?" Trent said.

"The play I'm producing has run into a few snags. Some of the backers have pulled out. It's incredibly difficult to get financing these days. No one wants to take a chance."

"I'm sorry." Trent shook his head. "What money are you talking about?"

"Ruth," Gil whispered. "Please...not now."

Ruth shrugged. "He's going to find out sometime, sweetie."

"What money?" Trent said evenly. His gaze flicked between Gil and Ruth. His fingers curled around the edge of the desk. He gripped it until his knuckles bulged. "Somebody had better start talking. *Now*."

"Quinn and I loaned Gil quite a bit of cash last year," Ruth said. "To pay for repairs on the inn, which, I might add, is looking lovely. Can't say I care much for the color of those pansies out front, but yellow and black has never been my—"

"Please, don't do this, Ruth," Gil begged.

"Someone had better start talking," Trent said. He glanced at Donald in the lobby, pacing up and down, staring out the front window. "And make it fast. I have somewhere I need to be."

Ruth's honey-brown eyes, almost identical to Selena's, hardened. "Why, I'm calling in the loan, dear heart. I want my money back. And I want it back now."

****

Annabel sat in the wicker rocker and gazed across the road to Sourwood Hill. She knew she was still in shock, but the funny thing about being in shock, other than having oatmeal for brains and shivering like a Chihuahua, was you couldn't do anything about it.

A three-quarter moon hung low in the sky. Little clouds gathered around it slowly, filling up one vacant section of sky at a time. The smell of stale wood smoke lingered in the air, clung to her hair and skin as if she'd spent the last two hours in the back room of Bernie's Bar.

Her mind kept spinning out *what if's*. What if she hadn't hiked up Sourwood Hill? What if she hadn't fallen asleep? What if she had been in her cabin when the fire started?

She had to make a decision, and quick. And it always seemed to be the same one: should she stay or should she go? Either way there were consequences to face. How could she thumb her nose at Selena's threat? What would happen to her family? Her father had raised her to stand by her word no matter what. How could she ever face him if she reneged on her promise to Quinn? How could she face herself? What about her own safety? The warnings had turned ugly. And she was plenty scared. But after tonight, if she stayed at the inn, who could she trust?

Annabel's gaze drifted toward the sundial garden. Her mother had always wanted a garden like that, pretty and frivolous. She longed for her mother, ached for her mother's hand to reach out and make everything all right. If wishing hard enough could make a dream come true, she would wish for her mother to come floating across the meadow, riding in a giant soap bubble like Glinda on her way home to Oz. And if she had another wish, it would be to keep Quinn's promise without getting herself killed. And to know in her heart, beyond a shadow of a doubt, that Trent Sheffield was one of the good guys.

"There she is!" Rachel's squeaky voice traveled the length of the porch.

"Hey, sweet girl," Byron said. "Your room's ready. We've come to take you upstairs."

They pulled her out of the rocker and stood on either side of her, holding her elbows.

"I've loaned you some clothes and a purse," Rachel said, "and Byron and I raided the gift shop. We got you a bunch of T-shirts and a hoodie, and twenty packs of M & M's. I even got you a toothbrush. Which you're gonna need after all the M & M's."

"I hate the hoodie," Byron sniffed. "The inn's logo makes this place look like Tara after the Yankees left. All it needs is a picture of Scarlett whipping that poor horse across the bridge."

Annabel hugged them. "I'm glad you guys are here. I don't know what I'd do without you."

"You'd be fine," Byron said. "You're a survivor, remember? Just like Rachel. Just like me."

The three of them walked arm in arm across the lobby, pausing at the front desk while Donald handed Byron the key, then took the elevator to the third floor.

Annabel unlocked the door to the Rose Room. The four-poster bed had been turned down, and it was all she could do not to fling herself on it and pull the satin comforter over her head. A tray filled with soup, ciabatta bread, and two of Mrs. Rosetti's cannoli sat on the dresser. A bottle of chardonnay chilled in an ice bucket. Stacks of folded jeans and shirts had been piled on the velvet chair, topped with one of Rachel's tiny shoulder bags.

Annabel's eyes filled with tears. "This is great. You guys are the best."

"We should leave you alone," Byron said. "Let you get some rest. Will you be okay?"

Annabel nodded. "I'm good."

"Take a nice long bath," Byron said. "You look like 'Pig-pen.'"

"Pig-pen is a boy," Rachel said.

"Well, we can't all be perfect." Byron glanced at Rachel. "Hey, would you mind going on ahead? I just remembered there's something I need to talk to Annabel about. Privately. It'll just take a sec."

Rachel cocked one eyebrow at him, but didn't say anything. She just crossed her arms and looked at Annabel, waiting for her to nod that it was okay to leave her. It reminded Annabel of something Keisha would do.

Once Rachel was out of the room, Byron reached into his shirt pocket and pulled out a folded piece of notepaper. "Here," he said. "I think this is what you wanted."

She opened the paper and read the address. "Nolan Sheffield is living in Knoxville? That's not too far away, is it?"

"Only an hour and a half, according to Dave the Bartender. And, as we all know, bartenders know everything, and are never wrong."

"An hour and a half away. Wow." She looked up. "Trent has been searching for his father for months, and all the time, he was practically under his nose?"

"Life does have a way of having the last laugh, doesn't it?"

She kissed him on the cheek. "Thanks, Byron.

Thanks for doing this."

"Anything for you, sweet girl."

"And thanks for always being there for me. I couldn't have gotten through the last—"

"Shhhh!" he said. "That's what friends are for, right?"

She nodded. "Right."

"Who knows? I might have to ask you for a favor someday."

"All you have to do is name it."

"Uh, huh." Byron laughed. "That kind of offer always looks better on paper."

After Byron left, Annabel carefully folded Nolan's address and tucked it into the side pocket of her backpack. She flipped the door lock and smiled, imagining the look on Trent's face when she showed it to him. He would be so surprised. And happy. She would like to see Trent happy. And selfishly, she would like to be the cause of that happiness.

She'd been short with him, and she regretted it. He'd tromped up a mountain in the dark to look for her, then patiently, gently guided her back down when every instinct in his body had probably been screaming at him to do otherwise. Had she even said thank you? He hadn't known if the fire was under control, or if it had spread to the other cabins and was raging through the forest toward the inn. He must have been out of his mind with worry. And yet he had hidden it from her to stave off the bad news as long as possible and protect her hip.

He was definitely one of the good guys.

She went in the bathroom and peeled off her clothes, then filled the tub with hot steamy water. She shook out the gift bag, opened a new bar of cucumber aloe soap, and lined the miniature shampoo and body wash bottles along the edge of the tub. After a long soak, she reluctantly pulled herself out and snuggled into the terrycloth robe. It still didn't fit any better than it had the day Trent had come to her room to tell her he wasn't firing her. Hard to believe that had only been a week ago. It seemed like light-years.

She tore open the plastic sleeve on a new pair of Size Small men's boxer shorts and pulled them on. She wiped the condensation off the mirror with a towel.

A noise in the bedroom made her stop. She stood still and listened, her heartbeat pounding in her throat.

Had she heard something? Had the door just opened and closed?

"Gil, is that you? Did you bring me that amaretto?"

Nothing.

"Byron? Rach?"

She cracked open the bathroom door and peeked out.

The bedroom was empty. She must have imagined things. She was making herself crazy, getting spooked for no reason.

Her gaze shot to the locked door. A surge of relief washed over her. She wasn't crazy. She had flipped the metal latch the second Byron had left, just as she'd remembered. No one could have slipped in without a key. But who else had a key? The extra key to the Rose Room was at the front desk with Keisha or Donald. Trent and Gil probably had master keys. And Housekeeping. She'd seen the maid pull a ring of them out of her apron pocket.

Paranoid.

That's all it was. She was just being paranoid.

And yet, she couldn't stop the sickening wave of dread from rising in her chest.

Her gaze ricocheted around the room. From the dressing table, to the standing mirror, to the writing desk beneath the window.

She eased herself out of the bathroom and stood with her back to the wall. She held on to the corner of the dresser for support and squatted down to peer under the high bed. A small antique armoire, used instead of a closet, stood in the corner. The space inside it was too narrow for a person to hide in unless they were a hobbit.

Something was wrong. She knew it.

She stepped on the braided rug. The old fight-or-flight syndrome had begun to kick in, pulsing more adrenaline through her veins.

Her eye caught a sudden movement. It came and went, darting across her peripheral vision like a glint of black light. Her eyes searched the ceiling, the drapes, the reflection in the oval mirror. Up and down and back again. Over and over. Until the black light flashed again.

A scream lodged in her throat. Her heart thumped hard against her ribs.

A fat black snake slithered out from under the nightstand and curled its way across the polished hardwood floor.

****

Blood rushed to Trent's face. His mind raced in circles.

He couldn't seem to unclench his fists.

How could Gil not have told him he'd borrowed the money from Quinn and Ruth? Money that had been spent months before on insulation, plumbing supplies, rewiring, and a twelve-burner stove? Why had Gil let him believe he'd used his savings for the loan? And worse, how could he have allowed Trent to feel obligated to him, knowing how much Trent detested owing anybody? This wasn't something Gil had conveniently forgotten to mention, like making a D in Chemistry, or accidentally washing their Jockey shorts with the red Christmas napkins, it was a deliberate, premeditated lie.

Trent looked at Gil, then at Ruth, then took a long, deep breath to keep his brain from exploding. If he was going to get through this—and he had to or everything they'd worked for would be in the Dumpster—losing his cool could only make it worse.

He took another breath and forced himself to use his calm voice, the one he reserved for breaking up bar fights and reassuring creditors the check was in the mail. "Tell me, Ruth, what was the plan? You're a savvy business woman. Why did you loan Gil money when you knew he'd never be able to pay it back? So you could take away everything I own?"

"No," she said in a clipped tone. "I did it because Quinn asked me to. I could never say no to Quinn; you know that. She loaned Gil the money as a favor, and Gil didn't tell you because he didn't want you to know he'd blown all his savings on vodka stingers and pot."

"Gil?" Trent said. "Don't you have anything to say?"

Gil glowered at Ruth. "You and Quinn promised this would stay between the three of us. You *promised*."

"I know we did," Ruth said. "But Quinn is dead. And with Quinn gone, that just leaves me." She folded her hands in her lap. Her lacquered nails glittered beneath the desk lamp. "If I thought there was the slightest chance either of you would be able to pay me back without selling this godforsaken place, I wouldn't be here. But I don't. And from the looks on your faces, neither do you."

Trent didn't know where to direct the brunt of his anger, and he had plenty to parcel out. At Gil for accepting Ruth's money without telling him. Or at Ruth for relishing the situation she'd put them in. If Ruth had her way, everything he cared about would be under her control. If she took the inn from them, she could bulldoze it and no one could stop her. Even

Aunt Margaret's will, as convoluted and severe as it was, hadn't provided a way out. If he and Gil couldn't come up with the money, it was over.

Trent blew out a short breath. Christ, how Ruth must love finally having him by the balls. She'd been trying to punish him for leaving Quinn for the better part of a year, and she'd finally found a way to do it—through his brother, where it would hurt the most.

"Why are you here, Ruth?" Trent asked. "I know you're loaded, but why waste money on a plane ticket when you could have ruined us just as easily with a phone call or the price of a postage stamp?"

"I wanted to see my sister, if it's any of your business."

"And delivering the news to me in person, and seeing the look on my face, would be lots more fun."

Ruth smiled. "Well, there is that."

"How long?" Gil asked. "To pay you back—how long?"

"Two weeks," Ruth said.

Gil stared at her. "Are you serious? You know we can't do that."

"Don't look at me like a whipped puppy," Ruth said. "It's just business." She stood and picked up her purse. "How's that girl I sent working out? Quinn's friend? Is she still choreographing the floorshow for your little supper club?"

"You haven't talked to her?" Trent asked.

"Of course not. Why would I?"

"I just thought—" Trent stopped. If Annabel and Ruth had been in cahoots, Ruth would be gloating about it. Here's the proof he wanted that Annabel hadn't lied to him. She'd been telling the truth. Of course she had. Because she was Annabel, not Quinn.

Trent stood and folded his arms over his chest. "If we win the lottery in the next two weeks, where do you suggest we send the check? Are you staying at Phyllis's?"

"God, no!" Ruth said. "I'm at the Grove Park. I'm flying back tomorrow. I'm only here long enough to see if Selena is right, and my lunatic sister needs professional help."

"Have you been out to Quinn's grave?" Gil asked.

Ruth's gaze wavered for a moment. "I...I thought I'd try and go tomorrow morning. Do you want to go with me?"

"I can't," Gil said. "I'm just not ready yet."

Ruth looked at Trent. Her stretched duck lips curled into a wide smirk. "How about you?"

"Maybe next time," Trent said.

"That surprises me," Ruth said. "I thought you might want to pay your respects to the mother of your child."

"Stop it, Ruth." Trent's jaw clenched until he thought it would break. He'd hoped she might take pity on Gil's grief and back off, but he should have known better. This was Ruth's moment, and there was no stopping her. She'd waited too long for the right ammunition to slaughter him.

Ruth turned her full fury on Trent. "That tiny little life growing inside my beautiful Quinn. She told me you begged her to get rid of it. She said you never wanted either of them."

"That's not true," Trent said. "If that's what she said, then she was lying."

Gil's face had gone white. He held onto the desk like a prisoner waiting for the verdict to be read. "What are you talking about?"

"Tell him, Trent," Ruth said. "Tell him the truth. He loved Quinn. He has a right to know."

Gil took a step back. His face twisted in anguish.

Ruth turned on her heel and walked out, rattling the door behind her.

"God, Trent. What have you done? Was Ruth right? Was Quinn pregnant when she died?"

Trent wished he could make it all go away. He'd made so many mistakes when it came to Gil. But this one was the worst. He'd spent the last ten years trying to protect his brother from every heartache imaginable. And yet, here he was, crushing him.

"*Answer me!*" Gil cried. "Was Quinn pregnant?"

"Yes."

Gil's face crumbled. "And you...were you the father?"

"I don't know. She said I was, but I'm not sure."

"But you were screwing her, right?"

"I...yes."

Gil slammed his fists on the desk. "You said you were just friends. You told me that's all you were to each other."

"That's what you heard me say."

"And you just let me go on believing it. How long did it go on? While I was engaged to her? Were you screwing her the whole time?"

"*No!*"

"She wouldn't have sex with me. Did you know that? She said she didn't want to rush it, said she wanted to wait so it would be special. And all the time you were nailing her behind my back."

"It wasn't like that." Trent put his hand on Gil's shoulder.

Gil shrugged him off violently. "Then tell me what it was like. And I want the truth."

"Quinn and I were together the months I commuted to New York. You knew we were seeing each other then. Why did you think I kept flying back and forth every other week, to keep my piddling little job at Merrill Lynch?"

"Then you quit your job and stopped flying back and forth. Why? Did she dump you?"

"She found someone she liked better. I didn't say

anything because I knew the two of you were friends. It never occurred to me she would go after you."

"It's been over a year since you worked in New York. If Quinn claimed you were the father of her child, you had to have had sex with her at least one more time, right?"

The world was crashing in on Trent, one question at a time. And he couldn't do a damn thing to stop it.

"When did you and Quinn do it?" Gil cried. "While she was staying at the inn?"

Trent didn't answer.

"You did, didn't you?" His eyes burned into Trent's. "Where? In your room? In the Rose Room? In the carriage house? In the back of the van?"

"Gil, don't do this."

"No, I want to know. She was only here one night after we broke up. If you're telling the truth, then that's when it happened. How long did it take to talk her into it?"

"You knew Quinn. Do you really think anyone could have talked her into anything?"

"Where did you do it?" He grabbed Trent by the shirt front and pushed him back. *"Where?"*

"On Sourwood Hill."

"In the middle of December?"

"I didn't say it was fun."

Gil came at him with both hands. He smashed his palms against Trent's collarbone and shoved him hard. Trent fell backward against the desk, flattening the wire mail basket. The plastic pencil holder skittered across the floor. A sharp pain cut through his lower back.

Gil lunged at him and drew back his fist.

Trent steeled himself for the blow he knew he deserved. The pain in his brother's eyes pierced his heart.

Gil stared at him. His fist slowly dropped to his side. "You're not worth breaking my hand over. You're not worth *anything*." He shook his head. "You make me sick. I hope Ruth gets this goddammed place and burns it to the ground. Then I can be rid of you both."

Chapter 15

Annabel bit her hand to keep from screaming.

The snake curled around the bedpost and stopped. It had been baiting her for an eternity, slithering across the floor, coming to an abrupt halt, then suddenly on the move again.

Her heart beat wildly.

The snake darted underneath the bed.

Annabel took two running steps and heaved herself onto the high four-poster. She rolled over and grabbed the phone, then lifted the receiver to her ear. Dead as a mackerel.

She smacked at the buttons with her hand and waited, panic-stricken, for the dial tone to hum in her ear. She banged it against the table. Was it even plugged in? She seized the cord and tugged at the end until the unattached plug flew through the headboard opening and landed on the pillow.

A tiny rustling sound sent her heart racing back to her throat. "*Help me! There's a snake in here! Please, somebody, help me!*" she yelled. Over and over. Until her vocal chords rasped with fatigue.

There was no one to hear her. The third floor was separated from the rest of the inn by a long hallway, and made even more isolated by the blocked off stairwell at the far end.

If the snake slid under the bed rail and latched onto the mattress, could it reach her? Could it make it up the slippery bedpost? If they could attach themselves to swamp vines and swing through the air, a canopy bed would be cake.

Annabel's gaze flicked around the room. Her athletic shoes lay near the dresser, but she'd have to put her bare feet on the floor to get to them. The bricked up fireplace had a screen but no fireplace tools. The antique bedside table had no drawer.

Tall windows flanked either side of the bed. She put her foot on the bedside table and stretched until she could reach the curtain rod. She shoved it up and off the bracket, ripping the delicate lace, then slid the metal curtain rod through the hole. She held the rod in her hand, brandishing it up and down while her eyes searched the room.

The snake glided into view. It wound around the nightstand leg and stopped. Annabel dropped to her knees and leaned over the bed. She held onto the bedpost with one hand and pulled the rod back. The first strike hit the middle of the snake dead-on. The second, third, and fourth pulverized its head.

The door crashed open. *"Annabel?"*

"Leon! Be careful! Get some help."

"I did that already. Donald is—"

"Right behind you." Donald rushed into the room. "I brought a shovel. Leon said you were yelling about a snake. Where is it?"

Leon pointed to the dead snake. "That's a big snake," he said calmly.

Donald scraped the snake onto the shovel blade.

Annabel climbed off the bed. She threw her arms around Leon's thin shoulders and hugged him tight. His spindly legs wavered under her weight. "Oh, Leon, thank God you were here." She stepped back. "Why are you here?"

"Mr. Trent said I could stay here at the inn until Ham's not hurt anymore."

Footsteps thundered down the hall.

Trent appeared in the doorway, gasping for breath. "One of The Blondes said someone called for help up here." His hazel eyes turned to ice as his gaze shifted from Annabel to the flattened dead snake. It swung in the air, draped over the shovel blade like a limp black rope.

"She killed the damn thing," Donald said. "By herself."

"Go show it to Officer Vance," Trent said. "He's still downstairs."

"On my way," Donald said.

Trent touched Annabel's arm. His eyes glistened with tears. "Lady, are you all right?"

Annabel nodded. "Thanks for getting help, Leon. Ham would be so proud of you."

Leon grinned and nodded. "I did good, didn't I?"

"You did *very* good."

"I'm hungry," Leon said.

Trent laughed. "Mrs. Rosetti made pizzas for the firemen. Go on down to the kitchen and help yourself. And tell her I said to open the ice cream sundae bar."

"Sure thing, Mr. Trent!"

After Leon had gone, Trent closed the door.

He closed the gap between them in seconds, then gathered her into his arms. "Annie, Annie," he said hoarsely, rocking her back and forth. "This has got to stop."

Her hands wrapped around his waist and held him tight. She nestled her face into the warmth of his broad shoulder; breathed in his sweet, musky scent. The strength of his embrace sheltered her like a shield. She sighed and pulled him closer. It was the safest she'd felt since Ham had fallen through the ladder that morning.

He kissed the top of her head. "Have you eaten any of this food?"

"Not yet. I started to, but—"

"Don't touch it. Someone might have tampered with it." He gently pulled away from her and crossed the room. He lifted the wine bottle out of the melting ice, dripping a stream of water on the floor. He glanced at the clothes lying on the chair. "How long will it take to get your things together?"

"Not long. This is it."

"I'm getting you out of here. Tonight." He picked up the stack of T-shirts and jeans. "Stuff these in your backpack. I'm moving you down the hall to my room where you'll be safe until we leave." She started to speak. "Save it. We're leaving. And I don't care if you think I'm controlling or not. This is serious. This is my fault. I should have made you go before now."

"Trent, no. It's not your fault. And I don't really think—"

"Hush." He dropped the clothes on the chair and turned to her. He reached out and drew her to him, then slid his fingers along the contour of her jaw until he held her face in his hands. He looked into her eyes, then at her mouth, then lowered his head and covered it with his own. His lips moved against hers with an urgency that took her breath away. "I'm not losing you," he groaned. "Do you hear me? I'm not losing you."

"I don't want you to."

He kissed her again, slowly, sending a shaft of heat rocketing into her lower abdomen. Her heart swelled until she thought it would burst. He held her to him, rubbing little circles on the back of her terrycloth robe. The robe slid off her shoulder. Her breasts pressed into his chest, aching for him to touch them.

"This robe is fast becoming one of my favorite things," he said, grazing his lips across the tender spot at the base of her throat. He smiled, then clasped her to him again, as if she were the only life preserver he'd ever found with the power to keep him afloat.

"Don't leave," she murmured.

"I have to. I've got to take care of a few things before I can make this happen. But I'll send Keisha up. She'll stay with you until I get back. Then we'll figure out where we're going."

"No...no, I don't need Keisha. I'll be fine by myself. Everything's okay now. The snake's gone, and the—"

He gazed into her eyes. "Honey, will you stop being so bloody brave? You're making me crazy."

"I'm not being brave. I'm just faking it until you leave. Then I'm going to fall apart."

"Don't you understand?" he said. "My room, with Keisha standing guard, is the only place I can be sure you'll be safe. And I want to—I *have* to know you're safe."

"But Keisha might not want to—"

"Keisha will do whatever I ask. She's the best protection you've got. She knows how I feel about you, knew it long before I ever did. I trust her with my life, Annie. And I trust her with yours. Get dressed. I'll wait for you." He swung her backpack over his shoulder and picked up her toiletry bag.

Annabel went in the bathroom. She put on a pair of Rachel's jeans and a T-shirt, then scooped up her borrowed clothes and followed him into the hall. He waited while she closed the Rose Room door and slid the key in her back pocket.

She followed him down the hall to his room. It was larger and neater than she'd thought it would be, and more homey, like the staff cabins. A log headboard and footboard, carved with a rustic mountain scene, framed the huge bed. A family of bronze bears ambled across the top of an old steamer trunk. A tall oak shelf unit, crammed full of books and family photos, towered in the corner. The faint scent of his cologne seemed to float through the air.

"Make yourself at home," he said. "And try to

squelch that girl detective urge of yours and stay put until Keisha comes. Promise."

"I will. I—oh, God. Wait a minute!" She dumped the stack of clothes on the bed and grabbed the backpack out of his hands in one fluid motion. She unzipped the side pocket and extracted the note. "Here," she said, feeling a little breathless. "This is for you."

He opened the piece of paper and stared at it for a moment, then looked back at her. "Is this for real?"

"I hope so."

"But I don't understand. How did you...I mean, how did you—" He stopped. "I'm floored. Let me try that again. How did you—"

"Byron. He knows someone on the police force in New York, and I asked him to see if he could find your dad for me."

"And my father's in Knoxville, Tennessee? I can't seem to wrap my head around that."

"Maybe he's working there. They couldn't have traced him unless he's used a credit card or filed his social security number with an employer. I learned that from watching *CSI*."

He raised his head and looked into her eyes. His hands, still clutching the wrinkled piece of paper, found hers, and when he spoke, the deep, rumbling baritone she had come to rely on for unwavering strength had been reduced to a gravelly whisper. "You did this for me. With everything that's happened, with all you've got to worry about, you...did this for me." He opened his mouth to say something else, then closed it and shook his head, as if he couldn't believe what had just happened. He took a step toward her and enfolded her in his arms, then stood rocking her back and forth with his face buried in her neck.

"I could stay like this forever," she murmured.

"I know. But I have to go. It's getting late, and I

have to put this plan in motion to get you the hell out of here."

She pulled back and forced herself to smile. "Then go."

"It's okay, Annie. It's all gonna be okay."

"You sure about that?"

"Yes, ma'am."

"You're not going to say something inane like 'Trust me,' are you?"

He chuckled softly. "I had thought about it."

"Well, don't."

"Because you wouldn't believe it if I did, right?"

"Exactly."

He let go of her and straightened up. "Get your stuff together and wait for me. Take a nap. Get some rest. And don't tell anyone we're leaving. I want to get a good head start before anyone knows we're gone."

"Where are we going?"

"I don't know yet. I need to make a few calls first." He gave her a quick hug. "Don't worry, Annie, I'm going to fix this. I'm not sure how. But one way or another, this madness is going to stop."

****

Trent heard Eli yelling a string of obscenities before he made it to the parking lot. It had been a long time since he had heard the F, B, and C words used so creatively.

"Look what I found!" Officer Vance emerged from a thicket of rhododendron. He clasped the back of Eli's collar and a good portion of the scruff of his neck. "What do you think I ought to do with this little weasel? Take him downtown and book him for trespassing?"

"What are you doing here, Eli? Everyone's looking for you." An empty gunny sack hung from Eli's belt loop like a pelt. "Oh, Christ, Eli."

"I didn't mean nothin' by it. I wasn't gonna hurt

her."

"What's he talking about?" Vance tightened his hold on the squirming boy. "Calm down, son. Cut it out or I'll have to cuff you."

Blood hammered in Trent's ears. "Eli? *You* did it? You put the snake in Annabel's room?"

Vance grabbed the gunnysack and tossed it to the deputy. "Bag it. It's evidence."

"It was a joke," Eli cried. "I swear!" His pale green eyes widened in fear.

Vance jerked him forward. "Where'd you get the snake?"

"I found it. In the woods."

"Like hell you did." Vance's eyes narrowed. "Don't bullshit me, son. I know who you are. Your family's been warned about this before."

"I don't know what you're talkin' about," Eli said. The waistband of his baggy jeans hung below the tuck of his filthy plaid shirt. His narrow chin, sporting a cultivated patch of blond peach fuzz, jutted out defiantly.

Vance let go of Eli's collar, then jerked his arm up behind his back.

"Ouch!" Eli hollered.

"Have you and your granny been raising snakes again for that church you go to?"

"It ain't illegal to raise snakes." Eli's sullen mouth couldn't hide the tremor in his voice.

"No," said Vance. "But in the state of North Carolina it's a Class 2 misdemeanor to transport them unless they're contained in a closed box. That flimsy little gunnysack doesn't exactly look bite-proof." He shook his head at Trent. "Snake handlers. They know it's illegal, but it doesn't stop them. I ran a raid on that church a couple of months ago. Their preacher almost died from one of those snakebites. So, if you put a poisonous snake in that girl's room tonight, son, people 'round here might think you wanted to kill her."

"It was a joke," Eli sniveled. "That old snake couldn't hurt anybody. There ain't no poison in it. It's been milked."

"Milked?" Trent said.

"Yeah," Eli said. "It's the one Grandmama takes to church. Since Pastor Simcox got sick, we took all the venom out."

Gil joined them on the path. He held a plastic garbage bag at arm's length.

"That it?" Vance asked. Gil handed the bag to the deputy. "Well, we'll soon know how harmless it is, won't we, boy?"

"I'm tellin' the truth," Eli said.

"You'd better hope you are." Vance let go of him.

Eli rubbed his arm. "You grab me like that again and I'll tell my aunt. She'll sue you for—"

"For what? You're the one on thin ice, son. If that snake's fangs are full of venom, I'm slapping you with an attempted murder charge."

"Why, Eli?" Trent asked. "Why did you do it?"

"I told you. To scare her."

"But why?"

Eli pushed a string of matted blond hair back from his pimply forehead. He leveled his unrepentant gaze at Trent. "Because she's a bitch."

"Why would you think that?" Trent asked. "Annabel knew your Aunt Quinn. They were friends."

"I heard Aunt Selena tell my mom that if Annabel weren't here, she'd be your girlfriend. Then we'd get to move into the inn, and I could have my own room and a bike."

"Your own what?" Gil said.

"A motorcycle," Eli spat. "When you were with Quinn, you said you'd get me a motorcycle, remember? You promised me you would. Or are you lying about that too?"

"I said maybe." Gil's voice caught. "I said after Quinn and I were married, when you turned fifteen."

"I'm fifteen now," Eli said. "Where is it?"

"But Quinn and I didn't—we didn't—" Tears welled up in Gil's eyes. He looked helplessly at Eli. "I'm sorry. But things...change."

"Fuck yeah, things change," Eli said. "I'm fifteen and Quinn's kick-ass body is rotting like garbage in the ground."

"That's enough!" Trent said.

"I'm hauling you in, son," Vance said. "And if your aunt doesn't like it, she can take it up with the chief." The deputy clasped Eli's shoulder then led him, stumbling, to the squad car. "The fire marshal will be here in the morning with the arson inspector. They usually come together."

Trent nodded. "Do you think Eli set it?"

"I don't think so," Vance said. "But as hot as that fire burned tonight, I'd bet my eyeteeth somebody did. If that kid had anything to do with the fire, we'll soon find out. I'll make sure his skin and clothes are tested for accelerant residue. Don't worry. We'll get to the bottom of this."

After the squad car pulled away, Gil turned to go.

"Gil, wait," Trent said. "I know those were hard words for you to hear. Especially coming from Eli."

"Blow me."

"Gil, I know you're angry. I get that. But we're family. Sooner or later we're gonna have to talk about this."

Gil spun around. "You know what? I've heard that from you my whole life, and I'm sick to freakin' death of it."

"I don't want things left like this between us. Just let me explain."

"Explain what? Why you slept with the girl I wanted to marry? Why you got her pregnant?

Because if you want to explain all that just to ease your conscience, then I vote no."

"It only happened once. I know it was wrong, but she—"

"You got her drunk, didn't you? You know Quinn could never hold her liquor. You got her rotten, stinking drunk and took advantage of her."

"Actually, it was the other way around."

"You go to hell." Gil glared at him. "I loved Quinn. I *loved* her. But I would rather have seen her dead than end up with you." He turned and ran up the path toward the inn.

This time, Trent let him go.

How could he explain to Gil what he didn't understand himself? How the two of them could have been drawn to—what had Selena called Quinn?—a woman with no soul? A woman who seemed to derive pleasure out of pulling the rug out from under them? If he'd seen that part of Quinn when they'd first met, it would have saved him a boatload of heartache and regret. But he hadn't. He guessed the old saying was true: You see every bus except the one that hits you.

In theory, he couldn't blame himself for getting involved with Quinn the first time. It was unintentional, like catching a cold, or wrapping his arms around a tree covered in poison oak. He'd been naïve. He'd never loved a woman before. And Quinn had been a master at hiding who she really was.

Quinn had blinded people with her charm, mesmerized them with the sheer force of her personality. It swept them along, liberated them from their dull, uptight lives. They rarely noticed they were in over their heads until it was too late. But once the thrill had worn off, being around her became an addiction, an exhausting, continuous high that demanded to be fed. Leaving her was like coming down off of any high. The crash either killed them or scarred them until they hardly recognized themselves.

Trent kicked a rock lying on the path. It spun across the asphalt, landing smooth side up in the long, damp grass. He kept walking, with his hands shoved into the pockets of his denim jacket, watching the ground slide by.

Trent believed Eli had been telling the truth about Selena. Selena's whole life had been fueled by envy, and now she seemed as jealous of Annabel as she had been of Quinn. Resentment grew inside her like a cancer. If she was anything like her mother, it unsettled the hell out of him wondering what lengths she would go to rid herself of it.

How could he have misjudged her? Was that all he did? Misjudge people? When did all that bloody self-assurance about who he should trust disappear? He'd been wrong about Selena and Quinn. And Annabel. Oh, God, he'd been so wrong about Annabel. She was the best of the lot, and he hadn't even given her a chance. Thank God he'd come to his senses and had the courage to open his heart before it was too late. He had grown so tired of measuring and analyzing each emotion, of not trusting the women he loved. He was sick of being alone and bitter. He'd still feel that way if Annabel hadn't come into his life.

Annabel.

Annie.

The thought of her in danger made his blood run cold. It was up to him to keep her safe. Christ, he needed a plan. And he needed it now. A plan would calm him down, make the crushing fear of failure slide into the background where it belonged. But his brain was too tired to churn one out. He was tired of feeling helpless, tired of worrying about things he had no control over. Like the inn.

Screw the inn. It was toast anyway. And screw

losing it to Ruth-friggin'-Donovan. Gil and Annie—they were the ones he really cared about, the ones who needed his help. They were the ones he loved.

"Is the fire out yet?"

Trent glanced up, surprised he'd already reached the inn. Byron stood on the side portico—hatless, for once—puffing away on a tiny cigar. A stream of blue smoke curled toward Trent's face, but it hardly made a difference. The bitter, dank stench of wet charred wood hung heavy in the night air.

"It's out," Trent said. "But the woods are so close, one truck is going to stay until morning just to make sure."

"That's a relief." Beneath the gold glow of the porch light, Byron's white scalp glistened through his thinning hair.

"I figured you'd be with Annabel. After the snake incident."

"The *what*?"

Trent told him about Eli planting the snake.

"Well, the little shit." Byron ground out his cigarette with the toe of his leather loafer, then kicked it off the landing. "I guess I should go see how she's holding up."

"Rachel's with her right now."

"Still—"

"I'd like to ask you something."

Byron adjusted the pale yellow sweater he'd folded and tied around his neck. Preppie capes, Gil called them. Trent wondered how many men would actually wear one if they knew how stupid they looked.

"You're Annabel's friend," Trent said. "She confides in you. Do you have any clue who might be behind these so-called accidents? The fire tonight was—" His throat closed up. "She could have been killed. The attacks are escalating. Whoever's doing this has gone past just wanting her to pack up and go home. They want to hurt her."

"Then why don't you talk to the little shit who hid the snake in her room? Or the rest of Quinn's family? I hear her mother is barking mad."

"She is, but she can't walk ten feet without a cane. If she's behind this, someone would have to carry out her wishes. Someone who could sneak into the inn and the carriage house."

"What about her sister Selena? She showed up soon enough after the air blower turned on." Byron chuckled. "All that sawdust. Sounds like a prank I might have dreamed up in my youth."

"A *prank*? You think everything that's happened in the last two weeks has been a prank? What about the sawed ladder rungs? It took two hours of surgery to stick the bone back in Ham's arm. And the fire? When it started, Annabel was supposed to be in the cabin taking a nap. What about the bump on my head the size of a grapefruit? Oh, yeah, those were all great pranks."

"I only meant—"

"Don't you understand she's in danger? I'm worried about her."

"Bullshit. You just want to jump her bones."

"And this is what you're worried about?"

"Among other things," Byron said silkily.

Trent squeezed his hand into a fist. It was all he could do to keep from smashing it into Byron's smug face. His eye caught a movement at the window. Craig stood behind the lace curtain panel, watching them. "Looks like your new friend is getting impatient. Seems to me you've been too distracted since you came here to worry about much of anything."

Byron smoothed the crisp shirt collar beneath his cashmere sweater. He smiled at Craig and waved. "Well, I guess I deserved that. I must look awful to you, a man of my age cavorting with a young stud like Craig. But don't judge me too harshly. I only have a few good years left."

"Yeah, well, you can cavort with that fire hydrant over there. I don't care. The only thing I care about is Annabel."

Something flickered in Byron's pale eyes. "In that case, I'd suggest you keep a close watch on Rachel Finley. She may look fragile, but that broad can bench more weight than that strapping desk clerk of yours. And I don't care what Rachel says about forgiving and forgetting, she's had a major grudge against Annabel since the day she got booted from the second dance lead in *Moondance* back to chorus."

"Why would Rachel blame Annabel for that? Didn't Rachel lose her part because she showed up too stoned to dance?"

"Yes, she did. But it was our dear, sweet Annabel who ratted her out."

Chapter 16

"My money's on the old crone," Rachel said.

Annabel stopped folding jeans and peered over her wire frames. "Mrs. Wolcott?"

"The snake came from her backyard." Rachel sat cross-legged on the corner of Trent's bed. She looped one arm around the thick bedpost. "I bet Selena broke into your room and let it loose so you'll leave."

"No, Selena wants me to stay. She thinks the supper club will save the inn from going under. Which just goes to show you how little she knows about theaters."

"Yeah, they're not exactly moneymakers unless you're selling drinks every two minutes." Rachel wrinkled her nose. "But yuk! How can she own snakes? That is so gross. I bet she keeps them as pets. I bet she dresses them in little outfits and takes them to the mall. They probably sleep with her. Ten bucks says they're the *only* thing she can get to sleep with her."

"It might not have been the same kind of snake."

"It was exactly the same." Rachel pushed a long red curl behind her ear. "Gil showed it to me before he gave it to the police. No, I still think Quinn's mother is behind this. She's the kind of religious fanatic who'd off one of her own kids to save them from a life of sin. And you know how sinful dancing eight shows a week can be."

"Did you say sinful or painful?"

"Mrs. Wolcott was at the theater that night. The

guard at the Park Square—Granville—can't hear himself fart, and his eyesight isn't much better. She could have sneaked past him easy."

"And what? Hobbled up a flight of stairs? Then limped down the hall to my dressing room and planted a bottle of pills on the shelf without anyone seeing her? That woman couldn't sneak into Times Square on New Year's Eve."

"No, but Selena could. You said Selena's always been jealous of Quinn, of her looks, her life. Of Trent. Quinn stole him from her, remember?"

"Well, Selena thinks she did. That would be a motive, I guess. But there are too many variables. Selena wasn't a member of the company. How could she predict where people were backstage, or what they were doing at any given moment?" Annabel pulled the tag off a T-shirt. "I've heard Selena talk about Quinn's death, and she seems genuinely broken up about it. I can't believe she would kill her own sister."

"Maybe she didn't mean to kill her. Maybe she just meant to give her enough codeine to wreck her dancing and make a fool out of her in front of their mother and Freeman Saunders. Freeman was there, you know. Sitting eighth row, center." Rachel reached into her shirt pocket and pulled out a Marlboro.

"You can't smoke in here."

"I'm not. I just can't think without one in my hand."

Annabel stared at Rachel. "Freeman *was* there, wasn't he? I had forgotten that. Byron was a basket case before the show, worrying he hadn't warmed up enough and wouldn't dance well for the Great and Powerful Oz. Then the codeine hit me, and I started to feel dizzy. I think he was worried I'd screw up our number and Freeman would blame him."

"Maybe Selena knew he was going to be in the

house and tried to sabotage Quinn's chances of getting in his new show."

"How did she know Freeman would be there? We didn't know it."

"Okay, I'll admit that theory's a little farfetched, but *something* happened. Selena's not a very nice person—Keisha told me that. Didn't she convince Trent not to call the police after the air blower pelted you? And wasn't she the first one on the scene after it happened?"

"You think she could've moved an industrial blower by herself? It weighs a ton."

"Hell, Annabel, she's as big as a horse. All she had to do was shove it with one of those gigantic hips of hers then hide backstage until you crawled under the bandstand. There are layers and layers to that woman. And I don't just mean insulation. I've seen the way she looks at Trent, willing him to notice her, wounded and disappointed when he doesn't. And each time he ignores her, you can see this little flash of uncontrolled fury in her eyes that makes you want to go out and rent *Fatal Attraction* again." Rachel regarded Annabel solemnly. "You know, at this point, you'd be a fool not to suspect everybody. Even me. Do you suspect me, Annabel? Do you think I switched those pills to get back at you and Quinn for dumping me?"

"I hope not." Annabel sat on the end of the bed. Exhaustion wiped out the last remnants of the adrenaline blitz that had begun on top of Sourwood Hill. She smoothed a section of the dark Amish quilt with her hand, then leaned her head back against the headboard and closed her burning eyes. "I gotta tell you, Rach—I'm going a little nuts right now."

"You're making *me* nuts. Why did you put yourself in jeopardy like this? Why did you feel obligated to keep a promise to Quinn when she never kept a promise in her life?"

"That's what Trent wanted to know. But the truth is she kept one to me. One day we were rehearsing, and I collapsed. My hip just stopped working. Quinn got me outside without anyone seeing us, then used her Aunt Ruth's name to set up an appointment with the best orthopedic specialist in New York. Quinn was so kind to me." Annabel opened her eyes. "Don't look at me like that. I knew you'd look at me like that."

"Like what?"

"Like Quinn being kind to anyone was the last thing you'd believe."

"Maybe the second to last thing."

"Even if my hip hadn't crapped out on me, we both knew I was too old to dance many more leads like the one in *Moondance*. I wanted to hang on for as long as I could. I knew if word got out I had dancer's hip, they'd replace me that day."

"But everyone knew. We all knew."

"How did you know? Quinn swore she wouldn't tell."

"She didn't have to. Jesus, Annabel, you danced like a dream. The girls in the company envied the hell out of you. It didn't matter how old you were, or how little professional experience you'd had, you were what we wanted to look like when we danced. We watched every move you made. Do you think we wouldn't know if you were having trouble with your hip? Everyone covered for you. We adjusted our dancing to keep it a secret, especially Frank and Louis. They did most of your lifts."

"But no one ever said anything. All those weeks and—"

"No one wanted you to quit. We were all dancers. We had the same dream."

"Which is another reason for you to hate me, Rach. If I'd been more supportive of you, you'd still be in *Moondance*. You'd be going to Broadway next month with the rest of them."

"Or I'd be hiding out on the Lower East Side, waiting for my next hit of booger sugar. I think the universe has a different plan for me. Why would I want to dance back-row-chorus on Broadway when I can be the star at Fred and Ginger's?" She laughed and jumped off the bed, then did a quick time-step. "I *am* the star, aren't I? Please tell me I'm the star."

"You're the star."

"Good. Now, I've been thinking. If we scrub the jazz band for the first few weeks and use recorded music, we could open with three solid dance numbers by the weekend, and the club could start generating some income. There's not much left to do. The wait staff said they'd help paint if we gave them free tequila shots. If we can get the bar sinks hooked up and the chandeliers hung, we'll be—"

"Are you sure this isn't too much for you?"

"*No!* I feel strong. I feel good. I'm excited about the show. I really think I can do it justice."

"Then do it. Do it all. You can have my salary. I never wanted this job anyway. Let the floorshow be your creation. It'll be great."

"Really?" Rachel grinned, her face radiant.

"Yes, really."

"I'm not worried about Craig. His inflated ego might explode, but he learns dance moves really fast. Marva is great, but not as experienced. If she can't handle something, I can pick up the slack. Believe me, it'll be nice to be the one picking up someone else's slack for a change."

Rachel looked like the old Rachel again—confident and sassy, ready to take on the world.

"I think you're gonna make it this time, Rach."

"I hope so. I am so sick of wrecking my life." Rachel slid the unlit Marlboro back in her pocket. "And I've got you to thank. You and Trent and Gil, for letting me stay here." She grinned. "Speaking of

Trent."

"What about him?"

"You love him, don't you?"

"I...yes, I do. I love him." Her heart soared just hearing herself say it out loud.

"Well, I think he loves you too. You should have seen him tonight when you were missing. He went to pieces. I think he would have done anything to find you." She laughed. "God, I'm jealous. It must be nice having your own personal knight just hanging around, waiting to rescue you. All he needs is a white horse and a suit of armor. And a big lance." She grinned. "Or maybe he already has one of those."

"He'll find out one day that I'm more trouble than I'm worth." Annabel stood and moved toward the door. "Go on, Rach. I need to finish putting these clothes away and go to sleep."

"Trent said to stay until Keisha got here. She's out looking for Mrs. Richmond's dog."

"I know that dog. It's not lost; it's just screwing with Mrs. Richmond's head."

Rachel hesitated.

"It's okay," Annabel said. "Keisha will be here soon, and I've got a lot to process. I need a breather between babysitters."

"Okay. As long as you promise not to do anything stupid."

After Rachel left, Annabel took a deep breath. She had to stay strong in order to do what she had to do. She couldn't allow herself to think about the fire, or the snake, or the consequences her family would have to face if Selena followed through with her threat to stall Drew's loan. Right now, she had to think about Trent."

Rachel was right. She loved him. With all her heart and soul.

Which was why she couldn't let him risk his life

to keep her safe.

He was protective of her. He would never let her leave the inn by herself. Not until he knew she was out of danger. If the tables were turned, as long as someone was out there trying to hurt him, she wouldn't let him out of her sight either.

Trent's whole life was centered around the inn and his brother. They both counted on him. They both needed him. If he left, things would not only fall apart, they might never recover.

What did Quinn used to say? *Time to put on your big girl panties and get on with it.*

Annabel scooped up the stack of clothes and stuffed them in her backpack. She tied her jacket around her waist and checked her billfold for her credit card, offering up a prayer of gratitude that, out of habit, she'd put it in her backpack before leaving the cabin. She stood for a moment, wondering what Trent would think when he came back and found her gone.

She glanced in the oval shaving mirror and caught a glimpse of her haggard face. If Freeman Saunders could see her now, he'd cast her as a dancing corpse.

She gazed around Trent's room. It wasn't going to be easy to walk out; he was everywhere.

A lopsided ceramic cup with *World's Greatest Brother* painted on it sat on the dresser. She ran her fingers over his things—a stack of folded white handkerchiefs, an open roll of Tums, a scattered pile of change, a stack of Sheffield Inn brochures. She picked up a brochure and flipped it over. Trent and Gil stared up at her from the foyer. She slid the brochure into her purse.

She moved to the bookshelf and looked at the framed photographs. Trent and Gil in matching baseball hats. Gil walking across a stage, holding a diploma. She picked up a small square frame. Trent, probably around ten or eleven, stood with his hands on Gil's small shoulders before a huge tinsel laden Christmas tree. Even then, Trent's smile looked strained. His clear hazel eyes stared gravely into the camera, already filled with the weary, burdened expression of an adult.

Her heart caught hard in her throat.

She would miss him terribly. She was already missing him.

She threaded her arms through the nylon back straps and hoisted the heavy pack onto her shoulders. On his desk, she found a pad of paper and a pen. She scribbled a quick note so he wouldn't think someone had kidnapped her and propped it on his pillow. Then she glanced around the room one last time, etching the last fragment of him in her memory.

Four loud knocks on the door sent her heartbeat thrashing against her ribs like a trapped bird.

Keisha.

Dammit. Why couldn't Precious have stayed hidden five more lousy minutes?

"Who is it?"

"It's Trent, Annie."

She opened the door.

He stood leaning against the doorway. The sleeves of his blue cotton shirt were rolled up and wrinkled, his shirttail haphazardly tucked into the waistband of his jeans. Tendrils of dark hair curled over the back of his collar. A delicate web of lines etched the outer corners of his eyes, faint blue smudges shadowed the hollows beneath them.

"I thought you were Keisha," she said.

He flexed his arm with a fist. "Not with these puny biceps." He came in and closed the door. "I sent Keisha to her parent's house. She's been here since six this morning. I figure we'll get a few hours sleep, then leave. Getting out of this place undetected won't be easy, but—" He stopped. His glance shot past her, taking in everything at once—her face, the bulging backpack, the note on the bed. Panic darted across his face, but he recovered quickly. The muscles in his jaw tightened. She could see the gears in his head shift and turn.

"So," he said, finally. "You've decided to skip out on us."

"I don't skip anymore."

He opened a little refrigerator beneath a table she hadn't noticed, grabbed a bottle of water, and handed it to her. "You might need this if you're planning on hiking out of here." He sat in the wingback chair beside the window and pulled his shoes off, not looking at her. "By the way, Vance has arrested Eli for hiding the snake in your room."

"*Eli?* Did he set the fire too?"

"I don't know. They don't think so, but they're holding him on suspicion of arson and attempted murder until they're sure. He swears the snake was harmless. Vance has sent it to the lab to have it analyzed."

"That boy's brain is what needs to be analyzed." The quaver in her voice matched her trembling hands. She curled her fingers into fists to stop them from shaking. *Her teeth would be next*, she thought, clacking against each other like a pair of castanets.

He lifted his head and looked at her. "Aren't you going?"

"I don't know. I'm suddenly so tired I can't move."

Fatigue washed over her like a tidal wave. It soaked into her skin, turned her limbs to rubber, relaxed the muscles in her neck until they refused to support her head, and it occurred to her that if she didn't sit down, she would fall down. She let the backpack slide off her shoulders and swing to the floor.

"I'm...sorry. I knew I was spent, but—" Her body was fast taking on a life of its own. She swayed forward, then giggled softly because she couldn't control where she was going to land.

Trent crossed the gap between them and scooped her up. The water bottle fell on the bed. "Something tells me you're not going to be skipping out tonight after all."

"I told you," she murmured. "I don't skip."

Her head bounced against his chest. The feel of his soft cambric shirt and the sweet scent of his neck were almost too much to bear. It evoked every shred of comfort she could remember taking for granted...wrapping herself in a quilt on a raw, rainy night...watching her mother's storm candles burn, keeping the black wall of darkness at bay...hearing coyotes prowl the yard beside the chicken house and knowing she was safe inside, where even the large ones, the ones with the hunched backs and yellow gleaming eyes, couldn't get to her.

She thought he would lay her on the bed, but instead he lowered her into the brown leather chair beside the fireplace, so velvety smooth it felt like butter against her skin. He flipped the gas switch on the hearth. A row of flames raced across the stubby logs. The blaze rocketed up, then settled into a silent, perfect facsimile of a real wood fire.

"There," he said gently. "That should warm you." He dragged the matching ottoman to her chair and sat facing her, his lanky frame doubled over into an *S*. He rested his forearms on his knees and gazed into her eyes. His lips had pulled into a hard, drawn line, and when he spoke, his thick, liquid drawl did little to soften the words. "Were you really gonna leave without telling me goodbye?"

Tears sprang to her eyes before she could blink them back. "I wrote you a note."

"Listen, Annie, I'm not gonna force myself on

you. If you want to go alone, I can't stop you. But for your own safety, I think you should get out of here as soon as possible."

"Well, me too. Now that the fire's out and the snake has been caught, my job here is done."

He curled his fingers around her hand and squeezed. Warmth flooded through it like molten silver. "Stop it," he said softly. "Stop pretending you're not scared shitless, because I know you are. If you don't want me to protect you, then let me find someone who can."

She threw her arms around his neck. "I do want you to go with me. I do. I just thought—it doesn't seem fair to involve you in this. You've got Gil to worry about, and the inn. When word gets out someone has been sabotaging the inn, this place will clear out like rats off a sinking ship. I can't let you throw everything away because I need a bodyguard."

"You let me worry about that."

"But I don't want to be the reason—"

"*Shhhhh,*" he said, holding her close. "You are the reason. You're the only reason. Do you realize I wake up in the morning and can't wait for the rest of my life? Do you know what a miracle that is? So, get over the fact that you've involved me in this. I wouldn't have it any other way." He leaned back and looked into her eyes, then stroked her cheek with his hand. His lips grazed against hers, tender and yielding, gentle as a butterfly's wing. "Honey, I need to ask you something about the night Quinn died. Something I've been thinking about for a while."

"Okay."

"Do you know what was happening on the rest of the stage while you were trying to save Quinn from falling?"

"Byron said as soon as I started running, the cast automatically filled the empty space I'd left in line. It sounds callous, but it's what they're trained to do. I guess, at some point, they stopped dancing and watched me and Quinn."

"That's what I'm getting at. Everyone had their own perspective. I think you need to talk to the cast and crew again. I've been in enough theaters to know that secrets don't stay secret very long. If something else was going on that day, you can bet someone saw or heard it. And maybe, now that two months have passed, they might have gained some insight. I think it's worth a try. Clearly, there's something about that night someone doesn't want you to know. And the sooner we find out what it is, the sooner you'll be safe again."

"The stage manager—Murray—could get me the casts' phone numbers."

"Then call him tomorrow. The inn has an 800 number which will be active for about thirty-six more hours. Another expense I'm dropping, right up there with cucumber aloe soap and—"

"—one-size-fits-all bathrobes?"

He grinned. "No, ma'am. I'm keeping those."

He switched off the fire then stood and held out his hand. He led her to the bed. When she had snuggled into the thick cotton comforter, he pulled off her shoes and threw the Amish quilt over her. He lay down beside her, then reached up and switched off the beside lamp. The amber glow of a tiny nightlight fanned across the lower half of the far wall.

"You sleep with a nightlight?" she murmured drowsily, nestling her head into the warm hollow of his shoulder.

"It's better than barking my shins on the furniture."

"And it keeps the monsters in the closet."

"And it keeps the monsters in the closet." He pulled the quilt over her shoulder. "I set my phone alarm for two. We'll sleep for three hours then sneak out."

"And how will we manage to do that?"

"Down the backstairs, out the kitchen side door, circle through the woods till we reach the road. I moved my car. It's waiting just past the stone wall."

She idly rubbed the downy hair on his forearm. "Is this what they call the calm before the storm?"

"Something like that." He held her tight and pressed his lips to her forehead. The soft stubble of his beard raked gently against her temples. She curled her arm over his chest and closed her eyes, feeling sleep pull her down into dark, billowy softness.

"And Annie?"

"Umm?"

"Thank you. Thank you for finding my father."

Chapter 17

Nolan Sheffield put his beefy arm around Annabel's shoulder. He led her to a tiny hallway outside the kitchen where he had covered the walls with framed photographs.

"There I am doing Tevye in *Fiddler on the Roof*," he said. "One newspaper said I was as cuddly as Zero Mostel." He pulled his gray, fuzzy eyebrows together and twinkled his hazel eyes mischievously. "I know you're too young to remember Zero Mostel, but the man was an absolute genius. That's me playing Velasco in *Barefoot in the Park*. Nice little dinner theater, but the beef tips tasted like shoe leather."

Trent watched them and smiled. There was nothing Nolan enjoyed more than recounting war stories from his forty-odd years of playing every broken down regional theater east of the Mississippi, especially to a willing audience. Annabel *oohed* and *ahhed* in all the right places, encouraged him to sing a few bars of "If I Were a Rich Man," and looked duly impressed when he quoted the same tiresome reviews Trent and Gil had heard a hundred times.

Trent didn't mind. It bought him some time. The plan to walk in and demand Nolan agree to sell the lots hadn't panned out. Nolan had burst into tears when he opened the door and saw his son standing there. It seemed cruel to hit him with a request like that right off the bat.

Trent still couldn't believe his father had been

living in Knoxville, less than two hours from the inn. But that was Nolan Sheffield. One of the most unpredictable, exasperating men he'd ever known. Trent had been sure the man was either dead or lying face down in a gutter, and yet here he was, respectable as hell, holding down a prestigious job in the theater department at the University of Tennessee.

He appeared thinner, less bloated. He didn't look like the same man who could play the lead in a grueling three hour musical, drink cheap scotch until 5 a.m., then scarf down a family-size box of frozen waffles before passing out cold on the couch. He had always been a large man, almost as tall as Trent, and slightly overweight, with a larger-than-life personality to match his girth. He'd made a career out of playing the "big" parts, the one-man-show parts, the roles where he could make a tasty meal out of the scenery and get a five-minute standing ovation just for showing up.

Trent leaned against the doorframe and crossed his arms. He loved watching Annabel watch Nolan. She laughed at some droll remark Nolan had made, then watched him do a little time-step and gesture grandly to bring his point home. Nolan lifted an oval picture off the wall.

"This is a photo of Trent's mother in *Last of the Red Hot Lovers*. My Glynis. She was something, wasn't she? We fell in love in that show before the first read-through was over. Look at those dimples. She was a beauty. Everyone thought so. Especially the guy who played opposite her in *Two for the Seesaw*. Three months later, when she couldn't fit into her costume, I figured out why the love scenes with that lowlife looked so realistic."

"He has a name," Trent said.

"Julius P. Funk," Nolan said. "Who could forget that? Never did find out what the *P* stood for."

"Dad let Mother give Gil his last name because she thought *Sheffield* on a marquee would sell more tickets than *Funk*."

Nolan smiled. "Glynis always did have a practical side. Used to drive me crazy. You must have gotten that from her, Trent. I didn't mind giving my name to Gil. Glynis and I were still married, and by then it was pretty clear Julius P. wasn't going to step up to the plate."

"Does Gil know his real father?" Annabel asked.

"He met him a few years ago," Trent said. "The man was living in north Georgia, selling painted concrete sculptures by the side of the road. You know the ones I mean: two frogs sitting under an umbrella, a naked cherub peeing into a fountain, those god-awful things people buy on vacation then regret the minute they get home. Gil said the poor guy was delusional enough to think he was a real artist."

"What happened when they met?"

"Oh, Mr. Funk was very polite," Trent said. "He even shook Gil's hand when he left. Right after he told him to never come back.

"Gil was crushed," Nolan said. "Makes me wish I'd just let him go on believing he was my son."

"No, you did the right thing by telling the truth," Annabel said. "Lies always come back to bite you on the ass."

Nolan nodded to Trent. "I like her, don't you?"

Trent grinned. "I do."

Nolan's gaze drifted to another photograph. "*A Christmas Carol*," he said. "I loved doing that show. Such nice people. I never hear from any of them." He sighed heavily. "Just make sure all your friends aren't in theater, Annabel."

"Why not?" she asked.

"Because if they are, you'll end up being alone."

For a moment, Trent felt sorry for him. But then

he remembered, just as he always did when an unexpected wave of sympathy threatened to gloss over the past, that Nolan had stolen his childhood from him. Nolan could make all the excuses in the world, but nothing could change the fact that he'd treated Trent and Gil like unwanted pets, pushed out of a moving car and left on the side of the road to fend for themselves.

Trent looked at Annabel. He liked looking at Annabel. He couldn't seem to keep his eyes off her. Light from the streaked kitchen window settled across the soft contours of her face, making her eyes look more blue than gray. She smiled at him, but her eyes couldn't quite catch up. They looked tired, haunted.

The woman had guts. He'd give her that. She hadn't whined. Or cried. Or turned tail and run, even though she'd wanted to. She was still apprehensive about accepting his help. He could see it every time he caught her watching him. But he couldn't blame her for searching for a chink in the armor, making sure he was honorable enough to trust. And he vowed not to let her down.

Trent touched his empty belt loop. His phone was still hooked to the charger in the car. He needed to check in with Keisha, see if Vance and the fire inspector had found out anything. Once he got Annabel to his old college buddy's house in Charleston, and knew she was safe, he could look at his options and see whether or not he could afford to rebuild the cabin. Of course, if Ruth Donovan took over, it was a moot point anyway. But first, he needed to rebuild his relationship with Gil. All he'd wanted to do was spare the kid's feelings. Instead, he had injured them more than Quinn could have ever done.

He heard Nolan say his name and looked up. His father and Annabel had moved to the kitchen.

They sat at the small Formica-topped table, deep in conversation. He wanted to join them, but something held him back. Curiosity, maybe. Hearing what Nolan had to say about him when he was out of the room was too seductive to pass up. He wasn't really eavesdropping. The place was so small, the sound bounced from one side to the other like air through a wind tunnel.

"I knew Glynis wasn't up to dragging two little boys with her on the dinner theater circuit," Nolan said. "Living with Trent in the actors' quarters was hard on her, but even harder on him. When he wasn't at school, he was stuck in the corner with a coloring book and a handful of Matchbox cars. And no one wanted him there. Who wants someone else's kid hanging around backstage, getting into mischief because they're bored out of their skulls? They used to call kids like that theater brats."

"They still do."

"When Gil was born, Glynis promised she'd stay in one place long enough to give the boys some stability. We rented a little apartment outside Asheville, but by the time Gil turned four, she was so unhappy, she couldn't stand it anymore. She put them to bed one night, paid the girl upstairs to watch them, and took off for New York. She left me a note saying it was my turn to be the parent."

"I thought your sister raised them."

"She did. If you can call it that. Margaret convinced me they'd be better off staying with her in a Christian home. What else could I do? Theaters are no place for kids. Hell, they're no place for adults. Margaret resented Gil because in her eyes he was Glynis's bastard child. When I found out Trent was having to take care of him, the damage had been done. No thirteen-year-old boy should be saddled with that kind of responsibility. It changed Trent, killed the joy in him. I should have checked on them more. I never should have left them. And now, neither one of those boys trusts anybody, and it's my fault."

Annabel leaned forward in her chair. "Have you told Trent this?"

Nolan shook his head. "Margaret wouldn't even let them stay in the inn. She made them live in the old caretaker's cottage. When I found out how miserable they were, I sent Trent money so he and Gil could move to New York with Glynis. But it didn't work out. They'd built up too much resentment against their mother for leaving them. They stayed with her for a year while Trent finished up school, but they hated it. Then Trent met that girl, the one who died."

"Quinn."

"Right. I think she and Trent spent all their time bailing Gil out of jams. That boy was wild—still is—and had a temper to match." Nolan chuckled. "Funny, isn't it? Gil's not my natural son, but he's more like me than Trent."

Nolan unhooked three mugs from beneath the cabinet. He lined them up on the counter and plugged in the coffeemaker. *That's one thing that hasn't changed,* Trent thought. It didn't matter if Nolan was at home or in a hotel room in Poughkeepsie, he always kept a pot of coffee ready to go at a moment's notice.

"Then Margaret had a heart attack and died," Nolan said. "It really surprised me her heart gave out, because I didn't think she had one."

"Nolan," Annabel admonished gently.

"It's true," Nolan said. His eyes got misty again. "The minute we got back from her funeral, you know what Trent did? He packed up his stuff and moved him and Gil into the inn. Then he hired a bulldozer to level the caretaker's cottage. Turned the damned thing into a parking lot."

"Nothing like wiping out your past in an afternoon."

"That was the general idea."

"What happened to Glynis? I know she passed away."

Nolan nodded. "Stepped off a curb and was mowed down by a stretch limo taking some third-rate soap star to the Daytime Emmys. I don't even think he was nominated."

"I'm sorry," Annabel said.

"That he wasn't nominated? Don't be. That man couldn't act his way out of a flower garden."

"I'm sorry about Glynis," Annabel said.

"Me too," Nolan said softly. "And I'm sorry I didn't stay in contact with Trent. I've missed him so much. After I made an ass out of myself at Gil's graduation party, he banned me from the inn. Did he tell you that?"

"He told me how long he's been searching for you."

Nolan's gray, unkempt hair bobbed around his ears. "I heard that from one of my old landlords up in Jersey a few months ago. Said some guy claiming to be my son was trying to find me."

"And you never called Trent? Why not?"

"Good question," Trent said from the doorway. "Why don't you answer it?"

Nolan looked up at him. "I...I don't know why. I guess I was afraid to hear how much you hated me."

"You're my dad. I don't hate you. Sometimes I don't like you very much, and sometimes I want to bang your head against a wall. But I suspect you feel the same way about me."

Nolan's deep voice choked with emotion. "I'm just glad you're here, son."

Trent swallowed the knot in his throat and nodded. "Me too, Dad."

Annabel sniffed then smiled up at him, her eyes

shining with tears . She reached up and wiped the corner of her eye with her ring finger. "You guys are making me cry."

"You should have been in the audience when I did the graveyard scene in *Shenandoah*. There wasn't a dry eye in the house."

****

Annabel laughed, then stood and pulled her sweater closer around her. "I'm going to let you guys catch up while I get some air. Trent, can I borrow your cell phone?"

"In the car." Trent tossed her the keys.

She took the elevator to the ground floor of the apartment complex and walked across the weed-infested lot to the Sheffield Inn van. She climbed in, unplugged Trent's phone from the charger, and called Murray.

"Stage manager."

"Murray? It's Annabel Maitland."

"Annabel? Hey, girl. How are you? We thought you fell off the face of the earth."

"Only as far as North Carolina."

"That's far enough. We miss you, babe. When you coming back? I guess you heard *Moondance* is moving to Broadway next month. We get a two week break starting Monday."

"I thought you were breaking now. Byron said he—"

"Have you talked to him? How's he doing?"

"What do you mean?"

"He called in sick a few days ago. Said he had the flu. Totally freaked out the cast. They've been wolfing down Vitamin C and Zinc like candy. Tell him if he claims two more sick days, he'll have to bring in a doctor's excuse."

"I think he's on the mend," Annabel said lightly. She was touched their friendship meant so much to Byron, but why had he lied about having time off from *Moondance*? Why hadn't he just admitted he'd called in sick? Sooner or later, everyone called in sick. It was no big deal.

"I got about two more minutes."

"Can I ask you a couple of questions about the night Quinn died?"

"Yeah, but make it fast. I gotta set up."

"After the matinee, did you see anyone backstage who wasn't supposed to be there?"

"Just that one guy. But I told the police, and they didn't care."

"What guy?"

"The one who was hanging around the stage door. You know about that."

"No, I don't." Her heart picked up speed. "Who was it?"

"Dunno. Granville always looks the other way when the dancers bring in their boyfriends."

"Can you describe him?"

"Kinda good looking, I guess. Thick eyebrows, brown hair. He was wearing one of those long, all-weather coats. I already told the police."

"You said they didn't care. Why not?"

"Because he never made it upstairs. He's on the security camera—at least, part of him is—but he never went past the lower hallway. After I talked to him, I left. Granville said he stayed at the check-in desk."

"But somebody switched those pills. Maybe this guy gave the Curenol bottle to Quinn, and she carried it upstairs. Or maybe he came back later, and she let him in through the scene shop door. There's no security camera back there. He could have come in that way, couldn't he?"

"Yeah. I guess so."

"When you talked to this man? How did he sound?"

"He sounded Southern. You know, like Quinn

did when she drank too much."

A sinking feeling stirred the pit of Annabel's stomach.

"Was he young? How old was he?"

"Jesus, Annabel. I don't know. My age, maybe."

Gil? Could it have been Gil?

"Murray, why didn't you tell me about this mystery man when I talked to you before?"

"'Cause I thought he was there to see Rachel. Rachel always had guys hanging around the stage door. Probably bringing her drugs, as it turns out."

"Do you still have that old fax machine in the office?"

"I think so, why?"

"If I fax you a picture, would you be able to look at it and tell me if it's the man you saw?"

"Sure. I guess."

"What's the fax number?"

"Same as the Park Square number with the last two digits transposed."

"Thanks, Murray."

"If you talk to Byron, tell him Freeman Saunders' office called the theater, trying to get hold of him. They said Byron won't answer his cell, and his agent doesn't seem to know where he is. Hey, you're still going up for the part in Freeman's new show, aren't you?"

Annabel took a deep breath. It was time to deal with it. Time to speak the truth out loud and make it real. "No, Murray. My hip won't heal in time. Just don't tell anyone until I've talked to Freeman, okay? He should hear it from me first."

"You'd better tell him soon, babe."

She snapped Trent's phone closed and leaned back against the seat. Her head was spinning.

Could Gil really be the one who tried to kill Quinn? Was that even in the realm of possibility? What would have been going through his mind?

What could Quinn have said or done to push him over the edge? Knowing Quinn, it could have been anything.

Annabel tried to sort it out.

Gil had admitted going to see Quinn, but claimed they'd met in the alley behind the stage door. Why had he lied about going inside the theater? To avoid suspicion? Because he thought his image might end up on a security tape? Why would he want to kill Quinn? Could he have known she was pregnant with someone else's child? Did he give her a bottle of codeine-laced pills, hoping she would take them and miscarry? Or had she mentioned having a headache, and he snuck back later during the lull between the matinee and evening performance to plant the pills on her dressing room shelf, knowing it was a sure bet she'd take them?

Gil had a motive—jealousy. Even Keisha had mentioned how jealous and obsessive Gil was with Quinn. If he knew another man loved her, and had fathered her child, he might not have been able to accept it. He certainly had the opportunity, and knowing Quinn and her allergies as well as he did, it wouldn't have been too difficult to come up with a fail-safe method to snuff out her life.

Annabel shut her eyes. The world was closing in on her.

Had Gil staged the string of "accidents" that seemed designed to drive her away from the inn and stop her from learning the truth? She tried to think.

Gil had access to every part of the inn, and Keisha's trust. He could have intercepted Selena's message and known Annabel was going to meet her at the carriage house. One of the first things Selena said after she arrived was that she'd seen Gil walking back from the parking lot. He could have trashed the sheet music, set the trap for her to crawl under the bandstand, then taken the long way around and arrived just in time to see Selena and pretend he was coming from the other direction. A trek like that wouldn't be hard to manage for someone who ran laps every morning. He knew about the Curenol switch. He knew Annabel climbed the wooden ladder six times a day. He knew...everything. Even Rachel hadn't completely trusted him.

She opened her eyes and stared at the dashboard. The gravity of what she was planning to do settled on her like a steel weight.

Her heart ached for Trent. This would kill him. Gil was everything to him. Trent had raised Gil, protected him, loved him. If her suspicions were true, Trent would be devastated beyond belief when he found out the person who had killed Quinn was his own brother. And that the woman he had finally let into his heart was instrumental in proving it.

She had to find out, but how was she going to get a fax to Murray? An office supply store would do it, if she could find one nearby, but she would need an excuse to drive Trent's car. She couldn't tell him anything until she was sure, beyond a shadow of a doubt, that Gil was guilty.

She put the phone in her pocket and slid out of the van. She hated feeling so helpless, but there was nothing she could do until Murray looked at the picture on the back of the Sheffield Inn brochure and identified Gil.

Chapter 18

Trent had been sitting at his father's table for hours. Once Nolan began one of his longwinded monologues, he knew he might as well sit back and get comfortable. He thought he could distance himself from Nolan, hold the biting sting of resentment in check. He used to be good at that. But this time it wasn't working.

He'd waited for this meeting for over a year. All he had to do was mention the lots they owned and make Nolan understand how vital selling them would be. Nolan owed him that money and more for throwing him and Gil to the wolves all those years ago. But every time he started to bring it up, he couldn't follow through. This was a Nolan Sheffield Trent had never seen before—one minute, fierce and confident, the next, a lonely, middle-aged man with nothing to call his own but a seventeen-year-old Mustang and a few scrapbooks crammed full of newspaper clippings.

Long shards of yellow light traveled across the grease stained kitchen wall, then deepened into shadows. Annabel moved silently around the kitchen, making them sandwiches, pouring them cup after cup of strong black coffee. Trent didn't know if his hands were shaking from the caffeine or because his father had finally said the two words he'd been longing to hear for the past twenty-three years: "I'm sorry."

"I've been such a bad father to you," Nolan said.

"I was afraid I'd never see you again. But you're here, and you know what? Life is short. And I'm not wasting any more of it without you."

Months, or even days ago, Trent couldn't have swallowed any of it. He would have sworn Nolan was using every acting trick in the book to weasel his way back into Trent's life. But not now. He wasn't sure when everything changed. Or why, sitting across the table from a man whose hands were trembling worse than his own, he couldn't come up with a good reason why saving an inn was more important than having his father back.

The slate was far from being wiped clean, but once the hatred he'd held onto for so long began to dissipate, he was amazed how much room there was left in his heart. He felt like the kid at school who'd just won a ten-speed bike he didn't know how to ride.

Nolan glanced at the clock above the table and let out a yelp. "Oh, Jeez, I've gotta go. Callbacks are tonight. Twenty-nine UT seniors are waiting for me at the theater. And believe me, you do not want to keep a senior waiting. They can make your life a living, breathing hell."

He left in a flourish, which was how he usually made an exit, hugging them both, begging them to stay the night. "The couch makes a bed, and I've got one of those blow-up thingies around here somewhere." He dug around in his pocket and pulled out a key. "I'm not sure how late I'll be, so take this. You might want to go out somewhere. It's the only key I've got, so if you decide to leave, just drop it by the super's office."

Trent plopped onto the dilapidated sofa and stretched his legs out in front of him. Annabel sat in his father's Lazy Boy recliner. She ran her fingers across the worn upholstery, smoothed a web of loose threads.

"What do you say, Miss Annie? You want to stay

here tonight before we go on to Charleston? We could find the blow-up thingy and take turns using it as a trampoline."

"Now, there's a plan."

"What do you think of dear old Dad?"

"I think he's charming."

"He is that."

"You didn't ask him about selling the lots, did you?"

Trent shook his head. "I couldn't. He thinks I came here because I want him back in my life. He thinks I came to forgive him. I couldn't let him know that this morning I didn't have the slightest intention of *ever* forgiving him. But then, it just...sort of happened. Enough time has passed, I guess. He's old. I'm old."

"Yeah, thirty-six is ancient."

"I guess at some point, you have to let go of the bitterness or it will eat you alive." He grinned just to make her smile. She had the sweetest smile in the world, the sweetest lips, and his heart swelled when the corners of her mouth began to curl upward.

"I'm proud of you," she said. "And you know what else? I admire you."

"For what?"

"For raising Gil when you were only a child yourself. For having a tender heart. For forgiving your father today. You did forgive him, didn't you?"

"I'm working on it." His gaze shot to the window. "Hey, look. There's a full moon."

"Yeah, I've heard that one before. Then I get up and walk to the window, and some kid is standing across the street, bending over with his pants around his knees."

"Not this time." He drew the curtain back and switched off the lamps. White light streamed through the window. He held out his hand. "Moon dance?"

She laughed. "Are you sure that's moonlight? It looks an awful lot like the streetlamp out by the parking lot."

"Come on, dance with me. We'll take it slow."

"Because of my hip?"

"Because I haven't danced with anyone under seventy for the past two years."

"Don't worry. Dancing with me won't be much different."

In an instant she was standing in front of him, as if she'd floated up off the chair and materialized across the room, like a vision moving through space in the blink of an eye.

She put her hand in his, always smaller and warmer than he expected, then leaned forward and arched her back. She extended her right leg behind her, pointing it up into the air like a ballerina. She placed her hand on his shoulder and dipped backward, then ground her hips against his, moving from left to right. He caught his breath. "And you said you couldn't dance."

She twirled beneath his arm, out and back again. "I'm just showing off. I thought you said *you* couldn't dance?"

"My mother made me polka with her at the cast Christmas party."

"I had to square dance with my brother at the Harvest Hoedown."

He pulled her to him and lowered his head until his mouth was inches from her own. He smoothed back her hair, never letting his gaze waver from hers. He hadn't been around the block as many times as people would think, but he'd bedded enough women to know anticipation was everything. He watched her lips part, heard her soft gasp, felt a rush of breath slide across his cheek like warm velvet. He grazed her lips with his, light enough to excite them both, firm enough to let her know he meant business. He looked into her beautiful eyes, and it occurred to him he might want to spend the rest of his life looking into them.

They swayed gently back and forth. He looped his arm around her waist and followed her lead. He thought he'd be intimidated dancing with her, but she moved with such grace and joy, it was easy. "Tell me about *Moondance.*"

"It's the story of a girl who finally gets everything she wants. Then she dies."

"Oh, a comedy. I love comedies."

"Before she dies, the moonlight shining through her window revives her. And the boy next door—"

"Gotta watch out for those boys next door."

"He's been watching her from the fire escape."

"A stalker? This is a musical about a stalker?"

"Stop it," she scolded, laughing. "Do you want to hear this or not?"

He placed his right hand against the small of her back, took a step forward, then dipped her to the floor.

"Very nice," she said when he brought her back up. Her hands slid around his neck. "The boy next door, who is madly in love with her—"

"Aren't they always?"

"Of course. He sees her dancing in the moonlight and climbs through her window. They dance, make love, and she dies."

"That's the end?"

"No, then she rises out of her body and she and the boy dance off together. Right through the wall. It's a really clever special effect. Makes the audience gasp every night."

"Who was the boy? A ghost? An angel?"

Annabel stopped dancing. "He's whoever you want him to be. He's her destiny."

"I guess if someone believes in signs, believing in destiny isn't much of a stretch."

"I believe in both."

"I know." He nuzzled the tender spot behind her ear, then skimmed his lips along the scooped neckline of her blue cotton T-shirt. Her small, firm breasts swelled beneath his touch and he wanted to slide his hands under her bra, run his thumbs across her nipples, and feel them harden like the growing bulge in his groin. But he forced himself to take it slow. Scaring her off was not an option he was willing to risk.

"I wish I could have seen you in *Moondance*," he said.

"I wish I could have seen you polka."

He trailed kisses along the silky column of her throat, then pressed his mouth against her skin, raking it slowly along the ridge of her collarbone, savoring the sweet taste of her, the softness. Heat flared in his chest. His heart was breaking wide open.

He kissed her again. And again. Then glanced up and realized her big blue-grays were half-open, watching him. He'd only kissed a handful of women who kissed with their eyes open, and he had to admit he liked knowing they were there, in the moment. With him. When a woman closed her eyes, she could be anywhere—making her grocery list, deciding which color to paint the kitchen, pretending he was the hunky guy behind the bar they'd just left.

His hands stroked the contour of her cheeks. She moved her lips against his with a fervor that sent his desire into overdrive. As the kiss deepened, he slid his fingers around the nape of her neck and threaded them through her thick, short curls. She pulled her mouth away for an instant and rubbed her cheek along the soft stubble on his jaw like a cat. A low, guttural moan rumbled against his neck.

"Okay," she murmured. "Ignore the animal sounds. It's been a while."

He laughed softly. "That's okay. It's been a while for me too."

"Who taught you to kiss like this?"

"I'm making it up as I go along."

"Well, it's definitely taking my mind off things."

"Instant Novocain."

He began to devour her lips again, gently backing her across the floor until she was leaning against the wooden table in the dining alcove. He ran his hands down the side of her thin cotton blouse to the waistband of her jeans. He encircled it with his hands and, in one swift motion, lifted her up and deposited her, sitting, on the edge of the table. Her rear end hit the table with a *plop*, sending a low giggle burbling up from her throat.

****

Annabel loved watching his face, his mouth, his eyes, glistening in the moonlight, catching a peek at her between kisses.

He began to trail his mouth along the column of her neck again. Slowly. Each kiss sending a newly manufactured shiver racing the length of her spine, across her abdomen, down her legs. She held onto his broad shoulders and arched her back as his lips lazily retraced their path along her throat, hitting every nerve ending she possessed.

Oh, he was good, all right. Damned good.

"Annie," he whispered. He held her face in his hands and gazed into her eyes. "Are you sure you want to—"

"I'm sure."

"But so much has happened. You're vulnerable right now. I don't want to take—"

"Stop over thinking this and kiss me." She unbuttoned his cotton shirt and pulled it apart, then tugged at it until it came flying out of the waistband. "Getting there," she whispered. She kissed the tiny indentation at the base of his throat, nuzzling the soft patch of dark hair curling against the collar of his undershirt. "I want this. I want *you.*"

She closed her eyes and ignored the voice in her head begging her to stop before it was too late. The physical attraction between them had been there from the start, but if it was just a chemical reaction, like vinegar and baking soda, then wouldn't she be better off pulling back, not letting it go so far there would be no turning back? She knew she should measure the risk against the thrill, protect her heart from a break that might take a lifetime to heal. She should stop. Just for a minute. Just long enough to imagine what it would be like to open her soul to Trent Sheffield, let him touch her in ways no man ever had, then watch him walk away.

Which might happen sooner than she expected.

Once she got to his friend's house in Charleston, he would leave her and go back to the inn. Chances were she'd never see him again. And when he discovered that Gil staged the freak accidents and was either directly or indirectly responsible for Quinn's death, he wouldn't want to see her at all. Seeing her would remind him of all the things he would be desperate to forget.

She should be careful. And sensible. And smart.

But right now. With his soft lips and expert hands driving her to the brink and back. She didn't care.

She pulled her head back and looked at him. His extraordinary eyes, as clear and deep as lake water, smoldered in the moonlit room. The light from the window fell across his dark hair, illuminated his face like a work of art. He leaned over and pressed his mouth against the tender rise beneath her chin. The gentle tickle was more than she could bear. She let out a slow, rumbling giggle.

"Lady, you have a wicked laugh."

She wrapped her legs around his knees and

covered his lips with hers. "Just let me know if you need to come up for air."

"Not a chance," he said huskily. "I've wanted you since the day you climbed down that damn ladder."

He pulled her close, then gently pushed her back on the table, kissing her, sliding his hand beneath her shirt, searing heat across her skin. When his cell phone jangled inside Annabel's pocket, neither one of them noticed. On the fifth ring, he drew back. "That's gotta be Keisha."

She fished it out and handed it to him.

"This is Trent." He listened for a moment, and even in the pale moonlight, she could tell his face had gone ashen. "Why didn't you call me sooner? I'm on my way. As soon as I can."

He closed the phone and stood staring at the floor. His shoulders slumped, then rocked forward as if the air had been knocked out of him.

"Trent, what's wrong? What's happened?"

He raised his head. The panic in his eyes turned her blood to ice.

"There's been another accident. It's Gil this time."

"Gil?"

"Christ, Annie. They don't think he's gonna make it."

Chapter 19

Trent stood in the center of the room, looking left and right, as if he'd been plunked down in the middle of a field and couldn't get his bearings.

"What did Keisha say?" Annabel asked.

He ran his hand back through his hair, a habit she had come to know well. "Mrs. Rosetti smelled gas and called Keisha. Keisha cleared the Laurel Room and cancelled lunch. Then the gas company came and tested everything, but no leak. The staff couldn't get back in the kitchen until five, so Gil decided to do a pizza buffet."

"But what happened? How did he get hurt?"

"The pot rack fell on him. Keisha thinks someone tampered with the chain. Gil put the damn thing up even though Mrs. Rosetti can't reach it. He has to hang the heavy pots and skillets on it for her. They think that's what he was doing because some of the iron skillets were still lying on the counter."

"Did it hit his head?"

"I don't think so. Keisha said it threw him back. But it's wrought iron. The thing weighs a ton. And with all those industrial size pots and pans, it—it crushed his chest. One of his lungs collapsed. There are internal injuries, broken bones. He coded in the ambulance."

Annabel put her arms around him. "He'll be all right. He's young. He'll heal fast. Before you know it, he'll be thinking up some wild new scheme to drive you nuts." She pulled back and looked into his eyes.

"Listen to me. Gil's got a will of iron, remember? And he's got you."

"He'll be all right," Trent repeated softly. "He has to."

Annabel took his cold hands in hers. "Okay, here's the plan. You load up the car and write Nolan a note, and I'll run the key down to the super's office. I've got the same lock on my apartment door. All you have to do is lock it, then pull it shut when you leave. I'll meet you in the parking lot and we'll get on the road."

His eyes snapped into focus. "You're not going."

"Oh, yes, I am."

"You can't go back. It's too dangerous. Keisha said the guests are leaving in droves."

"It's my choice. Accidents are still happening at the inn whether I'm there or not. You have to go to Gil, but you're in shock. I don't want you driving back alone. And to quote a very stubborn man, who I have come to care for more than I ever thought possible, 'This is non-negotiable.'"

To her surprise, he didn't argue with her. She looped her shoulder purse diagonally over her chest and stood watching him for a moment before she closed the door. He picked up her backpack. He wasn't moving fast, but at least he was moving. His jaw had frozen into a rigid clench. The soft lips she had taken so much pleasure in were pressed together in a hard line.

Outside, she put herself in New York City mode, walking briskly along the pavement, cranking her peripheral vision capacity to the max. She glanced at the moon. Aunt Lou always said you could make a wish on a full moon, and if it came straight from your heart, it might come true. Annabel's wish would be for Gil get well and be absolved of Quinn's death, and for her father to get better soon, and her sister-in-law. Her wish sounded more like a prayer, but wasn't that what prayers were? Wishes with at least a snowball's chance?

Annabel found the door marked *Office*. Between the half pulled curtains, she could see the jagged, flickering light of a TV pulsating against the wall. She pushed open the door. A balding, middle-aged man sat on a plastic lawn chair, watching an old *Charlie's Angels* rerun. When the door banged behind her, he glanced up and did a double-take.

"Hi," she said.

"Hi, yourself." The man's gaze traveled leisurely over her body, stopping for a brief moment on her breasts, then, on a quest for greener pastures, she guessed, scanning the rest before finally settling on her ass. Back in New York, she'd spilled drinks on men for less.

"I'm dropping off Nolan Sheffield's key. He said he'd pick it up later tonight."

"Nolan Sheffield? You mean the old guy in 4-D? What are you, his daughter or something?"

"No, just a friend."

The man whistled through his teeth. "Holy crap. If he's got friends like you, I should be nicer to him."

"You should be nicer to him anyway."

"So the old fart in 4-D has a friend who's a real babe."

She started to point out that the old fart in 4-D wasn't much older than the creep she was talking to, but something on the shelf behind him caught her eye. "Is that a fax machine?"

"Yeah. And it works too. A buddy of mine gets *Penthouse*. He sends me pictures out of it, and I send him the ones from *Playboy*. We save a ton of money on subscriptions."

"How pragmatic of you."

"Huh?"

Annabel flashed him a smile. "Look...uh..." She glanced at his name plate. "Andy. Do you think you could fax something for me? I'd be glad to pay you."

She pulled the brochure out of her purse. A pang of guilt swept over her.

It seemed callous to send the photograph to Murray when Gil was in an Asheville hospital fighting for his life, an innocent victim, just like she had been. There was no doubt he had been the intended target. Didn't that prove he had nothing to hide? Didn't that prove he was innocent?

But how could she know for sure? For Trent's sake, she didn't want it to be Gil. She was doing everything she could to explain away his actions in New York, chasing shadows in the dark, hoping for a miracle. Was she so blinded by her attraction to Trent that she'd lost touch with reality? She felt awful Gil had been injured, but if he had lied about going inside the theater to meet Quinn, she had to know.

She looked at the back of the brochure. Her gaze lingered on Trent's face until it disappeared, curling and humming its way through the fax machine. Then she reached in her purse and dug out a ten dollar bill.

Trent was waiting in the van outside the door.

"Well, that took forever." She climbed inside and pulled the heavy door shut. "Are you sure you don't want me to drive? I'm a little rusty, but I'm willing to give it a go."

He shook his head, barely registering a response. Somewhere in the last ten minutes, he'd switched to automatic.

"I can't believe it's only eight o'clock," she said. "Feels a lot later, doesn't it?"

He nodded again, but she knew he hadn't heard her. His heart and mind were with Gil. She decided to leave him alone, let him handle his anxiety the only way he knew how—by shutting down. She'd watch for traffic lights and exits, stay vigilant the rest of the way home. If he wanted to talk, he knew where to find her.

He stopped at a gas station before they reached I-40. "I need to fill up and put some air in the back left tire. Gil said he thought it had a slow leak, and I don't want it blowing on us while we're crossing the mountain."

She glanced out the side window and watched as he lifted the nozzle from the pump. Why did guys always put one hand on the hood and shift their hip to the side like they were ordering whisky in a saloon? She'd laughed the first time Drew had done it. But when she'd mentioned it, he didn't know what she was talking about.

Her gaze drifted to a small pad of paper and pen lying on the center console. She picked them up and absently drew two vertical lines crossed by two horizontal lines. For a moment, she was in the backseat of her father's old Chrysler station wagon, playing Tic Tac Toe with Drew. She stared at the grid. Why did it look too large? She scratched it out and drew a small X below it. No, that was still wrong. What was she trying to remember? What kept niggling at her brain?

Trent opened the door and leaned down. "I'm gonna hit the restroom. Nolan's coffee has finally caught up with me. Need anything?"

"A bottle of water would be great. Want me to get it?"

"Nope. I'll bring it to you."

She looked down at the paper again and rotated it to the left until the X turned into a plus sign. She stared at it for a few seconds, then wrote a small O beside it to form the word *to*. Where had she seen a sign like that?

And suddenly she knew. In the forest. On Sourwood Hill.

Something about the sign had struck her as odd.

She tried to remember the exact wording—*Quick Way to The Sheffield.* Not *This* way or *That* way but *Quick* way. Why had someone taken the time to carve a sign like that on a tree? Why not just paint one and nail it up?

She tore off the paper and held it up. The capital letters jumped out at her.

***Q**uick **W**ay +o **T**he **S**heffield*

Q W + T S

Quinn Wolcott + Trent Sheffield.

She glanced up seconds before Trent opened the door, and quickly stuffed the paper in her pocket.

Trent swung his long legs beneath the steering column. He handed her the water bottle. "I know it's selfish of me, but I'm glad you're here. But first thing tomorrow, I'm putting you on a plane for South Carolina."

She leaned back. As the car left the glaring lights of the Gas and Go and immersed itself in darkness, she tried to sift through the thoughts reeling through her head.

Trent had been on Sourwood Hill with Quinn.

He'd probably made love to her there. But when had he carved their initials on the tree? While he was dating Quinn, or while she was engaged to his brother? And why? Wasn't that a little old fashioned? A little too middle school for a sophisticated guy his age?

If Quinn was meeting Trent on Sourwood Hill, and the attraction between them was so explosive they couldn't keep their hands off each other, why didn't they just get it out in the open and run off to Tahiti or something? It seemed a lot easier than hiking up that steep hill every day in the middle of December.

She knew why. Because if Gil ever found out, he'd never want to see Trent again. Trent would lose his brother. And Quinn knew Trent would never choose her over Gil.

Maybe Quinn wanted to get caught in order to break her engagement to Gil. She'd made sure Keisha saw her leaving the inn and probably presumed Keisha would tell Gil. Then all Quinn would have to do was sit back and wait for the fireworks to begin. The plan was simple, reliable. And there was nothing Quinn liked better than setting off a few fireworks. Or maybe it was a way for Quinn to exact her revenge. Quinn didn't like getting dumped by anyone. She did the dumping. If she wanted to get back at Trent for breaking up with her, having Gil discover they were meeting in the woods for fun and frolics everyday would certainly be one way to do it.

Of course, if Annabel's theory was correct, it had backfired on Quinn. Keisha had turned out to be someone Quinn couldn't play. She didn't tell Gil about Trent's afternoon liaisons with Quinn either to protect him from heartbreak or out of fierce loyalty to Trent. She defied Quinn by keeping Quinn's secret a secret. Keisha had probably never told a soul, until the day she told Annabel.

Annabel glanced at Trent. He steadied the steering wheel with the heel of his hand, his arm stretched out, his brows knitted together to form a double arched line. Her father had driven a tractor the same way. Each day he'd left his dying wife with his daughter and gone out alone, then driven his tractor for three solid hours whether the soybean fields needed plowing or not.

Trent drove in silence. Before they reached the first Asheville exit, he pulled off and phoned the hospital. If she was going to say something about the tree carving, she had better do it soon. Once they got to the inn, chances were he would disappear from her life forever.

He snapped his cell phone closed and guided the

car back onto the interstate. "Gil's holding his own," he said. "His condition has stabilized. He's still on a respirator, but they don't think he'll need surgery. That's all I could find out."

"Look, when we get to Asheville, why don't you drive straight to the hospital. Taking me to the inn will just be backtracking. I can call Byron to come fetch me."

"Are you sure?"

"Of course. You need to get to Gil as soon as possible."

Relief swept over his face. He reached over and curled his fingers around her left hand, then brought it to his lips and kissed it. "Thanks."

"Trent? There's something I—"

"*Damn*," he cried. "I don't believe this!"

"What's wrong?"

"Can't you feel that? The car's swerving to the left. I think the back tire's going flat."

"Do you need to pull off? Do you have a spare?"

"I think I can make it to the exit. I see a sign. Is that a Shell station?"

She could feel the car shimmy and thump beneath her. As Trent navigated the off ramp, a string of curses turned into begging. "Come on, baby, *please*. Only fifty more feet." By the time they clunked across the highway, the rim had begun to scrape against the pavement.

"I should have pulled over. This isn't gonna be fun."

"Can I borrow your cell to call Byron?"

He unhooked the phone from his belt and handed it to her.

While the attendant helped Trent change the tire, Annabel called Byron and asked him to meet her at the hospital. He didn't seem upset, or even surprised she'd gone off with Trent. After they hung up, she called Murray. With any luck, the play was still in intermission.

Murray answered on the first ring.

"Yo, Annabel. Jeez, babe, wish you were here. It's magic tonight. The audience is electric."

A twinge of longing pierced her soul, just sharp enough to make it ache with envy. She closed her eyes and pushed it away. "Did you get the fax?"

"I did. It was him."

"Are you sure?"

"Oh, definitely. It was him, all right."

Annabel's heart sank. She'd hoped for a last minute reprieve. She didn't want to believe someone as sweet as Gil could harm anyone, much less the woman he loved. He still loved Quinn. She saw it in his face, heard it in his voice every time he said her name. She had hoped against all hope Murray wouldn't recognize Gil. But he had. And it would break Trent's heart.

"That's right," Murray said. "The tall one. As soon as I saw him, I knew he was—"

"What do you mean, the tall one?"

"The tall one. Standing with his arm around the short one. He's the man on the security video. He's the one I talked to backstage."

"Oh, God," Annabel whispered. "Are you sure?"

"Absolutely. The tall man with the scowl on his face. I'd know him anywhere."

Chapter 20

"Maybe now we can get this show on the road," Trent said. "If the car doesn't blow up, we should be there in about fifteen minutes."

"I want you to pull over for a minute." Annabel's voice sounded as shaky as Mrs. Richmond's, but she couldn't help it.

"Over where? We're at a gas station."

"I don't care. Just move it anywhere. I need to talk to you. And I don't want you driving while I do." She eased the window down a few inches. The pungent smell of gasoline and grease pricked her nose.

"You want to talk to me *now*?"

"Gil is stable. He's going to be fine. You can give me two minutes."

Trent steered past the pumps to the side of the building, then parked in the shadows next to a row of scraggly privet hedges. He cut the engine. "Okay. What's going on?"

It never occurred to her not to tell him. If she'd felt afraid he might harm her, it would have been different. But she was a woman who lived her life looking for signs, following her instincts, listening to her inner voice. She hadn't always chosen the right path, or believed in the right person, but it was the only compass she trusted. And no matter how many warning bells went off in her head, the impulses in her soul told her she had no reason to fear Trent Sheffield.

She glanced out the car window. If she was wrong, the brightly lit gas station, teeming with truckers and tourists, blanketed her with a fleeting sense of security that even with her rotten hip, she would be able to bolt from the van and get to safety before he could stop her. The fact that she never considered calling the police or depriving Trent of the chance to vindicate himself, was either a testament to the gullibility of love or to her infinite, naïve stupidity. Most of all, she felt betrayed he'd ended up being someone other than who she thought he was. And angry at herself for putting her trust in a man she barely knew.

When she looked at him, a crushing sense of loss broke through the bitterness and clutched her heart. When she told him about the phone call to Murray, it would be like sailing off a cliff without a parachute. Once she hit bottom, things between them could never ever be the same.

"Annie," he said gently. "What's wrong?"

"You were there," she blurted.

"I was where? What are you talking about?"

"At the theater. The night Quinn died. You went backstage. You talked to her."

He gaped at her in stunned silence. "How do you know that?"

"The stage manager recognized you. He talked to you. Your face is on a security tape."

"How do you know he recognized me? Oh, God, Annie. What have you done?"

"I faxed him your picture. The one on the back of the brochure."

He stared at her. The lights from a moving truck slashed across his face like the sweeping beam from a lighthouse. Except for the muted rumble and whine of a sixteen wheeler, all she could hear were the ragged breaths he took. In and out. Until she thought she might scream.

"Are you saying you think I killed Quinn?"

"No...I don't know. I thought it was Gil. Gil said he talked to Quinn in the back alley after the matinee. When Murray told me he'd seen a man at the check-in desk, I thought Gil had lied. I thought Murray was going to identify Gil's face on the tape. And when he told me it was you, I thought—"

"You thought what? That I dropped Gil off at Grand Central, told him I was going to a museum, then made the taxi go around the block and take me across town to the Park Square Theater to see Quinn?"

"Did you?"

He didn't answer. His steady, wounded gaze held hers without flinching.

"Trent, did you?"

"Yes."

"Why?"

"I had a good reason." He snapped his head around, adjusted the rearview mirror, and started the engine. "Not that it's gonna matter a hill of beans to you. You've already put me on trial and convicted me."

"Please don't drive," she begged. "I know I'm upsetting you more than you already are, and—"

"And nothing. I'm a control freak, remember? If you think I don't have enough self-control to get us to the hospital in one piece, then you don't know me very well." He yielded briefly at the highway entrance then stepped on the gas and barreled into the merge lane.

"I don't," she said.

"Don't what?"

"Know you very well. We only met two weeks ago, remember? That's not a lot of time to build up trust." She glanced at him sideways. "Other things, maybe. But not trust."

"So, you want me to tell you why I went to see

Quinn in New York? You want me to explain myself in case you're riding in the car with a murderer?"

"Yes."

"I went because she asked me to. She didn't ask it she demanded it. Which never goes down well with me. I didn't want to go. I was afraid Gil might find out. But then I thought that maybe, just maybe, I could drive some sense into that brain of hers and make her cut Gil loose once and for all. She didn't want Gil, but she couldn't stand for him not to want her. When he'd finally begin to accept the fact she was gone and try to move on, she'd call him, or text him, or e-mail him—anything to make sure he was still thinking about her. It got so bad, Keisha and I started screening his calls at the inn. But you can't screen calls on someone else's cell."

"Why didn't you just talk to Quinn on the phone? Why did you have to go see her?"

"Because that was her condition."

"Or what?"

"Or she would abort our baby."

The word *baby* shattered the air.

Trent was the father of Quinn's baby. Annabel had known all along it was a possibility, but why did it hurt so much to hear him say it out loud?

She stared at a streak of white dirt on the windshield. "How long had you known?"

"That she was pregnant? Not until she called. She knew how much I want kids of my own. I thought she'd made it up to hurt me. She said if I didn't care enough to show up in person to discuss our child's future, she would assume I wanted her to get rid of it.

"Didn't care enough?" he cried hoarsely. "Christ, I was thrilled. And I couldn't tell Gil. I couldn't tell anyone. No one knew Quinn and I had—"

"—had sex?"

"If you can call it that."

"You made a baby together. What else would you call it?"

"I'm not sure. Insanity on my part. Revenge on hers. Except for the possibility of fathering a child, I've regretted it every day of my life since."

"Then why did you do it? Were you still in love with her?"

"No. Not at all. And I have no excuse. Even when I realized that Quinn was poison, I couldn't resist her. She was like a freight train coming at me. I could see the light in the distance, hear the whistle, feel the tracks vibrate beneath my feet. I knew I only had seconds to get out of the way. But every time, before I could make a move, she leveled me."

"I saw the autopsy report. Quinn was two months pregnant when she died. So if you fathered her child, the two of you were together while she was engaged to Gil."

"I know, but—" His deep baritone rumbled so low, she had to strain to hear his reply. "No, you're right. They were engaged. See? I'm a bigger asshole than you thought."

Annabel made herself look at him. "That's probably true. But if there's an explanation, I'd still like to hear it."

He glanced at her. She could see the pain reflected in his eyes. He quickly turned his head and fixed his gaze on the road, as if he couldn't stand to see her faith in him crumble bit by bit.

"Quinn never loved Gil," he said. "I don't even think she liked him. But he was crazy about her. When I asked her why she was bothering with him when she couldn't care less, she just laughed and said, 'It's for you, Sheffield. So you can watch us being happy.' When we met on Sourwood Hill, she said she wanted to talk about Gil. I thought I could convince her to give him up. But when I got there, she was waiting for me with a blanket and two thermoses of hot buttered rum. She showed me the initials—our initials—she'd carved on one of the trees, and I knew I had walked into a viper's nest."

"So what did you do? Get drunk?"

"No, I got shit-faced."

"What about Quinn?"

"I don't think she drank anything. She said she was breaking up with Gil because she still loved me. Then she took off her coat. And her sweater. And her...well, you get the idea. Next thing I knew, she was gone and I was barfing up pizza and 151 rum."

"When did you alter the initials on the tree?"

Trent's head swung around. "You saw them, didn't you? When you hiked up there and fell asleep."

"Yes, but it took me a while to figure out what they meant."

"I went back the next day and added letters to change the initials to a sign. I was still pretty hung-over, but I was panicked Gil would see them and know what I'd done."

"When you met Quinn at the theater, what happened?"

"She was triumphant I had shown up. I think she needed to reassure herself that she still had some power over me. That was essential to her, you know—having power over people. I begged her to keep the baby, said I'd bring it back to North Carolina and raise it myself if I had to. She said the only way she would give me the child was if I promised never to challenge its paternity. So I left."

"You left? Why?"

"Because I knew she was bluffing."

"Quinn never bluffed a day in her life. Bluffing wasn't a part of who she was."

"Are you kidding? Bluffing was *all* she was. She deceived everyone she met. You included."

Trent turned into the Mission Hospital parking lot. He pulled into the nearest space and slammed on the brake. Annabel jolted forward.

He jumped out and banged the door shut, then started walking.

"I don't agree," Annabel said, hurrying to keep up. "Quinn didn't water down her opinions. She always had the guts to say what she thought, and since—*will you slow down!*"

He slowed his pace and waited for her to catch up.

"And since I seem to be the only person who liked anything at all about Quinn, let me just say that speaking her mind was one of the qualities I admired most. It was always something I wished I could do."

"Oh, I think you're doing pretty well," he said.

"Why didn't you tell me you saw her? All those times we talked about the night Quinn died, and you never said a word."

"Because I knew you'd believe the worst. Looks like I was right."

"When people hide things, it usually means—"

"—they're guilty?"

She didn't answer.

"You don't believe any of this, do you? No matter what I say, you'll still think I went backstage and—God knows how, because I sure as hell don't—managed to sneak past the guard and find my way upstairs. Then put a Curenol bottle full of codeine on Quinn's makeup shelf on the off-chance she might have a headache, tiptoe back downstairs, and wait for her to bite the dust. Sounds plausible except for the fact that no one knew she was allergic to codeine."

Annabel circled around him. "Everyone keeps saying no one knew Quinn was allergic to codeine. But the fact was Quinn was allergic to practically everything. Any number of over-the-counter and prescription drugs would have done the trick."

"Then tell me, detective. Where did I get hold of codeine-laced Curenol?"

"I don't know. Prescription pills are everywhere. When a doctor prescribes a painkiller for something, no one takes them all. And no one ever throws the leftover pills away."

"So you think I've been stockpiling painkillers just in case I needed to kill someone?"

"No." She reached out and touched his arm. The knotted muscle in his bicep felt like rock. "Please, Trent. I'm not accusing you. I'm just trying to understand—"

"—where all that bloody self-control was when I needed it? Trust me, Lady, I ask myself the same question every day." He jerked his arm out of her grasp. "But what difference does it make now if you understand me or not? You've got all the evidence you need—Murray's testimony, my face on a security tape. Just tell the police where I am, and I'm sure they'll be more than happy to arrest me."

"Will you stop?"

"Oh, I'm sorry. Do you need a motive too? Then I'll give you the short list and make it easy for you. You can tell them I killed the bitch so she would stop screwing with my brother's head. Or you can tell them I did it because she threatened to tell Gil she'd screwed *way* more than my head. Or—here's a good one—tell them I didn't want my baby, and murdering Quinn was a way to get rid of both of my problems in one fell swoop. I'm sure you've thought this all out, written it down in a little notebook somewhere."

"Trent, stop it! I don't have a—"

"Christ, Annie. If you believe I'd harm a pregnant woman—or any woman—then you must believe I'm capable of anything. Do you think I locked you under the bandstand and turned on the blower? Do you think I sawed the ladder rungs, hoping the woman I was falling in love with would crash through and blow her hip apart? Do you think I whacked myself on the head? Set fire to your cabin? Rigged the pot rack chain so a ton of wrought iron would fall on my brother?"

"I don't believe any of those things, but Murray said—"

"Screw Murray! You want a witness? Then ask the guard who stands at the stage door."

"Granville."

"Yeah, ask Granville. He was standing five feet from us. He heard every word Quinn and I said."

"Look, I know you're angry. And hurt. But you've got to understand I don't know who to trust."

"Well, it ain't me, is it?" He held his hands up, palms out, and stepped back. "You know what? I don't have time for this. I have to get to Gil. If you think I killed Quinn, then fine, think that. Call the police. Tell them whatever the hell you want to tell them. Call up Mrs. Wolcott and tell her you've found the guy who sent her daughter off to glory. *Tell everybody*. You'll be wrong. But if it'll make you feel better, go ahead."

"Trent, I'm sorry."

"Christ, Annie, don't be sorry. You're right. You don't know me. And except for that fascinating little interlude on my father's dining room table, I don't know you either. You believe in signs and destiny? Well, me too. I should have seen the friggin' handwriting on the wall the second I met you. I should have followed my gut and sent you packing."

Byron was suddenly standing beside them. "What are the two of you arguing about?" he hissed. "I could hear you across the parking lot." He pushed his tan fedora back on his head and shifted his gaze from Annabel back to Trent. "She's upset. What did you say to her?"

"I'm not sure it's any of your business," Trent said.

Byron pulled himself to his full height, which was still a good four inches beneath Trent. "You made her cry, you jerk. So whatever's going on here *is* my business."

"I'm not crying," Annabel said. She put her hands on her cheeks and was shocked to feel them damp. "I'm just tired. It's been a long day."

"Get your stuff," Byron said. "We're leaving."

She walked back to the van and stood waiting for Trent to press the unlock button on the remote and let her in. When she heard the door click, she slid it open, scooped her backpack off the seat, and slung it over her shoulder. Then she turned around. Trent was standing alone under the streetlamp with his arms folded across his chest, watching her. She had a sudden flash that this would be the last image of him she would ever see. The one that would sear itself into her brain the rest of her life.

She wasn't going to think about what they'd said to each other. Or why she couldn't throw all her doubts out the window and blindly trust him. She would have plenty of time to relive those moments later, on those lonely nights when sleep eluded her and left her curled restlessly in the corner of Aunt Lou's porch swing, staring at the moon.

She started walking toward him, avoiding his eyes, closing the gap between them one measured step at a time. A sharp breeze ruffled her hair, lashed against her face like wind off the ocean. She wanted to run to him, feel his strong arms wrap around her and hold her close. She wanted to feel his heartbeat beneath her cheek, pounding as loud and as fast as her own.

But she couldn't.

She didn't believe he'd tried to kill Quinn, but

she couldn't trust him. Not completely. And he would never understand why. Not when he'd pushed aside all the misgivings he'd had about her and granted her the chance to prove she wasn't like Quinn. He'd wrestled with his feelings for her, but in the end, he'd made the conscious decision to open his heart and trust that she could be trusted. Why couldn't she do the same for him? Because he'd held back information about the day Quinn died? Because he'd been too weak to say no to Quinn when his brother was in love with her? Because the mistakes he'd made seemed too significant to forgive? Because she was afraid of being disappointed?

Okay, he was flawed. Wasn't everybody? Didn't people choose their partners based on the number of flaws each one thought they could tolerate? Why couldn't she just let go and trust him?

Her heart was breaking. What was wrong with her?

She pulled at the silver chain around her neck until her fingers closed around her lucky buckeye. If it held any powers at all, it would get her through the next few minutes with her dignity intact. She would have to speak to him, tell him goodbye. After everything he'd done to keep her safe, she couldn't leave without thanking him.

Ten more steps and she'd be beside him. Eight more and she could reach out and touch his face. She kept her head down. The cowardly part of her couldn't bear to glimpse the expression in his eyes to see if they registered disappointment or relief.

She handed her backpack to Byron.

Trent reached out and caught her hand. "Annie, I'm the one who's sorry. I'm sorry we never had enough time together. I'm sorry you can't...I'm sorry. But I want you to know that whatever you decide to do with the information you have, I'll understand."

"Give my best to Gil," she said around the knot

in her throat.

"I will." His grasp tightened around her fingers. "When are you leaving the inn? Do you want me to call Keisha and have her book a flight for you?"

"No, thanks. I'll rent a car. You gave me your friend's address. I'm leaving tonight, right after I see Rachel. I feel bad I didn't say goodbye to her."

"So, this is it, then?"

"This is it."

At the last moment, she lifted her head and looked at his beautiful chiseled face, the profound sadness in his eyes. God, she would miss those eyes.

He glanced at Byron. "You'll take care of her?"

Byron nodded and smiled. "I'll take care of her," he said softly. "You can count on that."

Annabel pulled her hand from Trent's and backed away. Then she turned and moved out of the circle of light, leaving his life as abruptly as she'd entered it.

She wouldn't let herself look at him again, so she had no way of knowing if he watched her follow Byron across the parking lot to Craig's car or if he'd turned and sprinted through the front entrance. Trent liked things orderly and predictable. She hoped he might have stopped for a moment and glanced back over his shoulder, permitted himself a fleeting last look to wrap up the Annabel segment of his life in a neat, tidy package.

One last picture to file in his memory.

One last memory to carry in his heart.

Chapter 21

Annabel leaned her head against the car window and closed her eyes. Exhaustion burned behind them.

"You said you were leaving tonight," Byron said. "I'm glad you've finally come to your senses."

"Just for a while," she said wearily. "Just until things calm down at the inn and innocent people stop getting hurt." She looked over at him. Lights from the oncoming cars cut across his face in three-second intervals. "I'm getting closer to the truth, though. I can feel it. And I'm not giving up. I'll never give up."

"I never thought you would."

Byron drove through Asheville in silence. Emptiness pushed against Annabel's chest, making her heart ache until she wanted to cry out. Driving through the Blue Ridge Parkway usually made her nervous, but even the treacherous hairpin turns and switchbacks couldn't penetrate the numbness that enveloped her.

They turned into the Sheffield Inn's long driveway. Byron helped Annabel out of the car and walked with her toward the inn. The warm night had coaxed the remaining guests outside to sit in wicker rockers on the wraparound porch. A few were milling around the Laurel Room patio, drinks in hand. In the distance, she could hear them chattering softly, but the mood seemed somber. They'd probably seen the ambulance take Gil away and knew the latest catastrophe to befall the inn might just be its last.

Byron loosely draped his arm around Annabel's shoulders. He'd done it dozens of times before: standing backstage, strolling through Times Square, ambling around Soho on their day off. It was such a comforting gesture, tears stung the corners of her eyes. Part of her wanted to give in to the sorrow, just put her head on Byron's shoulder and sob.

He stopped beside the gazebo to let her rest. "What happened tonight? I got that you're breaking it off with Trent, but I didn't really understand what he'd done."

Her eyes filled with tears. "I love him, Byron. I love him more than I ever thought I'd love anyone. But I can't trust him."

Byron whistled through his teeth.

"I talked to Murray tonight. I faxed him a picture of Gil and Trent, and he recognized Trent's face. Trent was backstage the day Quinn died."

"You're kidding. And you confronted him? What did he say?"

"He's got a string of excuses. And I want to believe them all, but—"

"—you can't."

She shook her head.

Byron hugged her to him. "Cheer up, sweet girl. He might be telling the truth. The person I'd think twice about trusting is Rachel. Don't you think it's strange she showed up here the minute she got out of rehab?"

"It was part of her twelve-step treatment. She was making amends."

"I don't care. What about the grudge she held against Quinn? Quinn took away her part *and* her best friend, then destroyed what little self-respect she had left. You know Rachel blamed you and Quinn for everything she lost. The stress must have sent the poor girl scuttling back to her drug dealer before the ink was dry on Quinn's new contract."

"Stress wasn't the only reason Rachel took drugs. It's never that simple."

"Whatever." Byron rolled his eyes. "Rachel and Quinn had a huge argument when Rachel showed up stoned for the matinee."

"You heard them arguing? You've never told me this."

"Quinn said she was sick of Rachel messing up every number she was in, and if Rachel didn't go home and let one of the swings take over, she was calling the producer."

"I was probably in the warm-up room at the same time telling the dance captain Rachel wasn't in any shape to go on. She was getting extraordinary risk pay for dancing on top of that giant platform. It was dangerous as hell. I had to say something, even though I knew she would hate me for it."

"But she never knew it was you who talked to the dance captain. All this time, Rachel thought Quinn got her sent home, not you. That changes things a bit, don't you think?"

"I guess so." Annabel shifted her backpack to the other shoulder. "But if Rachel's guilty, when did she switch the pills in Quinn's bottle? She left before the matinee."

"She had time. What people keep forgetting is that Murray didn't escort Rachel out. He waited for her at the stage door while she went to get her things. All she had to do was dig her codeine stash out of that revolting tampon box then stop by your dressing room on her way out."

"So you don't think it was an accident? You think Rachel was sober enough to know what she was doing?"

"Yes. She hated you both. She did it for revenge. I'm not sure she meant to kill Quinn, but she knew getting you both blitzed on codeine would wreck your dancing."

"But—"

"No *buts*, Annabel. Rachel wanted you and Quinn to suffer. And I think the police should know that."

****

Trent stopped in front of Gil's room and took a deep breath. He'd paced the halls for ten minutes, waiting for the respiratory technician to finish her examination.

The nurse behind the glass enclosure had barely glanced up when she told Trent he could go in. She hadn't known what kind of courage it would take for him to see the brother he'd raised, lying mangled and helpless in a hospital bed. Or maybe she did. Maybe that was the reason she'd sounded so curt and indifferent. It couldn't be easy giving family members permission to go into their loved ones' room and face their worst nightmares.

Trent pushed open the heavy door and peered inside. Something told him he'd better assess the situation and get over the shock before he let Gil see his face.

He stood for a moment listening to his brother breathe. The respirator was gone; Gil was breathing on his own. But his lungs sounded like the old gas furnace at the Sheffield, wheezing and rattling with each forced blast of hot air.

Gil lay on his back. His left arm, covered in a white plaster cast and formed into a rigid *L*, nestled into a pillow beside his chest. Portable monitoring machinery surrounded his bed. A plastic bag swung from an IV trolley, dripping clear liquid into a vein on the back of his hand. A green oxygen tube had been clipped beneath his nose.

Trent had seen worse. Somewhere. On TV, maybe.

The left side of Gil's face was swathed in narrow bandages. One of his eyes had completely swollen shut. Puffy, bruised flesh obliterated his cheekbones and lips. Some kind of greasy ointment had been smeared over the cuts, leaving red and black streaks stretched across the bridge of his nose.

Gil opened his good eye and squinted at Trent. "You never could sneak into a room," he rasped. "Even when I was a kid, and you checked on me at night, I could hear you coming a mile off."

"And after I'd gone, you'd turn your flashlight back on and read another comic book."

"You knew about that?"

"Hell, yeah, I knew. I did it just to let you think you were getting by with something."

"How do I look?"

"Like Rocky, just before he started yelling for Adrian."

Gil tried to lift his head off the pillow and groaned.

"That's not a good idea," Trent said. "I'm under strict orders by the lovely Nurse Ratched to only stay five minutes. And that's if you don't talk or move."

"Aw, what fun is that?" Gil took a series of short labored breaths ending in a wracking, gurgling cough. "God almighty, this sucks. I could talk a lot better if somebody would get this freakin' anvil off my chest."

"Stop talking, then."

"Can't," he whispered. "I want you to know I'm still mad at you. And that I'm glad you're here."

"You were lucky, but if your lung collapses again, they might have to operate. I don't think you want that, do you?" Trent knew he sounded like a father spewing advice to a ten-year-old, but he couldn't help it. He'd fathered Gil too damn long to stop now.

"Hey," Gil said. He reached out and grabbed Trent's wrist, then curled his fingers around it until the oxygen sensor clip dug into Trent's palm. Relief flooded through Trent. He hadn't expected Gil's hand to exhibit so much strength. Maybe Annabel had been right. Gil was young and strong. If he stopped being so damned stubborn, and did what the doctors told him, chances were he'd bounce back in no time.

"You need anything?" Trent asked.

"Yes, I've got to tell you—"

"Don't talk."

"Got to tell you."

Trent leaned over and put his ear close to Gil's mouth. "Okay, kid. Tell me one thing, then you have to rest. What is so all-fired important it can't wait until—"

"It was Byron."

"What?"

"I saw him leaving the kitchen before the pot rack fell on me. He was holding a bag in his hand."

"What kind of bag?"

"Dunno. Some kind of purse-thing. It was jangling like there were tools in it. I went in, and all the heavy skillets were spread out on the work station. I thought it was strange, but I started hanging them back up, and—

"You're sure it was Byron?"

"Oh, yeah. I came in from the Laurel Room just as he was going up the back stairs. I didn't see his face, but I knew it was him. Nobody walks like he does."

"No. Nobody does."

Fear gripped Trent's stomach. His mind began to reel.

Annabel had left with him. Annabel was with him now.

Trent pulled his cell phone out of its holster. He

pushed the speed dial number for the inn and waited. Each hollow ring cut through his soul. *Why didn't Keisha or Donald pick up? Where was everybody?* He scrolled down and keyed in Keisha's number. After a few rings, it went to voice mail.

"It's Trent," he said. "Find Annabel. She may be at the inn. Find her now and don't let her out of your sight. She's in trouble, Keish. I'm on my way."

He snapped the phone closed and stared at the wall. The image of Byron standing in the parking lot, smiling complacently, blistered across his brain. What had the son of a bitch said? *I'll take care of her. You can count on that.*

"I'm glad I remembered to tell you about Byron," Gil said sleepily. He closed his eyes. "I'm glad you took Annabel someplace safe."

"Sleep tight." Trent kissed Gil on the forehead, something he hadn't done since the kid had left grade school. "And hang in there. I'll be back before you know it."

Trent turned and bolted from the room.

How could he have been so blind? How could he have let her leave with him?

Blood pounded in his throat. Adrenaline coursed through his veins, blocking out everything but the drive to reach her before it was too late.

He barely noticed the squeak and slap of his athletic shoes echoing through the hall like a string of firecrackers. Or the nurse shrieking at him to slow down.

The only thing he heard was the roar of his pulse crashing in his ears.

And the loud, thundering beating of his heart.

Chapter 22

"I don't know, Byron. I still can't believe Rachel would harm anyone. I don't think she's capable of it. She's been so open since she's been here. We've talked about the bad feelings between us. We've talked about Quinn. I don't think she's hiding anything, I think she's—" Annabel stopped. She took a step back and stared at him.

"What's wrong?"

"How did you know Rachel hid her stash in a tampon box?"

"Everyone knew it."

"No...they didn't."

A sickening wave of terror welled up inside her. Blood pulsed against her throat.

"Annabel?"

"It was you, wasn't it?"

"Don't be silly."

"No. It was you. You stole the codeine tablets from Rachel and switched them."

"You're crazy."

"All this time I thought—" She stopped and tried to grasp what was happening. "Oh, God, Byron. Did you really kill Quinn? But why? Why did you do it?"

"Let's go for a little walk," Byron said.

Annabel's gaze darted to the inn. She could never outrun him. Her hip wouldn't last two minutes, and they both knew it. She opened her mouth to scream.

"Don't even think about it." Byron spun her

around and twisted her arm behind her back. He threw her purse and backpack on the ground and kicked them under a rhododendron bush. "I'll come back for those later. After you're gone."

Byron shoved something hard against her ribcage.

"Is that a gun?"

"Of course, it's a gun. I live in New York City, for God's sake. Did you think I wouldn't have a gun?"

"Byron, what—"

"Shut up, sweet girl, and keep walking. Right past those nice old people on the porch. And if you say a goddammed word to anybody, I'll kick your hip so hard, you'll never walk again. You know I can do it. I could kick the spurs off a pair of boots if I wanted to."

"As long as there was a twenty-year-old chorus boy sitting in the saddle."

Byron chuckled. "Well, at least you haven't lost your sense of humor."

"Go to hell."

"I'm going to miss you, Annabel. You're one of the few people left in this godforsaken world who can still make me laugh."

Annabel stumbled along the path toward the inn. Her heart knocked against her ribs. A line of cold sweat ran across the back of her neck, down her spine. She tried to turn and look at him.

"Straight ahead."

"You're not going to shoot me, Byron. Not in front of all these people."

He pressed the gun into her shoulder blade. "To the right. Around the porch to the side entrance."

"Isn't that a little risky? Aren't you afraid Rachel will be out there smoking?"

"Not tonight, she won't. She'll be sitting in the bar, pouring her little heart out to Craig. One strawberry daiquiri at a time."

"Is that how you managed it? With a little help from your friend Craig?"

"Managed what?"

"The accidents, the threats."

"I left the Curenol bottle on your porch to see how paranoid you were. Craig helped with the fire, but I rigged the pot rack and the ladder myself. I can't believe I sawed the rungs. It was just so...butch. What a disappointment, though. I was sure you'd break your neck."

Her mind tried to comprehend what he was saying, and why he was doing this. But it kept hitting a brick wall.

"How did you rig the blower? I thought you didn't arrive at the inn until later."

"I'd already been in North Carolina for two days, staying at that nice Comfort Inn right off the Parkway, under an assumed name, of course. I'd follow you down to the supper club, dodge those idiot carpenters. You never even saw me."

"But I talked to you on the phone."

"Isn't technology wonderful? You thought I was in New York, and I was less than seven sweet miles away."

She had begun to limp. "Please, Byron. I have to rest."

"Tough."

He must have realized if her hip gave out, he would have to carry her. He stopped beside the bottom stoop. "You've got thirty seconds. I want this over with."

"But how did you get inside the supper club?" She tried to take the weight off her right leg, relax her lower back. The pain in her hip burned through to the bone.

"I stuck a wad of duct tape in the padlock hole." He started to laugh. "When that carpenter—the retarded one—tried to lock it, it fell open. He tried six or eight times. Then he just stood and stared at it like it was the Rosetta stone. It was hysterical."

"And you were hiding inside when I went in?"

"Stage right, next to the curtain pull. The same place we always made our entrance from in *Moondance*. You know what a sentimental guy I am. Then I hightailed it up to the inn. That was hard, but once I met Craig, things got easier. He's been a great help."

"What did you promise him, Byron? A job dancing on Broadway? Or a job dancing on Freeman Saunders' lap?"

"Craig is so star struck, I could have promised him a job scraping gum off balcony seats and he would have done it. Craig's cute, but he's a little wild and dangerous." He laughed. "But that's how I've always liked my chorus boys—a little wild and dangerous."

"You'd better be careful, Byron. He might turn out to be one of those people who gets up in the morning and shoots his whole family because there's no peanut butter in the house."

"Break's over." He grabbed her arm and twisted her around. "Up the steps—*go!*" Pain shot through her pelvis, ran the length of her legs. She bit her lip to keep from crying out.

He opened the door and pushed her inside, then guided her down the short hall to the lobby. Her head jerked to the left, hoping to see Keisha or Donald, but the room was deserted.

Byron steered her past the open cage elevator, past the bar, past the staircase. She turned and craned her neck to see if Rachel and Craig could see her, but no one was there. Dave had already turned out the bar lights and left. Even the Laurel Room looked abandoned. No one was dancing. No music drifted across the dance floor into the lobby.

"Looks like the place is empty," Byron said. "I

guess everyone got little spooked after they bundled Gil off in the ambulance."

"Why did you have to hurt him? He never did anything to you."

"I needed you here to finish this, and the only thing that would bring Trent running back was if something happened to his brother. I knew you'd come too. I knew you'd never let him make the trip alone."

"How could you know that?"

"Because you love him. Or you think you do, which is just as bad. I'm guessing it's only a raging case of misplaced lust, but who knows?"

Annabel forced herself to take a deep breath. She tried to stop trembling. She had reached the end of the line. Byron was going to try to kill her. And if she didn't calm down and start thinking clearly, by the time he got her to his room, it would be too late.

Think, goddammit.

She tripped on a tear in the carpet and pitched forward. Byron loosened his grip.

She could pull away from him and dive behind one of the high-backed Victorian sofas. Drop and roll. She'd done it dozens of times onstage. It used to be easy before her hip had turned to mush.

Through the glassed-in front door, she could see Mrs. Richmond standing on the porch. If she screamed, Mrs. Richmond might turn around and realize what was happening. Then call Donald or Keisha. It could happen.

Byron tightened his hold on her arm. "I wouldn't do that. Unless you want me to shoot the old witch, and her little dog too."

Annabel had no choice but to keep silent. She couldn't risk harming Mrs. Richmond. If Byron could poison Quinn and put a bullet through Annabel's back, he'd have no qualms silencing Mrs. Richmond.

Byron shuffled her up the back stairs. He

shoved her into the dingy hallway. She banged against the wall.

"Byron, *please!* My hip is killing me."

"No," he said quietly. "I am."

His tiny yellow teeth were all she could see beneath the deep shadow of his hat brim. She clung to the chair rail and plastered the side of her body against the wall.

"Why are you doing this?" she cried. "I didn't know you killed Quinn. You were the last person in the world I suspected."

"I didn't kill Quinn. At least, I didn't mean to."

"Then why did you switch the Curenol with codeine?"

"Because it was meant for you, sweet girl. It was for you all along. I didn't want to kill you—not then, anyway—I just wanted to make you sick enough to fall on your face in front of Freeman Saunders. He was there, remember? Sitting out front, nodding to the VIP seats like he was royalty. You were the one I wanted to take the codeine, not Quinn. Although, I must say, *Moondance* has been a helluva lot nicer without her."

"But we didn't know Freeman was coming until right before warm-ups."

"I did. I overheard the house manager talking to him on the office phone. She said Freeman was coming to watch the two of us and decide which one he wanted for his new dance piece. I was sure he'd choose you. Then I remembered your poor little hip, and how you couldn't get through a performance without a handful of ibuprofen. I knew Quinn kept a bottle of Curenol on the shelf next to your ibuprofen. Curenol and Curenol-C look almost identical, so I put the ibuprofen in my pocket and topped off Quinn's Curenol with the five I had from an old groin injury plus the ones I stole from Rachel. I figured you'd knock them back without even noticing the switch."

"I did," she said softly. "We both did."

"If those damned paint fumes hadn't given Quinn a headache, she never would have taken the Curenol."

"And she'd still be alive."

"Well, yes. But if I had to accidentally kill someone, I'm glad it was a vicious bitch like her. The world's well rid of her."

He started backing Annabel down the hall.

"This is insane," she cried. "Look at this limp. I can't dance Freeman's show. I can't dance *any* show. My hip is shot. My career is over."

"But I know you, Annabel. And I know what a fucking little trouper you are. You'd find a way to do Freeman's show if they had to carry you out on a stretcher. The only thing standing between me and the lead in a Freeman Saunders show is you. His new show will be my *Moondance*. It will make me famous."

"You're already famous."

"But I want to be famous with the people who count. The lead in Freeman's show will shoot me to the top. I've never been at the top. This is my last chance to find out what it's like."

She glanced down the hall. Byron's room was at the end, a few feet past the Rose Room. The Rose Room key was still in her jeans pocket. If she could distract him long enough to knock the gun out of his hand, it might buy her enough time to get to her room and unlock the door.

"What makes you so certain Freeman will pick me?" she asked.

Byron laughed. "Of course Freeman will pick you. He's obsessed with you. I think he wants to *be* you, though for the life of me, I can't see why. You're too tall. You're too scrawny. And you're too damned old."

She took another step back. "You're five years older than me. What does that make you?"

"A little desperate, my dear." The silken tone in his voice unnerved her. "In two months I'll turn forty. The good parts have dried up. I haven't been cast in a lead in nine years. I'll never have another chance like this."

"After coming here and meeting Trent, I wouldn't have danced the part anyway," she lied. "He loves me. We want to be together. And now that I know I can trust him, I'm going to stay here at the inn with him."

Byron's eyebrows shot up. "Are you now?" He curled his upper lip back from his gums. "Then Trent is going to miss you. We all are."

Her gaze dropped to the gun barrel pointing at her chest. It wasn't the small firearm she'd expected, something Byron could carry discreetly in his man-purse. It was huge and black and ominous. If he pulled the trigger, he could blow her through the back wall.

She edged down the hall. Her fingers slid across Trent's door, then Gil's.

Amber light from the wall sconce spilled onto Byron's felt hat, throwing an impenetrable shadow across his gaunt face. He lifted his chin, and for an instant she glimpsed the cold, cunning expression in his eyes.

"I thought you were my friend," she said. "I trusted you. You've always said you had my back."

"And I've always said you trust the wrong people. You should have listened to me."

"Please, Byron. You don't have to do this. The part is yours. I'll never be able to dance again."

"Just keep moving. Down the hall, past my room."

She glanced anxiously behind her. "The stairwell is missing."

"Exactly."

A burst of adrenaline shot through her. She stepped back and kicked her left foot as high and as hard as it would go. The toe of her athletic shoe made contact with the spongy underside of Byron's hand, thrusting it upward. The gun flew into the air.

"*Damn you!*" He held his bruised hand to his chest and dropped to his knees, groaning. All at once he was up again, scrambling and crawling toward Gil's room after the gun.

Annabel ran down the hall. Pain blazed through her pelvis. It penetrated the muscle like a fiery barb. Jagged gray lines danced around her peripheral vision. For a moment she thought she was blacking out.

She fumbled in her back pocket for the key.

Oh-God-oh-God-oh-God.

Her fingers closed around the grooved metal shaft. She pulled the key out. Her hands shook so violently, she couldn't fit it into the lock. She pushed against it, crying out loud for strength, then wiggled it until it yielded and turned.

All at once, Byron was there. He seized her arms and thrust her ahead of him. She couldn't defend herself. She'd felt the power of his upper body strength before, every time he'd lifted her above his head like she was made of cotton candy. He rolled her around. The butt of his gun banged against the sharp flange of her shoulder blade.

"*Stop it!*" she screamed. "*Let me go!*"

He kicked at her with his foot, making contact just above the back of her knee. "How does that feel? Not so good, huh?"

They staggered past the *Do Not Enter* sign.

"*Byron, no!*"

He lifted the plastic tarp and shoved her through the opening into the construction area.

Her body slammed against a vertical piece of

wood, expelling the oxygen from her lungs. She held onto a wooden crossbar, blinking like a mole in the dim light, then scooted along the ledge as far and as fast as she could. She huddled in the shadows and tried to silently shift her weight to her good leg. The stagnant air smelled like plastic bags and moldy wood. She took her glasses off and tucked them in her shirt pocket, afraid the reflection on her lens would give her away.

Byron's silhouette filled the doorway. He took a step toward her and stopped, then turned his head, searching for her. He brandished the pistol in front of him, but couldn't keep it steady. She must have kicked his hand harder than she thought.

Stacks of uncut boards lined the ledge along the perimeter of the opening. The board she held onto was nailed to a scaffold extending down to the main floor.

She watched the doorway. Byron had stopped moving. The only sound she could hear was the quick, muted swish of her own breath.

"Where are you?" he cried.

Annabel's heart thudded against her ribs. Once he spotted her, it was all over but the screaming.

She held onto the scaffold with one hand and bent her left knee as if she were doing a plié, then slowly lowered herself to the ground. She slid her fingers beneath a long piece of baseboard molding and gently lifted it. *Keep your eye on the ball, Annabel.* Drew had drilled those words into her whenever they lobbed unshelled walnuts over the fence with a stick. *Eye on the ball.*

She fixed her eyes on the gun. Then pulled her arm behind her shoulder and gave it all she had.

The molding whooshed through the air. It smacked Byron on the elbow, missing the gun completely. He screamed and fell back. The gun clattered across the floor. It spun toward the edge of the stairwell then fell into the chasm.

"Enough!" Byron picked up the molding and broke it over his knee. He threw one of the pieces down and gingerly stepped over the debris until he stood beside the scaffolding. He gripped the board with both hands and smacked it against the wood, over and over, until the structure above Annabel began to shift.

She clambered onto the support joist and looped her arms around the cross board. If she tried to jump and missed the ledge, she would never survive. All she could do was hang on and pray the bracing held when she fell.

The scaffold swayed to the side, then buckled.

The sound of splintering wood bounced off the walls, drowning out her screams. The joist swung sideways through the air with Annabel riding it like a pasture gate. Plaster dust roiled up from the floor. It permeated the air, coated her throat with powder.

Byron lunged for her and missed. His hands grappled the air, fighting for balance. At the last second, he dove back to the ledge, landing near the wall.

The web of scaffolding lay jumbled across the missing stairwell with one of its legs thrust up through the center. Annabel landed on top, hunkered over the plywood raft. She wrapped her arms around the wooden mast, not daring to move her legs, and peered down.

Two caged utility lights swung languidly over the black hole. One false move, and the wobbly structure could topple, sending her plummeting to her death. For the moment, she didn't have to worry about Byron. He couldn't get to her if he tried. No one could.

He stood on the ledge with his hands on his hips. "You can't stay there forever."

"Why not? I've always wanted to live in a tree

house."

"Give it up, Annabel!"

"Bite me!"

He picked up a scrap of wood and hurled it at her. She flinched and ducked her head as it smashed into the wall behind her.

"Someone will come," she said. "They'll hear us and come."

"No, they won't." Byron took off his hat and smoothed his thinning hair back from his face. "This end of the hotel is totally separate. Craig and I tested it last night. We threw sandbags into the hole, and no one heard a thing."

"Do you think you're going to get away with this?"

"Why not? There's a big hole in the floor. You took a wrong turn on your way to the kitchen and fell in. Everyone knows how unsteady you are on your feet."

He picked up another piece of wood and threw it at her. The wood flipped over in the air and bounced off the landing.

"If you want me dead, you're gonna have to do better than that," she said. "Maybe you should have taken up baseball instead of dancing." Her left leg was beginning to go numb.

He scooped up chunks of plaster and began lobbing them at her. "You and Quinn—God, you bitches! I hate you both. And Rachel. She's all squeaky clean and sober now. It won't be long before she's back in New York trying out for Freeman Saunders. Yeah, Rachel had better start counting her days. Because that bitch is next."

He threw a block of wood at Annabel's hip. "Bulls eye!" Sharp ripples of pain radiated through her side. "Actually, I did play a bit of baseball. For one summer. My father made me."

Annabel fought to stay conscious. If she passed

out, she would let go. And if she let go, Byron Patrick would dance on her grave.

"So, is that what you're doing? Picking off your enemies one by one?"

"Well, I hadn't planned to. But it's working out so well, I'd be a fool not to consider it."

She tightened her grip on the mast. "Then you'd better go after Craig next. Because the minute he finds out you can't make him a star, he'll tell everything he knows."

"Craig's in too deep to turn on me." He picked up a piece of crown molding. "This one looks long enough, don't you think? Let's see if it will reach you." He walked to the edge and poked the rubble like he was stoking a dying fire. The pile of scaffolding listed to the side.

Annabel's heart lurched.

Byron grasped the wood in both hands. He tapped it against the ground and took aim.

The air around her seemed to thicken. Time slowed to a crawl. The sound of her breath roared and swooshed in her ears, as if she'd leapt off the high dive and plunged into the deep end of the pool. It was out of her hands. Everything was out of her hands. And just like that, an incredible feeling of peace washed over her, calmed her, cradled her. Whatever happened, she knew it would be all right. If she fell, she would hit her head on the way down. The lights would go out. Simple as that. It would all happen in an instant. She would never know what hit her.

Annabel clung to the mast. She pressed her cheek against the coarse wood and closed her eyes. Trent's face swam before her. Smiling. Grinning. Happy. Loved. *Too bad she couldn't hang around to spend the rest of her life with him,* she thought.

Too bad she couldn't hang around.

Chapter 23

"That's mine, Tinker Bell."

In one swift motion, Keisha grabbed the board from Byron, took hold of his shoulders, and kneed him in the groin. Before he could double over, she pulled her fist back and punched him hard in the face. Blood streamed from his nose. He fell to the ground, holding his crotch, crying like a little girl.

"Damn, that felt good." Keisha turned and looked at Annabel. "You okay?"

"I can't move. I'll fall again."

"Hang on. We'll get you out." Keisha flipped Byron over and yanked his arms behind his back. "Trent's right behind me. Cops are on their way. That sucking Vance should have been here by now."

Trent appeared in the doorway. *"Where is she?"*

Keisha pointed to the middle of the stairway. "Out there."

"Oh, Christ!" He glanced at Byron. "Can you handle him?"

"Are you kidding? This little shrimp? He's not so tough. Are you, Tink?"

Byron whimpered a string of obscenities and tried to get up. Keisha pushed him back down with her knee. "Not gonna happen, old man."

Trent unfastened his leather belt and pulled it off. He wound it around Byron's wrists while Keisha held them. "That should hold him until Vance gets here."

"Where the hell is he?" Keisha said. "You called

him before you left the hospital."

"I don't know." Trent walked to the edge. "Annie? Annie, talk to me. Are you all right?"

"I think I'm slipping," Annabel said in a small voice.

"We have to get you off that piece of wood."

"Excellent idea," she murmured. "I'm not sure I can hold on much longer."

Trent looked around. He grabbed an orange extension cord lying coiled beside a box of nails. "If I throw you this cord, can you catch it and tie it around your waist?"

"Not sure," she said. "I'll try."

He looped the cord like a lasso and flung it across the chasm. She put her hand out to catch it. As the wood beneath her began to move, she jerked it back. The plug bounced against the platform and fell away. Trent reeled it back in.

"I'm sorry," she cried. "I can't let go. If I do, it's going to fall out from under me."

"It's okay, baby," Trent said. "Just hang in there. We'll figure something out."

"The ladder," Keisha said. She pointed to the far side of the ledge. "See it? Up against the wall? If we lay it across the hole, it'll reach the other side. We have to lock the rungs, though. It's aluminum, but I don't trust it."

"You've got to help me," Trent said. He tossed her the end of the extension cord. "Get his feet."

Keisha tied Byron's ankles and rolled him over near the wall. "Oh, darn," she said. "You're bleeding all over your pretty cashmere sweater."

Byron answered her with a wail.

Keisha and Trent skirted the perimeter of the ledge.

"Damn," Keisha said, glancing at the collapsed scaffold. "Tell me again why you used the old potting shed lumber to build the scaffold instead of renting a metal one?"

"Money," Trent said. "I was too cheap to spend the money. And now look what's happened. This is all my fault."

"No, it isn't," Keisha said. "You want to blame somebody? Blame the creep with the blue balls, crying in the corner."

Trent held the end of the extension ladder while Keisha used her massive arms to walk it to the ground. Her muscles bulged, sweat broke out across her forehead, but she never made a sound. They slid the ladder apart and locked the rungs, then scooted it with their feet until it lay across the stairwell like a bridge. Keisha shoved it toward the middle, a few feet from Annabel.

"Can you jump onto it from there?" Keisha called. "I can't get it any closer."

Annabel stretched out her hand. She could almost touch the metal stile. "I can reach it, but I don't think I can jump. The wood underneath me keeps moving. I can't steady my left leg, and my right one won't work anymore."

"I'll crawl out and bring her back," Trent said.

"Are you sure?" Keisha asked. "I can—"

"No, I'll do it."

Keisha nodded. "You want to slide a board on top of the rungs? Might make it easier to sit on."

"I'm afraid of the weight," Trent said. "I'll crab walk across. Just hold the end and don't let it slip."

Keisha knelt beside the edge and held the ladder with both hands. "Gotcha covered, boss."

Trent took off his blue oxford shirt and threw it to the side. He tucked his white T-shirt in the waistband of his jeans, emptied his pockets, and checked the ties on his athletic shoes. Then he swung one leg over the ladder and sat on the rung facing Keisha. He began to scoot, moving backward from one rung to the next.

"Be careful," Annabel whispered. "Oh, please, *please* be careful."

It terrified her to watch, but she couldn't look away. She was more afraid for him than she had been for herself. His bravery fueled her soul. Adrenaline surged through her veins, giving her the strength to hold on. Giving her the courage to keep watching him no matter what.

The dancer in her took over.

She'd trained for years to soar across a stage. If she could leap fearlessly into Byron's arms, the arms of a man who wanted her dead, then she could fly across hell to reach the man who was risking everything to keep her alive.

By the time Trent got to her, she had managed to pull herself partway up the mast and shift the bulk of her weight to her left knee. She was confident she had enough upper body strength to heave herself up and out toward the ladder. She also knew she had only one chance to do it.

"I know how to do this," she said. "Are you feeling lucky?"

"I'm here with you, aren't I?"

"Then put your right foot on the rung in front of you and wrap your left leg around the ladder. And sit up straight. When you catch me, your back muscles will be doing most of the work. They'll keep you on the ladder while your arms break my fall. If we were onstage, I could show you."

"You can show me later," Trent said. "And tell me if I did it right."

"If we're still alive, you did it right."

"Right."

"When you grab my arms, push on the rung with your foot. It will give you leverage. When you catch me, I'll try to place my left foot on the ladder, but you'll have to help me swivel around. I'm going to feel like dead weight."

"I'll take you anyway I can get you," he said.

She looked into his eyes. The power of his gaze steadied her. "Ready?"

"Yes, ma'am." He wiped his hands on his jeans and grinned. "Aren't you glad I'm one of those guys who works best under pressure?"

"On the count of three. Don't look down."

Annabel pushed against the mast with her hands and shoved down with her knee. The platform rolled beneath her weight. She catapulted up and raised her arms. When Trent caught her, the side of her foot pivoted against the ladder stile, twisting her in the air. His arms went around her torso, slamming her back against his chest.

Pain exploded in her hip. She cried out.

"I'm sorry," he said. "I'm trying not to hurt you. Just relax. I've got you. Keep as still as you can. We're goin' in."

She curled her fingers around Aunt Lou's buckeye, still hanging around her neck, and offered up a silent prayer. Then she leaned back and took slow, deep breaths while Trent crab walked her back to the ledge, one agonizing rung at a time.

Keisha pulled Annabel off Trent's lap and held her steady until he could climb off the ladder. He scooped her up and carried her through the doorway into the hall, then knelt on the floor and gathered her into his arms.

Pain pushed through her legs and pelvis like a firestorm, devouring her body, going from raw, throbbing heat to ice cold and back again. Her eyes slid back in her head. "Trent?" Her voice sounded distorted and far away, as if it belonged to someone else.

"It's okay, Annie. Hang on. I hear the sirens."

"Trent, thank you."

"My pleasure," he said. He hugged her to him and rocked her.

Annabel blinked up at him. "I'm passing out now," she said.

"Get help!" Trent cried. "*Keisha, go now!*"

Annabel drifted in and out of consciousness. She felt Trent's lips graze her forehead, his hand stroke her hair, her cheek. She felt the warmth of his arms try to hold the searing pain at bay, heard him whisper, "Annie," over and over in her ear.

She knew the hallway was full of people she'd never seen before, bending over her, touching parts of her body she couldn't feel, calling her by name. She knew her mother was standing beside her.

Annabel closed her eyes.

The last thing she remembered before they loaded her onto the stretcher, before the medicine they'd shot into her arm pulled her down into sweet, painless oblivion, was Quinn's face. It wasn't smiling, or even frowning, really. It was just there. In the days to come, she would think of it as a sign, something to help her believe with all her heart that wherever Quinn was, she was at peace.

Annabel smiled and squeezed someone's hand. "We got him, Quinn," she whispered. "We got the bastard."

Chapter 24

Annabel folded the letter from her father and slid it back in the envelope. She'd read it six times in the last half-hour. By now she had every word memorized.

Four rapid-fire knocks on the door made her heart swell with anticipation. *Trent.* She'd know his knock anywhere now. She and Keisha had finally persuaded him to go back to the inn and sleep. For the past two days, he'd camped out in the hospital, dividing his time between her and Gil, refusing to leave their sides.

He poked his head around the door and grinned.

"Get in here," she said, laughing.

He walked in and took her breath away. He'd shaved, trimmed his hair, probably talked Keisha into ironing his jeans. His unbuttoned tweed sport coat covered a crisp white shirt. The scuffs on his athletic shoes had magically disappeared.

He pulled a bouquet of pink tulips from behind his back like a magician.

"They're beautiful," she said. "You're kind of beautiful too."

"Gil says hello. Nurse Ratched is gonna wheel him down later this afternoon for a visit. He bribed her with two tickets to Fred and Ginger's. Who knew the old bat had a deep, abiding passion for torch songs and tap numbers?"

"Only Gil."

"And Rachel sends her love. She's rehearsing

nonstop, getting ready for the big opening this weekend. I watched a little bit of it before I left, and she's really something."

"I know. She'll be great."

He pried the plastic lid off the water pitcher and stuck the tulips inside, leaving them a little lopsided. "Actually, the flowers are from Mrs. Richmond. Keisha said she picked them from the flowerbed next to the gazebo. But I figure it's a fair trade. Precious has kept that patch fertilized for months."

"Any news about Craig? Have they found him yet?"

"About two hours ago, somewhere in Pennsylvania. Vance called just as I was walking out the door."

"God, what a relief."

"They found indisputable proof Craig started the fire. His fingerprints on the brim of his top hat were saturated with accelerant. He must have set the fire then raced back to rehearsal. You know the hat I'm talking about?"

"Craig's lucky top hat."

"Looks like its luck just ran out."

"Well, he's not getting my buckeye."

Trent rolled the IV trolley to the side and sat on the edge of her bed. "How's the hip?"

"The old one or the new one?"

"The one made of oxidized zirconium."

"Ah, that one. Well, it's going to take some getting used to, not to mention three or four weeks on a walker and a cane. But I'm becoming very fond of it not hurting."

"I have something for you." He pulled an envelope from the breast pocket of his coat.

"No, there's something I want to give you first." She reached under the blanket and took out her father's letter. She opened the envelope and handed

Trent a bank statement.

"What's this?"

"My dear old dad, who's having *his* hip replaced next week, sent this to me. It's a lot of money, isn't it? All those checks I sent home every month for four years—my father never used a penny. He cashed the checks and put the money in a trust account for me. I guess I underestimated his pride. And his stubbornness."

"And his love."

"I want you to take some of this money—no, wait, don't make a face. I know you won't accept it as a gift."

"The lady's finally getting to know me," he said, smiling.

"But what if we make it a permanent loan? You can pay me back whenever you can. Take forever if you want. It should cover Ruth's loan with interest, get her off your back and save the inn. Save the innkeeper," she added softly.

"My turn. Nolan showed up at the inn today with this." He handed her his envelope. She opened it and stared at the amount on the appraisal sheet. "Whoa."

Trent laughed. "Nolan wants to sell the lots on the south side of Peg Leg Mountain. It was his idea. Although, I think Keisha might have put a big bug in his ear about the inn's finances, or lack of them. There's a developer who's very interested."

"That's great."

"Nolan and I wanted to give you enough money to get the bank off your father's back. Save the farm." He picked up her hand and kissed it. "Save the farmer's daughter."

Her eyes filled with tears. Happy tears. The kind of tears Aunt Lou said would keep her heart from drying up and cracking like a parched cornfield.

He pulled her to him and hugged her tight. "I love you, Annie. You know that, don't you?"

"I know I love you."

"Good. Then you won't mind if I give you this." He pulled out another envelope.

"How many of those do you have?"

"Keisha's been doing a little research for me." He shook out a stack of loose note paper.

"What's this?"

"Hip replacement success stories." He picked up a few of the papers. "Suzanne Farrell, world famous ballerina, returned to the stage to dance again in her early forties. Jimmy Connors, world famous tennis player, back on the court six weeks after his hip replacement."

"I don't play tennis."

"Doesn't matter." He started dealing the note paper across her bedspread like playing cards. "Here's a dance teacher in Atlanta. A salsa dancer in California. A stripper in Vegas—she continued doing *many* things after her surgery."

Annabel laughed.

"The point of all this is they kept on doing what they loved. Every one of them. I'm not saying it'll be easy, I'm just saying it can be done. And I'll be beside you every step of the way." He smiled, filling her heart with joy. "Because Lady, you're my destiny."

He took both her hands in his and held them to his heart. She could feel it beating.

"Annie, tell me what you want." His sweet southern drawl softened each vowel. "If you want to dance on Broadway, I'll do everything I can to make it happen."

"You hate New York."

"Then I'll just have to un-hate it."

"What if I want to stay here?"

"And dance?"

She put her arms around his neck and pulled him close. "I'm not saying I'll never want to dance again, but right now, I think I want to teach."

"Salsa to seniors?"

"And performance jazz to kids who have the same dream burning inside them that I had, but can't afford it. Would the inn sponsor a program like that?"

"Hell, yes." He nuzzled the tender spot behind her ear. "The inn would sponsor lap dancing lessons if you're giving them."

"I didn't know the word *hell* had two syllables."

He laughed softly. "Are you making fun of my accent?"

"Yes."

"You'll make a wonderful teacher."

"You'll make a wonderful father." Annabel took his face in her hands and kissed him gently on the lips. "Because life's too short not to make someone's dream come true. Don't you think?"

"Oh, yes, ma'am. Just tell me where to sign up."

A word about the author...

Rebecca lives with her husband in the beautiful, misty mountains of East Tennessee, where the people are charming, soulful, and just a little bit crazy. She's been everything from a tax collector to a stay-at-home mom to a house painter to a professional actress and director. When she's not churning out sensual romantic mysteries with snappy dialogue and happy endings, she likes to travel, go to the Outer Banks for her ocean fix, watch old movies, hang out at the local pub, and make her day complete by correctly answering the Final Jeopardy! question.

Visit her at www.rebeccaleesmith.com.